THE CAPTAIN'S WIFE

Top: Eiluned Lewis, studio photograph, early 1950s.
Bottom: Eveline Lewis, mother of Eiluned, on her
86th birthday, 4 September 1957

THE CAPTAIN'S WIFE

BY
EILUNED LEWIS

Edited by
KATIE GRAMICH

HONNO CLASSICS

Published by Honno
'Ailsa Craig', Heol y Cawl, Dinas Powys
South Glamorgan, Wales CF6 4AH

First published by Macmillan & Co Ltd, 1943
This edition © Honno 2008

© Introduction, Katie Gramich

British Library Cataloguing in Publication Data
A catalogue record for this book is available from
the British Library

ISBN 13: 978 1870206 983

Published with the financial support of the Welsh Books Council

Cover image: Veer Europe
Photographs from *A Companionable Talent* (Finchcocks Press)
by Eiluned Lewis, with kind permission from her estate.

Printed in Wales by Gomer

CONTENTS

INTRODUCTION

Eiluned Lewis (1900-1979)

Eiluned Lewis was born and raised in rural Montgomeryshire. One of four children, she used the experiences of her early life as material for her best-selling 1934 novel, *Dew on the Grass*, republished by Honno in 2006. Both Lewis's parents were well-educated and cultured people – landowners, JPs, and holders of Masters' degrees. Her mother, Eveline Lewis (née Griffiths), was a particularly remarkable woman in her time, a Welsh-speaker from north Pembrokeshire, former county school headmistress and close friend of the playwright J. M. Barrie. Eiluned Lewis herself was educated at boarding school in Wimbledon and at Westfield College in the University of London and thereafter joined the editorial staff of the *Daily News* and later the *Sunday Times* before her marriage to Graeme Hendrey in 1937. In later life she wrote extensively for *Country Life* magazine. She and her husband travelled widely to Europe, India, Cyprus, and elsewhere but settled in rural Surrey, with frequent holiday visits to Wales.

Lewis produced three novels in all: *Dew on the Grass* (1934), *The Captain's Wife* (1943) and *The Leaves of the Tree* (1953). She was also a poet, publishing two volumes of verse, namely *December Apples* (1935) and *Morning Songs* (1944), as well as interpolating poems in her prose works. Her essays and rural sketches written for *Country Life* were collected in the volumes *In Country Places* (1951) and *Honey Pots and Brandy Bottles* (1954). Surrey forms the setting for her third novel, *The Leaves of the Tree*, but both her first novels are set in Wales and it is clear that, despite living for many years in England, she continued in a sense to define herself as a Welsh writer, formed by her Montgomeryshire upbringing and her Pembrokeshire antecedents. This is reflected in her essays and broadcasts, which frequently focus on Wales, and in the topographical book, *The Land of Wales* (1937), co-authored with her brother, Peter Lewis. She also edited and wrote a personal memoir in the *Selected Letters of Charles Morgan* (1967); Morgan was a prominent Anglo-Welsh novelist of the mid twentieth-century, married to the Welsh novelist, Hilda Vaughan. Again, these connections reinforce the suggestion that Lewis, despite her long residence in England, continued to regard herself as possessing a Welsh identity.

An historical novel in time of war

Whereas Lewis's first novel, *Dew on the Grass* (1934) was based on memories of her own childhood in rural Montgomeryshire, her second, *The Captain's Wife* (1943), draws on the memories of her mother, Eveline Lewis, whose childhood was spent in Pembrokeshire in the latter years of the nineteenth century. This novel, written during the Second World War when Lewis was living in rural Surrey, thus takes the author and her readers on a nostalgic return journey of the imagination: to Wales, to the experience of childhood, and to the 'other country' of the past.

Like its predecessor, *The Captain's Wife* was immediately popular, being reprinted twice within a matter of months. Quite apart from its literary merits, one can see clearly how the tone and subject of the book would have appealed to a country at war. The poem which acts as an introductory epigraph is redolent with nostalgia or *hiraeth* for a lost past. Its continual questioning ('Are they still there? Shall I find them again?') is reminiscent of war poems such as Rupert Brooke's 'The Old Vicarage, Grantchester' but Lewis's poem is more consolatory. She answers her own questions, reassuringly: 'the children [still] play/As the children played there yesterday.' Conjuring up a vivid image of a particular place, St Idris in Idrisland (a scarcely disguised St Davids in Pembrokeshire), the poem and the novel as a whole suggest a sense of timelessness, of survival and continuity. Moreover, the novel's early allusion to the repulsion of the French invasion by the women of Fishguard also adds to the sense of a history of a doughty people not easily vanquished.

Lewis manages both to emphasize the difference and distinctiveness of the Welsh in her opening pages and subtly to suggest their continuing participation in a cohesive British identity. Partly this is achieved, as Diana Wallace has suggested in her essay 'Mixed Marriages,' through the novel's linguistic hybridity. Lettice Peters, the eponymous 'captain's wife,' for example, 'spoke English to her husband and children, Welsh to her servants, and both in turn to her farmer cousins…but she could never repeat a word of the Bible in anything but Welsh.' Although this linguistic flexibility has definite class and cultural implications (Welsh is the language of the lower classes and of Nonconformist religion) it does, as Wallace suggests, afford a 'positive view of the hybridity which goes to make up the varied peoples of the British Isles [and] might also have contributed to a sense of national unity during wartime.' (Wallace, p. 182). The Peters family itself reinforces this notion of a cohesive national identity composed of migrants who now belong in Wales, for Captain Peters' grandfather was a Scottish immigrant, and even Lettice Peters' family, who have lived in Nantgwyn farm for generations, trace their ancestry back to West Country people fleeing England during the Monmouth Rebellion.

Mother and Daughter
As in her first novel, which was much praised by critics for its almost uncanny evocation of the perceptions of a child, *The Captain's Wife* also demonstrates this ability of Lewis's in her delineation of the experiences of the little girl, Matty. The novel subtly alternates between the perspectives of Matty and her mother, Lettice, creating a fictional world seen tellingly from two, often contrasting, points of view.

The novel begins by mapping the features and limits of six-year-old Matty's 'world', ranging from the kitchen to the yard, the garden, back lane and 'staircase' up to the hedge, which leads down towards the sea. It also presents us with Matty's dreams of the future: how she will live in a cottage by the sea and care for her three brothers, since she sadly acknowledges that, being a girl, she will not be able to go to sea as they will. Lewis reveals the way in which a young Welsh girl in the year 1880 is only too well aware of the restrictions placed upon her by her gender and yet, even at this age, she is attempting to plan and take charge of the course of her own life. Lewis's free indirect style takes the reader very close to Matty's thoughts and idiosyncratic way of seeing the world, so that we empathise with her 'great longing to be a boy', which for her means the freedom to travel and to become part of that enticing, embracing other realm of the sea.

Having lived in a house 'subject to a woman's rule' on account of the absence of Captain Peters at sea, Matty's world is turned upside-down by her father's return; here, the dual perspective of the child, who can barely remember what her father looks like, and the mother, who has longed for her husband's return, is particularly poignant. Matty's first view of her father is an estranged one: a man standing behind her mother 'tall as a house, filling the narrow landing and towering above Mamma ...a great fair-haired giant with laughing blue eyes and a yellow beard.' This somewhat ominous description is redolent of Matty's unspoken fears, since she has recently been comforting her little brother, Philip, with 'a story about a giant', who decapitates a saint, though the story ends happily with the saint having his head restored to his shoulders without even a mark on the neck where it has been cut off. Matty clearly fears the masculine, paternal threat to her female-centred world (as does Philip) but she trusts, in her made-up story, that the world will return to its former, perfect state. In the second chapter, the narrative perspective shifts from Matty to her mother, Lettice, who is overjoyed that her 'handsome, lavish, fearless' husband is safely home for the summer; even Matty notices that 'Mamma…was laughing more often than not these days.'

The narrative perspective is further complicated since the narrator herself is clearly situated in the 'present' of the early 1940s, looking back on the family history of some sixty years before, and occasionally reflecting explicitly on the temporal and often cultural gap between 'then' and 'now'. This doubling perspective is one often adopted by novelists who set their novels in the recent past. For most of the novel the narrator remains silent about the present, sustaining the realist illusion that the events of the 1880s are happening in the here and now, with the result that when that illusion is suddenly broken, the effect on the reader can be quite dramatic. One example of this occurs in Chapter XIV, where the generous Uncle Dan buys Matty an inappropriate gift of a sealskin muff just like her aunt's. The narrator throws off her cloak of concealment and exclaims: 'Dear, warm-hearted Uncle Dan! How odd that your present should survive when so much has perished. You with your curly beard and your warm life have been dust these fifty years…But the niece to whom you gave that ridiculous present…possesses it today, and her grandchildren like to snap the fastener and poke their fat fingers into its soft fur.' The 'niece,' Matty in the novel, is identifiable as Eveline Lewis, the author's mother, while the reference to her grandchildren underscores the sense of an unbroken familial heritage.

The lives of women and girls
The alternation between Lettice and Matty as centres of consciousness in the novel is particularly appropriate for a novel which is based on the relationship between a real mother and daughter, Eveline and Eiluned Lewis. As Diana Wallace puts it, 'This is … a *matrilineal* and familial history.' (Wallace, p. 180). Moreover, the novel is peopled by a whole

range of aunts and cousins and maidservants who are as close as family members, so that it embraces the experiences of a wide range of women, not just those of mothers and daughters. Indeed, Lettice, who is particularly close to her unmarried sister, Martha, reflects that 'it was the unmarried sisters... who kept flowing the stream of continuity; not the ones who, like herself, went away and bore children...Old maids kept the essence of life.' Lettice herself is a woman well used and well able to run her own household in the absence of 'the master of the house.' Small wonder, then, that 'in her secret heart she found the rules of a man-made world faintly ridiculous', reflecting that 'she did not go so far as to think that she would run the world better than men could do, but she was quite sure that she would run it differently.'

In this way Lewis's novel calls into question some of the norms of early twentieth-century patriarchal society, not least in its representation of unmarried and older women. In fact, the representation of a character known as 'Old Nannie' in the novel may well be regarded as a direct refutation of Caradoc Evans's notorious story 'Be This Her Memorial,' in his 1915 collection, *My People*. In the latter 'Old Nannie' is so poor, disregarded, and humiliated by her community that she dies a horrific death being eaten by rats; in *The Captain's Wife*, 'Old Nannie' is the retired nurse who is revered and cherished by the men whom she had cared for as babies: 'None of Mrs Tudor's brothers ever came to the house without running upstairs to see Old Nannie. One was a parson, one a doctor, and yet another a Q. C., who was said to have a fierce way with witnesses up in London. But he was a very humble man when he climbed the stairs and knocked on Old Nannie's door.' Similarly, Nansi Richards, a poor old woman of the village is still held in high esteem, partly because it was not 'forgotten that Nansi's mother had helped to keep away the French invasion.' This is a society which values women and acknowledges their strength and ability, again perhaps just as valid a portrait of the 1940s as of the 1880s.

Despite the nostalgic tone of the text, Lewis makes it clear that women's lives even in the past were not always idyllic. Lettice's anxiety and dread when her husband's ship is overdue is vividly imagined: 'the time of waiting for John to come home seemed to Lettice a season of drought...it was as though the very roots of her nature were parched.' This is the role which Gillian Clarke in her seminal poem, 'Letter from a far country' (1982) speaks of as the traditional female role in rural Wales: 'The minstrel boy to the war has gone./But the girl stays. To mind things./She must keep. And wait. And pass time.' (Clarke, p. 46) and of course it is the very role that the young Matty resents, reflecting frequently on 'the miserable unfairness of being a girl.' The novel ends with two unexpected deaths and both Lettice and Matty in mourning, echoing the experience, surely, of many female readers in 1943, yet the novel carefully ends on a note of hope for the future.

A sense of place
Just as the sealskin muff is a material object which links familial present and past, so too does Lewis's atmospheric evocation of place suggest a sense of continuity, not just between the 1940s and 1880s, but stretching much further back as far as prehistoric times. The opening of the novel, couched in the present tense, reads like a travelogue, introducing the reader to 'the sea-girt land' of 'Idrisland', or north Pembrokeshire. The emphasis is on the unexpectedness of this rather bleak and wind-swept landscape; it is as if the narrator is setting out from the start to correct readerly preconceptions about Wales and to focus our attention on the real, the authentic: 'The city of St Idris lies many hilly miles from the railway station, but they are not the hills that anyone expects to find in Wales.' This place is established as remote and austere but also magical, mysterious, for natives and visitors alike. It is characterised by the sea, which surrounds it on three sides and is a place where

religion is as 'native as the rocks taken hence to be the sacred stones of Stonehenge.' Again, the author cleverly conjures up a place of difference, which is yet deeply interfused with the rest of Britain.

St Idris, the 'village that boasts itself a city,' the nearby coast at 'Silversands,' and the rural hinterland where Nantgwyn, the old farmhouse with its 'Flemish chimney' is situated, are all lovingly described. Looking down over the city is the rocky outcrop of 'Carn Idris,' where Matty climbs with Ivor and her cousin Harry, looking down with awe on the panorama below – 'it was all there, everything that made her universe.' It is not smply an intimately known landscape, but an historicised and mythologised one, containing echoes of a 'British camp,' a 'Roman city', and the 'lost land [of] Cantre'r Gwaelod.' The cathedral and the Bishop's Palace, too, are memorably described, evoking contrasting attitudes from Matty, who regards the cathedral precincts as an exciting playground, and Lettice, who is consoled by the peace and beauty of the cathedral's interior. Stone House, where the Peters family live, overlooks the ancient 'grey Celtic cross, worn with centuries of wind and weather' which, again, connotes a sense of survival, standing 'just as it had stood in the days when medieval pilgrims came thronging to St Idris.' Although Captain Peters when he returns from his voyages brings exotic presents for the family, presents like tricycles, 'such as the streets of St Idris had never before seen,' this incursion of modernity does not fundamentally alter this place which remains, in Matty's eyes at least, an 'enchanted country.'

In addition to the atmospheric evocation of St Idris, the family farm, Nantgwyn, is seen as encapsulating a particular sense of identity and belonging, especially for Lettice, who was born and brought up there. Towards the end of the novel, when it is clear that Nantgwyn is likely to be sold, the narrative makes clear how central the family home has been in Lettice's orientation of herself to the world: 'For the rest of her life

Lettice, who despite her sea voyages was deplorably vague about the points of the compass, would fix the relationship of North and East by remembering that if she stood with her back to the stables at Nantgwyn then the sun rose on her right hand over the sycamore tree.' In this way, Nantgwyn ('white spring') is situated at the still centre of Lettice's bodily compass, and remains unaffected by her physical journeys away from home.

Maritime fiction

Although Lewis herself was from the landlocked county of Montgomeryshire, she succeeds in creating a highly atmospheric, intimately felt setting of a 'sea-girt land' whose interdependence with the sea is everywhere apparent. Historically, coastal Wales, including Pembrokeshire, has had a strong tradition of maritime trade and industry and this historical dependence on the sea has also been reflected in Welsh fiction. Allen Raine, one of the founders of the twentieth-century tradition of Welsh fiction in English, wrote a number of maritime fictions based on the setting of the south Cardiganshire coast. *Torn Sails* (1898), for example, focuses on the sail-making industry which involved large numbers of Welsh women and men in the late nineteenth-century before the demise of sail. In fact, *The Captain's Wife* is set at the temporal cusp when the age of sail was dying away, to be replaced by the age of steam, as reflected in the contrasting careers of Captain Peters (still devoted to sail) and Uncle Dan, plying a steamer across the Atlantic. Lettice's anxieties about her husband are compounded by his determination to stick to sail: 'If only John were not so obstinate…about refusing to go into steamships. Why should he cling to sail, when everyone said that the future lay in steam?'

Interestingly, Aled Eames's brief bilingual history of 'the twilight of Welsh sail' includes extensive extracts from the journal of a Captain J. Peters who sailed on the four-

masted iron barque *Metropolis,* built in Portland Oregon in
1887. By 1913, though, as Eames observes, 'Peters left the
Metropolis to study for his master's ticket which he obtained
at Liverpool …and so embarked on a distinguished career
in steam.' (Eames, p. 55). Eiluned Lewis could hardly have
been familiar with Captain Peters' unpublished journal but her
representation of the life and anxieties of the 'captain's wife'
indicate an intimate, probably familial, knowledge of the real
experiences of characters such as the first mate of the barque,
Metropolis. For Welsh-speaking readers interested in reading
the journal of a real 'captain's wife', Eames has also published
a book (*Gwraig y Capten*) on women's roles in Welsh maritime
history which includes extracts from the journal of Ellen
Owen, who sailed the Atlantic with her captain spouse in the
late nineteenth century, and whose experiences are reminiscent
of those recalled by Lettice Peters in *The Captain's Wife*.

The dangers of the sailor's life are brought home in the
text with the dramatic shipwreck of the *Mystic Tie*, described
in Chapter III. The death of the small 'black boy' arouses all of
Lettice's maternal instincts and empathy and yet her reflections
as he lies before burial in the Cathedral are inevitably governed
by the racist and imperialist ideology of her day (and, indeed,
the 1940s): 'Strange fate that had brought the dusky savage
from his African village to lie between those sweeping
Norman arches in the company of saints and prelates…' Yet
these unexpected connections, strongly linked with the history
of British imperialism and a salutary reminder of Wales's
full participation in that chequered history, are everywhere
apparent in the novel. Lettice herself, for instance, remembers
journeying with her husband down the West African coast,
while even in the Nonconformist chapel vestry where she
attends choir practice, there hangs 'a brown map…of the
mission-field in the Khassia Hills of India.' Similarly, Captain
Peters' ship, the *Zouave*, (whose name itself is based on a
French colonial regiment with its roots in Algeria) is burnt

in the Indian Ocean, while Matty is entranced by seeing 'the world's shipping in the great highway [of the Mersey, in Liverpool]. Big liners and little tramps, dredgers and lighters, schooners and barquentines, with the Chinese crew washing their clothes and the brown Lascars coiling ropes and running barefoot on the decks...' Thus, Idrisland may indeed be 'many hilly miles from the railway station,' yet its inhabitants are connected with the furthest-flung parts of the world through the intricate criss-crossings of trade and empire.

In a talk broadcast on the Welsh Home Service on 8 July 1959 entitled 'Welsh Influences Abroad' Lewis speaks of her own experience of being both a traveller to diverse parts of the world and, paradoxically perhaps, a person who is very attached to home. Interestingly, she ascribes this outlook to a family tradition, one which she explores in *The Captain's Wife*. For, as she states in 'Welsh Influences Abroad':

> One side of me is very stay-at-home Welsh. The sort that is homesick if it loses sight of its own hills, and regards Paddington Station as the door to Paradise. The other side of my family includes some rolling stones. As I wrote this down, I looked at a faded photograph of a pillared house in Howrah, Calcutta, where my grandmother bore her first child in 1866. She was a sea-captain's wife from Pembrokeshire, and her first voyage was with a cargo of salt. When I go into one of those houses in Pembrokeshire or Cardigan, with a model of a ship on the sideboard, and a photograph of Shanghai or Sydney Harbour over the mantelpiece, I know that I belong there. (*A Companionable Talent*, p. 69)

Conclusion

All the preoccupations of *The Captain's Wife*: family bonds, marital love and fidelity, motherhood, hope, religious faith, a sense of continuity of tradition from generation to generation, are clearly themes with especially poignant reverberations in time of war. In that sense, the novel is a consolatory one, whose elegiac yet hopeful tone is apt for the time in which it was first published. On the other hand, its unusual focus on matrilineal inheritance, its proto-feminist concerns, and its emphasis on the often neglected domestic, familial and maritime experiences of women and girls means that it is a novel which still has the ability to speak directly to contemporary readers.

Katie Gramich, *Cardiff, June 2008*

BIBLIOGRAPHY

Clarke, Gillian, *Collected Poems* (Manchester: Carcanet, 1997)

Eames, Aled, *The Twilight of Welsh Sail/Machlud Hwyliau'r Cymry* (Cardiff: University of Wales Press, 1984)

Eames, Aled, *Gwraig y Capten* [The Captain's Wife] (Caernarfon: Archifdy Gwynedd, 1984)

Evans, Caradoc, *My People* (Bridgend: Seren, 1995; original ed. 1915)

Gramich, Katie, *Twentieth-Century Women's Writing in Wales: Land, Gender, Belonging* (Cardiff: University of Wales Press, 2007)

Lewis, Eiluned, *Dew on the Grass* (Dinas Powys: Honno, 2006; first ed. 1934)

Lewis, Eiluned, *The Leaves of the Tree* (London: Peter Davies, 1953)

Lewis, Eiluned, ed., *Selected Letters of Charles Morgan* (London: Macmillan, 1967)

Lewis, Eiluned, *A Companionable Talent: Stories, Essays and Recollections*, selected by Glen Cavaliero (Goldhurst: Finchcocks Press, 1996)

Lewis, Eiluned and Peter Lewis, *The Land of Wales* (London: Batsford, 1937)

Wallace, Diana, '"Mixed Marriages": Three Welsh Historical Novels by Women Writers,' in *Moment of Earth: Poems and Essays in Honour of Jeremy Hooker* ed. Christopher Meredith (Aberystwyth: Celtic Studies Publications, 2007) pp. 171-184.

TO

GRAEME HENDREY

Are they still there? Shall I find them again?
The small, grey city, blurred by rain,
The geese and the donkey with patient gaze,
The milk-mild air and the timeless days,
The winding roads that lead to the sea
And the sense of all eternity?

Yes, they are there and still you'll find
The Saints are waiting, for Saints are kind
And well contented to lay their bones
In a place so blessed that even the stones
Break into praise, when the pilgrims come
Chanting the carols of Christendom

Down in the Close the hoarse rooks call ;
Valerian grows by the Palace wall
Where once proud bishops held their feast.
Cold in the their tomb lie prelate and priest
And warring princes whose features are lost,
Swords at rest and tired legs crossed,
While still by the river the children play
As the children played there yesterday.

The Sea-girt Land

The city of St. Idris lies many hilly miles from the railway station, but they are not the hills that anyone expects to find in Wales. Rather does the road dip continually into little valleys with a stream at the bottom of each, and then climbs out again to make its way across the sea-girt promontory. On one side is the blue outline of distant mountains, and rising beyond St. Idris – the village that boasts itself a city – stands the sharp, volcanic chain of rocks led by Carn Idris; but no woods or gently swelling fields soften the austerity of the land.

The farmhouses scattered far and wide have an equal simplicity. Only in their colouring, pink, white and apricot, does fancy creep in; yet the design seldom varies from the square front with windows on each side of the door and a row of windows above, like a child's first attempt to draw a house. If more rooms are wanted the house grows a little longer, but the pattern does not change.

A bleak country, then, you say, stone-banked and treeless, and so it can be on days of winter gale when the urgency of the wind is like feet running over the land, kicking up and flinging down the churns that stand drying in the farmyards, and turning itself at night into a witch's fury. So too it can be on motionless days of mist, wrapping sea and land in silence, while the lighthouses utter their endless warning.

Yet this country casts a spell on strangers, and holds the natives in so fast an enchantment that they cannot escape it, all their lives long, so much is it in their blood, pervasive as the milk-mild air and the all-conquering sea. For the sea surrounds three sides of Idrisland, and whichever road you take out of the city will lead you to it in the end.

Lettice Peters, concerning whom this story is written, could never keep the sea out of her life for long, though she would have liked to do so sometimes. In her day it claimed men from every family. Sailors, farmers and preachers they were: even the fields they tended ran to the margin of the cliffs, and the boom and murmur of the Atlantic mingled with the hymns and prayers rising from the whitewashed chapels they built on their own lands.

Perhaps it is true to say that Idrisland, more than most places, remembers its Creator. Religion in this country is native as the rocks taken hence to be the sacred stones of Stonehenge. The light that pours from the sky, reflected back by sea and shadeless land, so that even the wild flowers have a rare depth and intensity of colour, is like the clear faith of its people.

That faith built the great Norman Cathedral, on the place of a far older shrine, hewed the stones from the lilac rock of the sea cliffs and laid it in a little valley at the foot of the city, hidden away from pirates and sea-rovers. Its square tower has an air of grey simplicity; the long straight lines of the roof match the countryside. But as the land decks itself with a rapture of wild flowers and the sea spills its treasure in countless secret bays, so this great church with a plain exterior is all beautiful within.

Close to the Cathedral stands the ruined Bishop's Palace, fantastic as a fairy tale, and between them runs a little stream, smothered in a water-weed and the legends of Christendom. There are times, under the May moon, when the Cathedral is silver and the Palace dull gold. Next day they have changed parts: it is the Palace that flashes with magnificence, the light catching the parapet of delicate arches which top its walls, with their checker-work of coloured stones, while the Cathedral has faded into the lilac dusk of a spring evening.

*

Lettice lived and brought up her children in a square stone house opposite the grey market Cross. She was a rigid but not a bigoted nonconformist, which meant that she went every Sunday to the Independent Chapel, standing bleak and upright above the old city wall; yet the rain washed gravestones of her forerunners from both church and chapel still lean today in the shadow of the Cathedral.

She lived in days that seem to us now incredibly peaceful and serene, yet her grandparents had helped to cut off the lead pipes from their Cathedral to cast bullets when the invading French landed a few miles away.

She wore crinolines and smoothly parted hair in her youth, which had given place to frills and ringlets by the time of this story. She spoke English to her husband and children, Welsh to her servants, and both in turn to her farmer cousins who filled the house on Fair days, but she could never repeat a word of the Bible in anything but Welsh.

She had travelled round the world but preferred her own city, and although the coming of the motor car has brought some changes, she would not find it very different today.

St. Idris has outlived many convulsions in men's history, and still each year the wild flowers return to the sheltered banks of the lanes, and the children of the new generation still smell the heady wine of flowering gorse along the cliffs as they run joyfully to the sea.

Chapter 1

Matty's Holiday

On the last day of June 1880, the Stone House at the corner of the Cross of St. Idris was in a state of bustle and excitement. It was usually the quietest and most orderly of houses, in so far as any place that holds four children can be said to be quiet and orderly. If the master of the house, Captain Peters, had been more often at home, life would have been more stirring, but he was so frequently away at sea for such long absences, stretching from winter to summer and back to winter again, that the house had fallen into the quiet mood of a woman's rule.

Mrs Peters, with her two excellent servants, Marged and Catherine Jane, ordered the days to suit herself and the comings and goings of the children. Ivor and Archie, the two elder, attended Dr. Prout's school near the Cathedral ; Matty had recently joined the troop of boys and girls who ran every day to Miss Carlyle's school at the foot of the hill, and little Philip still trotted at his mother's skirts. Except when relations called in before driving back to the country from St. Idris there were few disturbances.

But on this summer's day the house was topsy-turvy, and no one felt it more keenly than Matty as she stood on the steps of the back door above the periwinkle bed and looked ruefully across the yard. For today was a whole holiday at Miss Carlyle's school, and as this was Matty's first quarter (no one ever spoke of a 'term') it was the first whole holiday of her life.

Ivor and Archie were for ever talking of their holidays and considered Matty too babyish to join in the conversation. But now her day of days had come and Mamma had promised, a whole week ago, that she and Philip should have a picnic at Silversands with Shoni Shoemaker's donkey cart.

Alas for these fair hopes!

Matty had wakened early that morning in the little room over the front hall, where she slept alone, and sitting bolt upright in bed had immediately seen that the sun was shining on the roofs of the houses on the opposite side of the Cross. Dressing herself with difficulty but determination, she slipped past her mother's door and the room where Ivor and Archie lay abed. Catherine Jane was washing the front steps and Marged was in the kitchen 'balling' the culm fire and tossing the egg-shaped pieces from one hand to another. She called out in Welsh to Matty, 'Are you going to wash your face in the dew that you are up so early?'

Matty ran out into the sunny yard, past the mounting block under the two sycamore trees, and the hooded well where the big ferns thrust up their green fists, past the little stable, the outer kitchen and the culm-house, and opened the door into the garden. But she did not wait here.

The path ran between a vegetable patch and a flowerbed where the red and white 'York and Lancaster' roses were mixed with fat peonies and crimson fuchsia trees leaned over the beds of lettuce and parsley. At the far end of the long narrow garden was an arbour overgrown with sweetbrier where Matty loved to bring her favourite story books, but today she did not linger there. Instead she lifted the latch of the garden door, a pointed Gothic door with a faintly ecclesiastical air, and stepped into the Back Lane.

The Back Lane was not forbidden country but it was the beginning of all adventure. To the right lay the path to 'Hannah the Milk', where the children were sometimes sent for an extra jug of cream; the other way led to the sea, to Crab Bay, their favourite place for everyday bathes.

Matty did not follow either of these roads; she had her

own cherished plan, a ritual kept for special occasions. First she sought her 'Staircase' – a series of small footholds in the grassy bank in which only Matty's eyes could perceive a sequence and design. They carried her up the bank, to the little path which ran along the top and was used by grown-ups in winter to avoid the muddy lane below. But in the late spring and summer months grown-ups inexplicably chose to walk on the road, and the 'hedges', as the grassy banks were called in the country round St. Idris, were left to delight the children who never set foot in land or field if it were possible to run aloft. Certainly the children had the best of the view, and all the flowers as well.

When primroses and violets had vanished summer brought the high tide of wild roses and convolvulus, dog daisies, blue scabious and flaming poppies. They were all there that morning of Matty's holiday, though the great gorse bushes, round which she jumped to avoid scratching her bare legs, had not yet given out their sweetness to the morning sun.

The day was so clear that Matty could see every landmark of her world. There were the green leaves of the sycamore trees behind the Stone House, the pampas grass in the middle of the lawn next door belonging to Mr Daniels Jenkins, and all the huddle of white and grey houses that stood round the Cross and toppled down the hill to the Cathedral towers; a broken arch which was part of the ruined Bishop's Palace, and the dark rocks of Carn Idris. Beyond and round the green country was the enchanting, never-forgotten sea, caressing the headlands, whispering to the little bays and calling all day to the children to come and play on its shores.

Matty had almost decided that when she grew up she would build herself a house on the edge of Crab Bay, for since she was a girl and could not go away to sea as her father did and as Ivor and Archie would do one day, the next best thing was to live close to the sea and hear it pounding on the rocks as she lay in her cupboard bed at night, and open the door to find it again when she woke each morning.

When Ivor and Archie came home from their voyages they would visit her, and she would pack their sea chests for them when they went away. But Philip would live with her always and would have another little cupboard bed in a corner of her room. By that time of course their parents would be so old that they would both be dead and Matty would have to be both father and mother to Philip.

Just as she was thinking about all this she noticed Mr Rees Parry's geese in the next field and altered her course, because she hated geese and the haughty way in which they stretched their necks at people. Turning along another bank she ran towards the sea with the wind ruffling her hair.

She was glad that the picnic would be at Silversands today because it was so far off and it meant hiring Shoni Shoemaker's donkey cart. Mamma had sent her down to Shoni's the day before to ask for Moses, the best donkey. Catherine Jane would come with them too, for she loved picnics and was a great help in finding firewood and getting the kettle to boil. Marged would stay at home to give the boys their tea when they came home from school, but she had baked yesterday and made Matty and Philip two little loaves of crisp bread to eat at the picnic. They would stow their bathing clothes and towels as well as the baskets of food and the big kettle in the bottom of the donkey cart, and set out in good time so that they would have as long as possible on the sands. It was a pity that Ivor and Archie would miss such a treat, and yet she felt it very important that she and Philip should have a holiday all to themselves. It would show the others that although she and Philip were the youngest they were babies no longer.

The sun was growing hot on Matty's back, so she sat down on the bank and watched Mr Rees Parry's cow scratch herself on the big stone standing upright in the middle of the field. The stone was placed there just for scratching, since there were few trees round St. Idris, and Mr Rees Parry's cow was taking full advantage of it.

Matty smoothed her sprigged cotton frock and pulled up her white socks. Her black elastic-sided boots were powdered yellow by the buttercups, and looking at them Matty wished once more that Mamma would give her a pair of yellow tan boots. If only she could possess those and a puggaree on her hat like the summer visitors who came to stay at St. Idris, she fancied she would be completely happy.

After she had said the words 'completely happy' to herself she wondered if they were quite true. Would there still be something left to wish for, even when she was wearing a puggaree and yellow tan boots? Was there not always her great longing to be a boy, so that she could go away to sea? There was another wish too, her desire that she might be as beautiful as the day. But in this respect she had suffered a grave disappointment when recently she had slipped into her mother's room and picked up the mahogany-backed mirror. Standing with her back half turned to the looking-glass, as she had so often seem Mamma stand when she was arranging her curls, she had succeeded in seeing, for the first time in her life, her own nose and chin in profile.

Whether she had expected to see someone as ravishing as Rowena in *Ivanhoe* or as lovely as the lady Christabel in the illustrated works of Coleridge, she could never afterwards explain ; but what she actually saw filled her with mortification. In Matty's opinion she was utterly hideous and she vowed she would never look in a hand mirror again as long as she lived. She had taken the vow two days ago and she remembered it again this morning, a little sadly. Yet why she should have felt so bitterly deceived by her own reflection would have puzzled anyone who saw her sitting there, a slight, fair-haired child with steadfast grey-blue eyes, straight nose and resolute chin. But at this moment there was no need for resolution ; no need to tighten her lips and tilt her chin, for today was the crowning day of the summer, the sun was shining and it was a whole holiday. With that thought she jumped up and started to run back, for she was suddenly very hungry and knew that Marged would be stirring the porridge over the kitchen fire.

But when she stepped over the threshold of the back door there was no one in the kitchen, and she ran straight through to the dining-room, expecting to find her mother and all the family seated round the table. Again the room was empty. Ivor and Archie had evidently finished their breakfasts, for their chairs were pushed back from the table, but the plate and cup at her mother's place were untouched. Overhead she heard the sound of hurried footsteps and of drawers being opened and closed. It was all very puzzling and unlike home.

In the lobby she met Archie carrying a butterfly net and his school books.

'Where's Mamma?' she asked. Archie cocked his head on one side.

'Haven't you heard? Mamma's going away.'

'What do you mean, going away? She's not going away today.'

'Yes, she is, my girl,' said Archie coolly. 'She's going to a place called Dundee, hundreds of miles away from here, and I don't suppose you've the faintest notion where it is. You don't learn geography at Miss Carlyle's school.'

'We do learn geography,' cried Matty hotly. 'We learn it in a brown book with questions and answers on the same page and I'm more than halfway through already.'

'That's a pretty silly way,' said Archie in a superior voice, swinging his books to and fro in their strap. He went down the steps into the street, stopping to call back, 'Anyway, Mamma's going away and you don't know the reason why.'

Mamma going away! Speechless, Matty stood at the foot of the stairs, her world suddenly fallen into pieces. Why should she go today, today of all days? She must have forgotten the picnic, forgotten that Shoni Shoemaker's donkey cart was already ordered. If she had remembered for one moment that it was Matty's holiday she would never have done such a thing, such a cruel, heartless thing.

Up the stairs she ran, stumbling in her haste, and straight up to her mother's room. It was true, what Archie had said. In the middle of the room was Mamma's ark-shaped trunk, and kneeling in front of it was Catherine Jane, her arms full of clothes. Mamma herself was standing with her back to the door at the open wardrobe and was lifting down her best and prettiest frock, the cinnamon pineapple muslin, trimmed with little bows of brown velvet.

At that sight something like a sob rose in Matty's throat. 'Mamma, Mamma,' she cried, 'you can't be going away today!'

Her mother laughed her light, low laugh and dropped the muslin dress over her arm.

'Can't I?' she said. 'It all depends on whether Catherine Jane can get this trunk packed fast enough. The fly will be here in half an hour. Miss Richards is coming to look after you. Now run away, Matty dear, and don't worry us.'

Matty went slowly out of the bedroom and into the nursery next door. Philip was sitting at the table in the window and Marged was giving him his breakfast of bread and milk.

'Marged, why is Mamma going away? She's forgotten all about the picnic.'

'I daresay she has, missy,' said Marged, scraping round the bowl with the spoon. 'She isn't likely to remember a thing like that today.'

'But why? It's our whole holiday at Miss Carlyle's.'

'Now then, missy, be reasonable. How can you expect your mamma to be thinking about your holiday with papa coming home after all this long while, bless her heart!'

Matty stood silent in the middle of the nursery, her head whirling. Papa coming home! She knew she ought to be glad, she ought to be happy, but she couldn't even remember what he looked like, having a confused picture in her mind made up of memory, hearsay and the picture on her mother's dressing-table. And why, oh why, had it happened today?

Mamma had gone, bound on a long journey of several days for a strange, unfriendly place called Dundee to meet Papa's ship, and Nansi Richards in her black lace cap and with the mole on her chin had come to look after them. None of them loved Miss Richards much, though they had often heard Mamma declare how good she was and how trustworthy. She was small and bent and very precise. Her mother, it was said, had worn a red cloak and marched along the shore to frighten the French when Napoleon tried a landing in Wales. She used to tell how the people ran down the streets of St. Idris calling out, 'The French have landed!'

Matty got this story mixed up and imagined that it was Nansi who had marched to her country's aid. It was a consoling thought, after a sharp rebuke from Miss Richards for not wiping one's feet, that even the French soldiery had quailed at the sight of her.

Ivor and Archie came home to midday dinner and there was much talk about the voyage of the *Zouave*, and surmise as to whether Papa would bring back a monkey or a parrot. Ivor could remember that once he brought a monkey, which escaped from the house into the country and climbed in at the window of an old bedridden woman. She wakened to find it sitting on the bedpost, and never having seen a monkey in her life, thought she had died and the devil come to fetch her soul. Miss Richards shook her head over this story and hoped there would be no more monkeys, but Archie wanted a blue-nosed baboon and a chest full of gold bars.

'Matty, do you remember what Papa looks like?' asked Ivor.

'Of course I do,' said Matty stoutly.

'Well then, tell us what he does look like,' Archie demanded.

'I shan't,' said Matty, 'because I know you know, so why should I tell you?'

This was certainly a point scored, but Archie persisted, 'How tall is he? Is he taller than Mr Rees Parry? I don't believe you have the faintest notion of him.'

'Don't tease her, Archie,' Miss Richards interposed. 'You ought to be thankful that your dear papa is coming home to you, safe and sound, instead of wrangling among yourselves. Now it's time that you and Ivor were off to school again.'

Miss Richards meant to be kind, but without Mamma the house had lost its centre and mainspring. As though to make matters worse, Marged and Catherine Jane had a fever of cleaning and scoured the house from top to bottom to make it ready for the Captain's homecoming. Early in the bright, beautiful afternoon Shoni Shoemaker's son, Willie, came to the door to ask if the donkey cart were wanted, as his father had heard that Captain Peters' ship was home and Mrs Peters gone to meet him. So Mamma had even forgotten to tell Shoni!

Miss Richards said no thank you, no donkey cart would be needed today, and Matty stood at the nursery window watching Willie run across the square.

There were two windows in the nursery and from the corner one she could see past the worn stone Cross that stood in the middle of the street to the blue sea breaking far away on the rocks.

By now they should have been starting for the picnic, clip-clopping, clip-clopping past the houses and out into the country, between the green banks and the yellow gorse bushes. Mamma would be wearing her hat of leghorn straw and holding up her skirt in her hands. Catherine Jane would lead Moses, with Philip sitting proudly on the driver's seat holding the reins, and Matty would run along the top of the banks, calling out to the others all the things she could see.

The tears rose in Matty's eyes as she pictured this scene, but she fought them back, knowing them to be poor, despicable things, and asked Philip what game he would like to play. He chose 'driving to the station', one of their favourite inventions, and together they dragged out the 'horse' from his corner.

Now the horse was nothing more than a wooden stool which had been made by the ship's carpenter in the *Zouave*, and had a piece of brownish carpet nailed to the top. But it served the children as both steed and carriage, and on its sturdy, prancing form they would go long journeys to the places of their imagination. Today they played that they were driving to the railway station at Westford. Sixteen miles and seventeen hills they covered, just as Mamma had done that morning, stopping at Sarnau to call on Aunt Rachel, losing a shoe on Croesty Hill and having a new one fitted by the blacksmith with loud blowing of the bellows and sizzling of hot iron.

They had gone thus far on their journey when Catherine Jane appeared with dusters and brooms and announced that she wished to 'turn out' the nursery. So downstairs they went, a little dispirited, to the lobby which proved an even better place for a gallop. To and fro they pranced, the two of them astride the wooden stool, making it rock and curvet and bump beneath them over the polished boards.

'Children, children, whatever are you doing here? Don't you know that Marged has just finished beeswaxing the lobby, and here you come, messing and scratching it with your old stool!'

Here was Miss Richards in her sternest mood, and shamefacedly the two children dismounted.

'But why in the world do you stay indoors on such a fine afternoon?' Miss Richards went on. 'Can't you find a nice quiet game to play in the garden? Matty, take your little brother out of doors and look after him, and leave us to finish the cleaning. There's little enough time, dear knows.'

So it was that they went out into the yard, where Matty, standing above the periwinkle bed by the back door, considered the vanity of life and the wretchedness of her lot. Philip trotted to the empty stable, on his own devices, while Matty slowly walked to the old mounting block, where it stood between the two sycamore trees. Its platform of grey weathered stone made a perfect stage, and here Matty would recite long poems, waving her arms after the fashion of Eisteddfod competitors. Often she would strut up and down the narrow stage, enacting scenes of her own invention and taking the part of each character in turn. But today she had no heart for such antics and stood moodily looking into the next door yard.

Mr and Mrs Dan Jenkins, with whom they shared the ferny drinking well, lived in a substantial grey house and had once kept their own carriage and pair. But now they were grown very old and fat and somehow less rich, and the stable at the end of their yard was as empty of horses as the sea captain's next door. Mrs Jenkins would occasionally call on Mrs Peters for a chat, and her unvarying remark on seeing any of the children was,

> *Where has pussy gone to?*
> *Pussy's gone away!*

— which she repeated in a high sing-song voice. Matty never knew the answer and had taken to running away, like Pussy, when she saw Mrs Jenkins approach. She saw her now at the far end of the garden, her white cap bobbing among the pea sticks.

But at this moment there was the sound of jaunty whistling and into the yard came Wallie Flanagan.

The Flanagans were an Irish family and the most troublesome in all St. Idris. If ever there were any rowdy trouble at a fair, or young men had up before the bench for stealing a goose, or taking the gates off their hinges on New Year's Eve, the Flanagans were sure to have a hand in it. Wallie was the youngest of the family and had not long left school.

He was prominent at all pleasure fairs, and was one of the boys who devoured a plateful of boiling pudding for a prize of sixpence, seated on a platform among the flares and merry-go-rounds, before the gaping crowds. He was a sharp featured youth with a cheeky tongue and had lately taken to delivering the weekly newspaper – the *Idrisland Gazette* – round the city in return for a few pence.

Now, in Matty's opinion, there were three desirable occupations: going to sea, keeping a bookshop and delivering newspapers. She had often wished that she might go round St. Idris, armed with a pile of *Idrisland Gazettes*, rapping smartly at all the doors and flinging the *Gazettes* deftly on to the doormats.

The reason for Wallie's coming to the back door instead of to the front steps of the Stone House was a piece of laziness on his part. He had just delivered a paper at the sweet and tea cake shop at the corner, and the shortest way from one house to another was through the back alley, past the Peters' ashpit. Here he now appeared and, marching up to the open door, slapped the *Gazette* down on the threshold and turned to go. Seeing Matty on the mounting block he grinned cheerfully and set off towards the Jenkins' house next door.

Matty jumped down from the mounting block, a new idea suddenly bubbling in her head.

'Have you lots more papers to do?' she asked.

Wallie nodded. 'Top of the town, Rees Parry's and Maesteg.'

Matty drew a deep breath. 'Can I come with you?' she asked. 'I could push them through the doors for you, you know.'

'As you like,' said Wallie, who was a mannerless boy.

'Then I'll come and bring Philip too,' said Matty and called, 'Philip, Philip, come quick, I've got a lovely plan!' Obediently Philip abandoned his occupation of sticking twigs in between the white pebbles round the periwinkle bed and trotted after Matty.

No one saw them go out of the yard and up the street with the graceless Wallie or it is probable that they would have been stopped and sent home again. But in the main street of the city only a dog or two lay basking, and the bushes of crimson fuchsia outside the cottage doors glowed in the afternoon sunshine.

Matty was enjoying herself. The aimless day had suddenly found a centre, and the pleasure of the adventure was so far quite equal to her expectations. Wallie was quite willing to hand over his duties and loafed along the road, whistling and occasionally shying a stone at a bird, while his two confederates pushed open the front gates of the houses and trotted up the paths to deposit their papers within the stout whitewashed porches, flanked by bushes of veronica and hydrangea.

Then they came to the end of the houses and turned down a lane to Rees Parry's farm.

Matty had already evaded his geese that morning, but in her present company they were less alarming. Round the corner of the pink-washed farm buildings they trudged and up to the door of the farmhouse, with its ivied well and sturdy Flemish chimney. Here for the first time a twinge of conscience seized Matty. She knew Miss Rees Parry, a rigid black-haired woman who occupied the Chapel pew in front of the Peters family on Sunday mornings. In fact, Matty knew precisely the shape and number of the jet ornaments on Miss Parry's bonnet and the twists and whirls of the braid on her cape, far better than did that lady herself.

Approaching the front door, she realised that she would not be completely happy if Miss Parry's black eyes fell on the ill-assorted party of Wallie, Philip and herself.

'You do that one,' she said to Wallie, and pulled Philip back behind the low wall.

'Afraid of the old girl?' asked Wallie impudently. 'All right, you watch me shy this one from here.' And he showed them how he flicked the newspaper on to the doorstep without troubling to open the gate.

After that they crossed the fields to Maesteg, a farm that Matty barely knew by name and whose people were unknown to her.

By this time Philip's short legs were growing tired, and although he manfully kept up a jog-trot beside Wallie's stride Matty knew that he had had enough. Crossing the fields meant climbing up and down the banks, and Wallie did not trouble to wait for them. He would spring on to the grassy top and jump down the other side, while Matty laboriously hauled Philip up beside her and then looked for a place where they could both slide down.

Philip's bare legs were scratched with gorse bushes and his socks stuck all over with burrs and goose-grass by the time they arrived, flushed and dishevelled, at Maesteg. The farmer was turning his cows out from the milking shed and took the paper from Wallie at the gate, nodding to the children and calling out in Welsh that it looked like rain.

There were indeed black clouds piling up behind Carn Idris, so that the rays of the sun struck like shafts across the bare country and dazzled the children's eyes as they followed their guide down a rutty lane that led past the farm.

'Where are we going now?' Matty asked.

Wallie glanced back over his shoulder. He was growing tired, he told himself, of two kids tagging along behind and thought he would put an end to the matter.

'I dunno where you're going, but I'm off to Craigclais to look for gulls' eggs. You'd better get home to your mammy, the two of you. So long!' And with that Master Wallie Flanagan hoisted himself over the bank and disappeared from their sight. They heard him whistling on his way.

Philip sat down firmly and suddenly on the grassy bank. 'I'se hungry,' he announced. 'I wants Catherine Jane.' Matty pulled him up gently.

'We'll go and find her,' she said, 'then she'll give you your supper. What would you like best for supper, Philip?'

'Jelly,' said Philip, surprisingly, 'I'd like yellow jelly.'

'Pink is nicest,' said Matty. 'I had a pink jelly at Aunt Hannah Williams' party – it was the most lovely thing I've tasted in all my life.'

'And I'd like a currant loaf,' Philip continued, 'and a sausage and a toffee apple.'

'But you couldn't have them all at once,' Matty objected prudently. Then she stopped short in the lane. Were they walking in the right direction? Maesteg lay behind them, but the lane had taken a sudden surprising turn leftwards, towards the sea, and seemed to show not the slightest intention of returning to St. Idris.

'Wait here a minute, Philip,' she ordered, and climbed up the bank to get a view from the top. There was nothing to be seen but fields. The bank was not a high one – it would be easy to pull Philip over it, and once on the other side Matty was sure she could find her way home.

So up, over and down came Philip and away they went across the next field, where their long shadows went before them through the grass and a few grazing sheep raised their heads to stare at the children. Beyond that field was another, a small hay field thick with sorrel, buttercups and white moon daisies. Matty knew well enough that they must not walk across growing hay, so they kept to the top of the bank till a gate forced them down. The gate did not seem to lead in the right direction and up they clambered again and round the second side of the hay field, and then, by an easy jump, down into a boggy meadow where yellow flags and kingcups were growing. They stopped to pick some of these and Matty got one of her shoes soaked in bog water.

Philip was now so tired that she started to tell him a long story about a giant, a saint and a spotted cow, half invention, half memory of one of the many legends of the countryside

– but she was growing tired herself and the story grew more and more mixed.

'What did he do when the giant cut his head off?' Philip asked.

'He put it under his arm and swam across the water to the other side.'

'But was it all right?' Philip put a hand anxiously round his own plump neck.

'Absolutely all right,' Matty assured him. 'He put it on again and there wasn't even a mark.'

'Then why did the giant cut it off? Wasn't he silly?'

'He didn't know when he cut his head off that the saint was good enough to mend his own head. Now we must go over this hedge. I'll go first and pull you up.'

'I don't want to climb over any more hedges – they're all prickly.'

'Oh yes, Philip, you must. Look, you go first this time and I'll push you.'

But this bank was not a kind one. There were gorse bushes on top and the other side was thick with nettles. Clambering down, Philip fell headlong.

'The wicked, nasty nettles,' he sobbed, 'they hurted me all over.'

Matty sat down on a grassy place against the bank and took Philip on her lap.

'Philip, we won't walk any more. I'll pretend you're my little boy and I'm your mamma, and then you'll go fast asleep.'

Phillip curled against her, comforted.

'And wasn't there even a little tiny mark where he stuck the head on again?' he asked drowsily.

'No,' said Matty, 'not even a little tiny one.' And with that assurance Philip fell asleep.

A white moth touched her face, but she did not move a hand to brush it away for fear she should waken Philip. She still felt sure that she could find her way home – a few more fields to cross, a few more banks to scramble over and they would certainly be there. Ivor and Archie must have come home from school long ago and they would be eating their suppers in the nursery. Matty had never before felt so hungry. But she knew Philip could go no further and she must never desert Philip.

Behind the bank on which they leaned something moved with a slow, tearing sound. Matty wondered if it were a cow or whether one of the saints might be walking about the fields, as they were said to do on summer evenings. But only good people met the saints and Matty was sure she wasn't good enough. If she were really good she wouldn't have gone walking with Willie Flanagan.

There was another thing troubling her. When Archie had asked her if she remembered Papa she had pretended that she did, but was she really sure? At the bottom of her heart she knew that she had no notion at all of how he looked.

Philip had grown very heavy and she longed to shift one of her arms, but she kept quite still, even when 'pins and needles' pricked it. She was Philip's 'little mother' and mothers never thought of themselves. The breeze thrummed in the gorse bushes overhead and far away a sheep bleated. Then the sky and hedgerow faded, blurred with the uncertain edges of evening, and Matty fell asleep.

The end of that day was never very clear in Matty's memory. Into a dream, where she and Philip feasted on pink jelly in the company of a headless saint, came two men carrying a lantern. It was dark, and she was cold and glad of the comfortable feel and smell of a coat wrapped round her. Hoisted into the arms of one of the men she fell asleep again, but awakened once or twice at the roughness of the way. Whenever she opened her eyes there was a bobbing lantern going in front with the other man and a bundle in his arms that was Philip.

After that came the bright light of the house and Miss Richards crying at the foot of the stairs. But this couldn't be the same day on which Miss Richards had scolded them both for riding their horse up and down the lobby. That must have happened yesterday or some other day. And Miss Richards must have forgotten, for now she was hugging them both. Her cheek was much rougher than Mamma's and Matty did not like the dampness of her tears. How long had they been lost? she asked when she was sitting on the kitchen windowsill a few minutes later, while Catherine Jane was taking off her boots and socks.

But Catherine Jane would say nothing but 'Oh duwch, duwch, whatever was it that came into you heads to run away like that?'

'But we weren't running away,' Matty explained, 'we were helping Wallie Flanagan to take round the newspapers.'

'Wallie Flanagan indeed! Isn't that just like the wickedness of that good-for-nothing boy!' Catherine Jane cried out, but Marged stopped her.

'Hush now, they're safe and unhurt, praise God. Here is some lovely gruel I have made for you, Matty fach. Eat it up now, cariad, and don't trouble your head with anything at all.'

Marged sat down beside her with the bowl and Matty obediently opened her mouth like a hungry bird in its nest. The warm bright kitchen glowed round them and made a pool of light in front of the fire where Philip was sitting in a bath with Miss Richards kneeling on the floor beside him.

Some days after this the Captain and his wife came home. They arrived in the evening, when Matty and Philip were in bed and Ivor and Archie had special leave to stay up late. From her little room above the hall Matty heard the fly stop before the door and saw the reflection of the carriage lights waver on the ceiling. She longed to jump out of bed, to rush down the stairs into Mamma's arms, but something held her there.

Suppose, after all, Papa was quite different from the picture in her mind?

She heard the clamour of her brothers, her mother's voice and a strange, deep one joining in and laughing great gusts of laughter. Then they were all coming upstairs, walking softly so as not to waken Philip.

In a flash she was out of bed, had flung open the door and run out to the landing. Mamma, her dear pretty Mamma, was hurrying towards her in a long dark cloak, her bonnet fallen back from her head, shining curls hanging on either shoulder. Behind her, tall as a house, filling the narrow landing and towering above Mamma, was a great fair-haired giant with laughing blue eyes and a yellow beard. Hugged close in Mamma's arms, peeping over her shoulder, Matty rapidly adjusted her ideas. There wasn't any beard in the photograph on Mamma's dressing table.

Her notion of Papa had been completely and entirely wrong. But she would never, no never, let Archie know!

Chapter 2

Nantgwyn

The Captain was home. The *Zouave* had gone into dock for overhaul and the long days of summer would be over before he sailed again.

Lettice Peters, his wife, hummed softly to herself about the house, and wakened each morning with a little start of joy. Remembering the calendars of her school days, where date after date was scored off with a neat stroke and a bold many coloured circle adorned the first day of the holidays; she wished that somehow she could reverse the process and spin out the days like a spider's thread, finer and finer, longer and longer, a silken rope on which to swing for ever.

The first visit to be paid, now that John was home, was to Grandfather Merion at Nantgwyn, the farm where Lettice had been born and brought up and where John Peters was as great a favourite as any son of the house.

Tom Pugh's wagonette and horses were ordered for two o'clock on a fine afternoon and the children made ready in time, the boys in their Sunday suits and clean collars, Matty in her fresh gingham, trimmed with curly braid, and a leghorn hat, Philip in his little tartan frock.

But the three eldest ones were nearly late on account of the presents which Papa had brought them from America – three glossy, top-heavy tricycles, machines such as the streets of St. Idris had never before seen. Ivor, Archie and Matty, circling the Cross among a group of admiring and envious children, were hailed with admonitions and threats that they would be left behind if they did not come in immediately and change their clothes.

Lettice had shaken her head a little ruefully over this latest extravagance of John's. She knew he could not really afford the presents he heaped on the family with so lavish a hand. The chests of tea from Ceylon were all very well, and so were the jars of preserved ginger and Chinese chow-chow, guava cheeses from Brazil and barrels of dried apples from California. All these were welcome additions to her store-cupboard.

But Lettice was not so sure about the chinchilla furs which he had brought this time for herself and Matty. Expensive furs were not suitable for a six-year-old child. Were they really suitable for Lettice herself, though her mirror told her how flattering were the soft, smoky skins to her fair colour and grey eyes? These thoughts, chasing through her mind as she dressed herself, were not really disturbing. She knew her good fortune in having such a husband. There was no one in the world like him, she thought exultantly – certainly she had never met anyone who could hold a candle to her handsome, lavish, fearless John.

'If I'd married a skinflint,' she said to herself, closing a drawer with a snap, 'I couldn't have borne it.'

The sound of wheels stopping outside announced the arrival of Tom Pugh's wagonette and she ran to the landing.

'Children, are you ready? Matty, come and let me see if you're tidy. Ivor, tell Papa that the carriage is here. Where is Archie, and has he got a clean pocket handkerchief?'

At last they were all packed into the wagonette, rattling cheerfully down the main street of St. Idris and out into the countryside.

The three elder children kept up a stream of chatter with their father. Why hadn't he brought back a monkey this time? What had happened to the cook's parrot which talked three languages? Had he heard about the rocket drill at St. Idris and how Ivor had persuaded Johnny Morris, the cox, to let him travel in the breeches buoy? What was it really like to walk about on a coral reef, and was it true that if you put both thumbs into a shark's eyes when it was biting off your leg it would let you go?

Lettice leant back in her seat, thankful that there was someone else, and that one so excellently fitted, to answer such questions. Philip's chubby hand lay in hers and she could feel the pressure of his small, firm body against her side. Of all her children he was the quietest and most easily pleased, a round, sweet apple of a child, as full of good sense as good humour. He had brought a toy monkey with him today, but was content to sit quietly by his mother, watching Tom Pugh's broad back and the wandering tassel of his whip as it flicked the flies off the horses' flanks.

Lettice breathed contentment. To be driving home to see her own people, John and the four children with her all in good health on a fine summer day, was the fullness of happiness. Watching the wind run over the silver oats and feathery barley, she knew without putting the thought into words that her life was brimful as the harvest fields, as though the tide were in everywhere – there beyond St. Idris Head where she could see the white waves break lazily on the rocks, here in the brimming fields and, last of all, in her own heart. Catching her husband's eye she smiled, and then turned her head because of the tears that came suddenly, why or wherefore she could not tell, to dim the scene.

A mile from Nantgwyn, in a dip of the road, stood a little whitewashed Ebenezer and three or four cottages, coloured in shades of apricot. In one of them lived William Bowen, a seafaring man with earrings and a grizzled red beard. He had served as steward to Captain Peters on many voyages and never missed an occasion to greet his homecoming. So now, as the horses trotted down the little dip, with a grinding of brakes, the red ensign of the Merchant Service fluttered on the flagstaff outside the Bowens' door, and drawn up on the road in front were Bowen, his wife and Old Richard, Mrs Bowen's father, once a tailor and now close on a hundred years old, with long white hair and beard.

'I see you've got it up, Bowen,' called out Captain Peters, glancing at the staff head.

'Yes, Cap'n. It's the one you gave me when I said goodbye to the old *Zouave* for the last time.'

Then out of the carriage they must all bundle to shake the family by the hand and tell Old Richard that he looked younger than ever.

'It isn't true,' thought Lettice, wondering how it was possible to appear so far away from this world and yet continue to live in it. But that was the accepted way of talking to old people and perhaps the only one; it saved the trouble of thinking things out afresh.

Soon it was time to repack themselves in the carriage and to take the last mile of the road that led to Nantgwyn, waving goodbye, as they trotted uphill, to the Bowens and Old Richard, leaning tremulously on his stick beneath the fluttering ensign.

Grandfather's people had lived at Nantgwyn for generations and there was a saying among the family that everyone born at Nantgwyn knew what was best – the best came from Nantgwyn. Not that the soil was noted for richness; the farms on this western end of the county could not compare with the fat land to the north and east; but everything that grew at Nantgwyn had a peculiar sweetness, shared even by the blackberries, the hazel nuts and the field mushrooms.

Lettice never came away without a basket of good things stowed in the carriage, and if the season of fruit and cream cheeses was past then there were home-made jams and perhaps a pumpkin to take back to St. Idris. Today she was glad to think that she had something to bring in return, two guava cheeses from Rio and a bag of Brazilian coffee berries.

The long, low building which lay before them as they turned into the home lane, with its Flemish chimney, a solid, round mass of masonry, rising in the middle, had housed the Merion family since the days of the Monmouth Rebellion when, it was said, a certain James Merion, escaping from the Bloody Assizes of the West Country, had landed quietly on the Welsh shore from a little coasting vessel out of Bristol.

Whether or no that was true, they were sturdy nonconformists, those early Merions, and many of the chapels of the district were built on their land. Farmer, preacher, preacher, farmer – often they filled both parts and the word of God was sown no less vigorously than the crops of oats and barley in the sea-girt fields.

Lettice could remember her father's father, a little man of almost frightening energy, coming in from the hay meadow to write a theological treatise. He was an old man then, but in his thirties he had been in charge of eight churches, three in Pembrokeshire, two in Montgomeryshire and three in Merioneth. They were separated by a hundred hilly miles and he would journey from one to another on a famous grey horse which was surely as doughty a campaigner as his master.

Sometimes the preacher's wife came too, riding behind on a pillion. Lettice often thought with envy of her grandmother, leaving the complicated house behind her to ride out with her man, setting forth in the grey dewiness of morning, following the old Roman road, Sarn Helen, across the uplands of Cardigan, seeing the woods and streams of Montgomery and coming after many days through a gap in the hills to a little chapel by the seashore in Merioneth.

Lettice, who in the first year of her marriage had followed John across tropic seas to strange cities, felt jealous of her grandmother, who could set out at morning and come to a night's lodging among friends, with her husband's broad shoulders going before, and the kindly Welsh tongue still sounding in her ears.

'But today I have everything that I can desire,' she said to herself as the wagonette drew up at the last gate and the children called out that they spied old Polly, the brown mare, and Cadwalader, the pet lamb, grown to a prodigious size.

They were all waiting outside the house; Father with his white hair, aquiline nose and high cheek bones, erect and handsome in his spotless cravat; beside him Martha, the only daughter left at home, and Jim, Lettice's favourite brother, with his sheepdog, Rattle, nuzzling his hand.

Between Lettice and her sister there was a close bond. 'How is it with you?' their eyes telegraphed before they had kissed each other. Already the children had swarmed round Uncle Jim, and now they were dragging him away to field and outhouse and all the places where he reigned supreme, Philip riding happily on his shoulder. Lettice watched them go and then turned to follow the others indoors.

They went through the little garden, full of hydrangeas, fuchsias and flowering currant bushes, under the square porch into the broad, low passage hung with whips and hunting crops.

To the left lay the big kitchen and Lettice would have liked to open the door and go straight in, as she had done in her childhood. But now that old Betti the cook, who had been there longer than anyone could remember, was dead, no one expected Lettice to run into the kitchen. She was a married daughter of the house, she who had been the youngest and the wildest, and she followed Martha down the wide, flagged passage, past the deep windowsill where stood now, as it had stood all through her childhood, one of those strange plants fashionable in the Pembrokeshire farmhouses. Its long, straight leaves sprang out on either side at regular intervals from a central stalk, and each leaf was carefully rolled up and tied with bits of coloured silk and wool, so that the plant resembled scrolled ironwork more than any living growth.

It was like Martha, Lettice thought, to carry on this odd bit of tradition. None of them, she knew, had liked that queer, tortured plant; Jim had often laughed at it and said it looked like an old woman in curl-papers. But now that Martha ruled the house there was no custom that she did not carefully preserve. It was the unmarried sisters, Lettice reflected, who kept flowing the stream of continuity; not the ones who, like herself, went away and bore children. Merely to bear children, she thought, was a scattering of energy. Old maids kept the essence of life.

By now they were in Penisha – the 'lower end' – the name always given to the comfortable living-room of the house, reached by two steps down, and Father had made her sit in one of the tall armchairs, though she would rather have slipped across to the window seat looking out on to the orchard.

Father was asking John about his voyage and John was telling the old man all the things that would interest and amuse him.

Then, as they talked of Australia, John's quick glance came to rest on one of the photographs hanging on the wall.

'That's Sydney Harbour, isn't it, sir?'

'Yes. My brother Tom sent it home from Australia twenty years ago, and that one, over the desk, is the house he built for himself.'

John got up to examine the two pictures.

'They're pleasant houses, those big ones outside Sydney,' he remarked. 'Your brother did well for himself, sir.'

'Oh, yes, Tom made a fortune and so did my brother Edward, when he followed Tom out there.'

'And you never wanted to go and make a fortune too?'

The old man turned his clear blue eyes on his son-in-law. 'I shouldn't know what to do with a lot of money,' he said simply. 'Great wealth would make it all the more difficult to lead the right life.'

But besides wealth, thought Lettice, there were such things as opportunity and adventure. Others of her grandfather's family had followed learning; she numbered professors and at least two Fellows of the Royal Society among her cousins.

Jim, in manhood, had put away all these ambitions, but in their childhood it was those framed pictures of the Australian houses that had beckoned to him.

'I'll go out there one day, and you shall keep house for me, Letty.'

How often he had said it! For Father's sake only Jim had waited at home, but Father never understood that. When all the others had gone, except Martha, it was Jim who stayed to help with the farm and quietly buried his dreams, while Lettice sailed round the world with another man.

Had Martha buried her dreams too? Lettice turned to look at her sister. That calm brow told no secrets, carried no complaints. Like Jim she had made her peace with the world.

Meanwhile little Matty had slipped away from the others, leaving them to make ducks and drakes over the shallow brook where it ran past the hay field, and had run indoors to the farm kitchen.

The kitchen at Nantgwyn was a place to dream about. The great Flemish chimney alone was as big as a little room, and only a small part of it was taken up by the fire. A settle in front cut it off from the rest of the room, making a little dark chamber where Matty could sit, and finding her usual corner seat within the chimney, could look up the great soot-lined walls to the patch of sky above.

On a rainy day the drops came pattering down and drove one away from this place, but today there was a square of blue at the top, while faint sunlight lit up the rough stones and mortar of the sides. No other occupant as yet shared the chimney with Matty, but she sat down to wait, sure that something would soon happen, as it always did in Grandfather's kitchen.

She had not been there long before there was a clip-clop on the paved floor and in through the open door came a little grey donkey. Matty knew her well; she was Jenny, the water-carrier, whose task it was, twice a day, to draw a hand cart along a rocky road to the well and bring back to the house all the water used for drinking and butter-making. Matty sat still and quiet as a mouse for fear she should startle Jenny and drive her away, but this was quite unnecessary.

With the friendliest, most confident air Jenny made straight for the chimney corner past the barrier of the settle, and stood in front of the fire, warming first one side and then the other.

'I belong here,' she seemed to say, 'I am a servant of this house, and its food and fire are mine by every law of hospitality and service. Who are you, little sister? By what right are you warming yourself at this fire?'

Matty would have liked to answer, but their conversation was cut short by one of the maids, a red-haired girl named Bronwen, who came in with a great cauldron of food for the calves and drove Jenny away.

'Deio! And what next, indeed?' she called out. 'Do you think it is December that you should be warming your sides all day by the fire? Out you go, my girl, into the field until you're wanted, and don't let me have any more of your fine airs.'

The little donkey walked away with an offended look, as though to say, 'You are only a common creature. I shall keep my conversation for those who understand it.'

Bronwen set her pot on the fire and smiled at Matty. 'No sense at all in that donkey,' she said, half apologetically. 'I don't mind the little lambs when they've lost their mothers. They're different, somehow, and they don't take up near so much room – all except Nellie.'

'Who's Nellie?' asked Matty.

'She was the lamb that Rattle adopted. You know our Rattle?'

'Of course,' said Matty, for who that knew Nantgwyn did not know the sheepdog, with his one eye of blue and one of brown?

Bronwen had taken a wooden bowl from a shelf, fetched flour and butter, milk and eggs, and now set about making light cakes for tea. But she went on talking while she rubbed the butter and sifted the flour between her fingers.

'He's clever, Rattle is! Would you believe it, he went blackberrying last summer and, you'll see, he'll be the first to find the ripe ones this year.' He goes trotting along the hedges, choosing the big berries. Even the ones above his head he gets by standing up on his hind legs and biting at them.'

'But what did he and Nellie do?' Matty persisted.

'They wouldn't be parted, just like two dear lovers,' said Bronwen sentimentally. 'Every evening they'd lie down together before the fire. That was well enough when Nellie was a little lamb, but when she grew big there was no sense at all. None of us could get near the fire with a great big old sheep couching there, as well as Rattle and all the other dogs, and the men coming in with wet boots and steaming clothes, dear to goodness!'

'So what did you do?' prompted Matty, never happier than when extracting a story.

'Well, the sheep were fastened up and Nellie with them, but that seemingly made no difference. Rattle and Nellie were there by the fire the same as ever, every evening. So at last your uncle gave orders to take the sheep to a far-off field, with high hedges, the way no one could climb them, and the gate all wired up so as not even a dog could get through a crack of it.'

'And did that keep Rattle out? I don't believe it did!'

A soft look came into Bronwen's eyes. 'There's something stronger than bolts and bars and high fences,' she said. 'One evening last autumn when it was raining something awful, Rattle wasn't there in his place with the other dogs. But just when we were all thinking of going to bed, there was a whining at the door and there were Rattle and Nellie waiting to be let in! Next day the men looked close at the hedges and gate but no one ever found how it was that Rattle got Nellie out.'

Bronwen finished her story and her light cakes at the same

time and came over to the fire to place them on the girdle, or 'plank', as she called it. At that moment the outer door opened suddenly, and Matty half expected to see Rattle and Nellie on the threshold.

But it was Gwen, the dairymaid, carrying two pails of frothy milk. She did not see Matty in her dark corner but called to Bronwen that Dickie Reynolds was home from sea again and had been seen hanging round Nantgwyn. No doubt it was Bronwen he was after and what did she mean to do this time? Was it not a shame to keep the poor boy waiting?

'That's foolish you talk. Get off with you,' said Bronwen. She was bending over the plank and Matty saw that her face was rosy, but whether it was from the firelight or because of what Gwen had said she could not be sure.

She wondered who was Dick, and what Gwen had meant by keeping him waiting. Would he have to stand outside in the yard like Jenny, waiting till he was wanted? But what was he waiting for and why should Bronwen keep him there? Matty wondered if this was one of the puzzling things she could ask Mamma to explain. The world, for her, was divided into questions that were answered and others that were turned aside with 'There's no need to worry your head over that. Now run away and play.'

But now the inner door, which was hidden from her, opened very softly, and a moment later Mamma herself peeped round the settle. She greeted Bronwen and wrinkled her nose with pleasure at the delicious smell of light cakes.

'What are you doing here, little mouse?' she asked Matty, sitting down beside her. 'Don't you want to play outside with the boys?'

'I like this best,' said Matty.

'So did I, always,' Lettice rejoined.

She took off her bonnet and leaned her head back against the polished wood of the seat. She had slipped out of Penisha to see what the children were doing and had been drawn as by a magnet to the kitchen.

Now, as her eyes travelled round the familiar room, she found it as good as ever. On the shelf above the long table stood rows of wooden bowls, white with scrubbing, in which at midday the farm hands took their broth, screened from the rest of the room by a wooden partition. In the centre of the room was the space in which all the busy happenings of the farm took place. The peace of the afternoon lay on it now, but it was here that buckets of calves' food were mixed and the beef salted down for the winter's use. With her mind's eye Lettice saw herself a child again, carrying the bowls of jellied oatmeal out to the harvesters, and helping with the candlemaking in the autumn when the great tubs of bullock's fat were melted down. She remembered that she had been allowed to hold the rod on which the twisted wicks were strung and to dip them again and again in the fat until they grew into shapely candles.

A feeling of lightness and airiness came to her as she thought of these things. How free from cares she had been in those days! Her mother and elder sisters may have been troubled at times. She remembered them talking of difficulties, sighing that the drinking well was so far from the house, and wishing that the dairy were more conveniently placed, so that the pails of milk had not to be carried through the kitchen twice a day. But Lettice, because she was the youngest child, petted by all the household, took these matters for granted. She would never have done for a farmer's wife, she said to herself now, and yet the life of a farm, moving steadily from season to season, was a perpetual reassurance. Lambing and harvest, living and dying; every birth a new sowing, and death itself but a gathering into barns.

Family and farm hands, in her childhood, were bound by their common tasks and shared a common leisure. She recalled the winter evenings in her grandfather's time, when the old man would sit in the midst of the company reading aloud in Welsh, the maids and the men servants gathered round this same hearth, the maids spinning wool and the young men carving wooden spoons to give to their sweethearts. Did they still carve them today?

'Tell me, Bronwen, has anyone ever given you a love spoon?' she asked. But Bronwen, blushing and laughing, shook her head.

'Mother has one of them,' she added, 'that Dad made when he was for courting her. A funny old spoon it is, with a wheel for a handle.'

'I'm sure your mother thought it the finest spoon in all the world,' said Lettice. Then she jumped up and pulled Matty to her feet.

'Run out, Matty, and call the boys in to tea. Bronwen's light cakes smell so good that I can't bear to wait another minute.'

In the 'room-bach', where tea was laid out, the family was gathered, with only just room for their chairs between the table and the wall, while the pinky-mauve lustre china reflected the level sunshine streaming through the low window. The table was laid with rich brown barley bread (so good that the homemade fruit cake seemed of no account in comparison), Bronwen's light cakes, honey in the comb and a flat tart of crisp pastry.

The children munched in a satisfied, golden silence, while their elders conversed.

Lettice told how the Bowen family and Old Richard had greeted them with the flag flying, and Father recalled that it was Old Richard who had made his first suit and those of the two brothers now in Australia. In those days the family tailor was itinerant, like the family shoemaker. From house to house they went, the shoemaker following the tailor, so that he might use up the scraps of broadcloth left over from the suits to make slippers for all the little boys and girls.

'It was the shoemaker, too, who brought the gossip,' said Father. 'Old Richard was never much of a talker.'

'No, nor a reader either,' added Jim, and exchanged smiles

with Martha.

'But surely he can't read at all,' Lettice exclaimed.

'That's just it,' said Martha. 'And now he's so old it's dull for him sitting indoors day after day in the bad weather, with nothing to do. So last winter Jim offered to go there once a week to read aloud from *Y Cyfaill*.'

'What's that?' asked John, whose Welsh was not a strong point.

'It's a weekly magazine,' Martha explained, 'rather a serious one as a rule, but just then it was running a serial story, in Welsh, of course, and Jim read it aloud every week to Old Richard.'

'You should have seen him relish it,' Jim put in. 'It was a good blood-and-thunder tale – crime, innocent suffering and a forged will, and goodness knows what else besides. I can tell you I put plenty of drama into the reading and Old Richard got more and more excited. He made all sorts of plans to bring the villain to justice.'

'And who was to carry them out? You, I suppose?' asked John.

'That's just it. When I found that Old Richard was expecting me to muster several of the farm hands and call in Evan Parry, the constable, to put an end to all the wickedness, I thought the matter had gone far enough. I reminded him that after all it was only a story and the incidents all imaginary.'

'I don't suppose he liked that,' said Lettice. 'No, Archie, you've had five light cakes already. Bread and butter next. What did Old Richard say then, Jim?'

'He was dumbfounded. 'Do you mean to tell me,' he shouted, 'that you have been wasting your time and mine by coming here, week after week, to read me something that isn't true? You ought to be ashamed of yourself!' And, d'you know,' added Jim with a little laugh, 'somehow or other I was. I'd been rather enjoying that story up till then, but I suddenly saw what a silly, hollow thing it was.'

'Is Richard really a hundred years old?' asked John.

'Just about, and the Bowens are close on seventy. That's the trouble,' said Jim. 'They're coming to the end of their savings. Mrs Bowen is often ailing, so there are doctor's bills to meet every now and then. Of course, they don't say a word and do all they can to hide it, but last winter I noticed how small their fires were, and I fancy that a joint of meat hardly ever goes into that house.'

'Their clothes are very shabby,' Martha added. 'Richard sits cross-legged mending his own suits, as though he were plying his old trade. I wanted to give him a good coat of Father's, but that would hurt his pride. 'What is one to do?'.

The quick tears had sprung to Lettice's eyes. 'That must be remedied,' she said firmly.

'Very well, but tell us how!' cried the family.

But Lettice only smiled mysteriously. 'I have an idea,' was all she would say.

On the way back to St. Idris, while the children played Up-Jenkins under the carriage rug, she was considering the case of Old Richard, and by the time Matty and Philip were tucked up in bed she had turned her idea into a plan.

Lettice's plan could not be carried out at once, and John had gone back to sea before it was accomplished. The first steps had been easy. She wrote to all the scattered members of the Nantgwyn family whose suits had once been made by the aged tailor, and gradually the cheques came in until there was enough to keep Old Richard in comfort for more years than he could hope to see. But when the moment came to lay siege to Richard's pride, she needed to walk warily. Remembering the 'surprise parties' of her American visit in the *Zouave*, Lettice decided that Richard should have a surprise party too.

Early one afternoon Tom Pugh's fly, with Lettice and Matty inside, drove to the Bowens' cottage. Lettice wore her prettiest bonnet, and had brought a basket containing bread, butter and a large batch of yellow tea-cakes, for which she was justly renowned throughout the family. The door of the little pink washed house opened, and when their visitors were recognised the ancient trio came to meet them: Mrs Bowen in her spotless apron, Bowen enquiring for the Captain, and Old Richard looking more than ever like an Old Testament prophet.

'We were wondering,' said Lettice, when everyone was inside the little clean kitchen, 'whether we might take tea with you today. We should like it very much, if it does not trouble you, and we have brought some provisions as you could not be expecting a party.'

Certainly they were not expecting a party, but you would never have guessed it from the charming grace with which they expressed their pleasure at the prospect. While Mrs Bowen was laying the white cloth on the table there was the sound of hooves and wheels outside, and up drove the Nantgwyn dog-cart with Jim and Martha in front, and more baskets under the back seat, a home cured ham and a farm cheese of which Old Richard was particularly fond.

These visitors too, it seemed, had had the same extraordinary idea of taking tea with the Bowens that afternoon. Two tables must now be placed together and chairs fetched from the bedroom to accommodate so large a party.

The best china was brought out from the corner cupboard, the fire encouraged with fresh sticks, and then they all sat down while Mrs Bowen poured out tea at one end of the table, and everyone talked politely in Welsh, since Old Richard did not know any English.

So far, so good. But the real problem was still before them. A certain nervousness was apparent among the guests and Lettice telegraphed to Jim with her eyebrows.

At that he rose to his feet, cleared his throat, and addressed the company. He thanked their hosts for the kind way in which they had welcomed their unexpected guests, spoke of the pride of the neighbourhood in its centenarian and the great pleasure they felt in taking tea with him this afternoon. His friendship with the Nantgwyn family had been long and happy, and the guests assembled today represented many others who would like to show their appreciation of a long and upright life. Such a life was a crown of glory: nothing that they could say or do could add to its lustre, but would he honour them all by accepting this little gift?

At this point Lettice left her seat and, smiling, laid on the table before him a beaded purse.

The guests held their breath. Would he take it? Would he refuse it altogether? If he opened it and saw how large an amount it held, would he take fright like a timid animal that refuses food?

For a time the old man sat motionless, then he raised his mild blue eyes, and with the pleased smile of a child who has been given a sweet, he said, 'Thank you.' The company round the table breathed again and the future was safe.

Lettice was well content. What nonsense it was, she thought, to say that money was an evil, though perhaps they had never had enough of it in her family to dread its power. Thinking of her children, she hoped that their lives would lie between the two extremes.

'Let them have enough to give to others. But never so much that they forget what it is like to be poor,' she prayed in her heart. Then the arrogance of her prayer overcame her. Who was she to ask God to keep her children from learning the lessons of life? It might be that the extremes of wealth and poverty were needed to perfect their character. Looking across the table at Matty she wondered what future lay before her daughter, even more unknown for a girl than for a boy, since the choice of a way of life did not lie with her.

All this time Old Richard sat wrapped in his dreams, paying no attention to the talk that ran merrily round the table. It was time, thought Lettice, to bring him back into the company and, turning to him, she asked if he would not sing to them. In his day Old Richard had been a noted singer and choir conductor, and now, without more ado he rose slowly to his feet, holding the edge of the table with his gnarled, trembling hands.

In a high, quavering voice, which occasionally broke but always recovered itself, he sang a hymn so old that no one in the room had ever heard it before. The long forgotten words wandered like frail ghosts on a melancholy air that seemed as ageless as the mountains and as desolate as the sea. As he sang tears filled his eyes and coursed slowly down his cheeks, but they made no difference to the song; the thin stream of ancient melody flowed on. He was like a bird singing in the rain for a grief so old that all the world has forgotten it.

Chapter 3

The *Mystic Tie*

The dining room of the Stone House was a pleasant place at breakfast time. Anyone seated at table could watch the comings and goings in the Cross without doing more than turn his head, unless he placed himself, as the Captain did, with his back to the window. Lettice, in the seat opposite her husband, had the best of it. Entrenched behind the coffee pot with its yellow frilled cosy, she could keep an eye on the happenings in the Cross, seeing them beyond John's broad shoulders, silhouetted against the light, and the four children seated before their bowls of steaming porridge.

But on this early October morning the only things stirring out of doors were the clouds which a south-west wind pushed briskly across the sky. It had blown all night and John had risen up to wedge the windows, which rattled and kept them both awake. Having secured them, he had come back to bed and immediately fallen asleep beside her, but Lettice lay awake for an hour or more, listening to the wind's buffets and trying to keep her mind from the thoughts which ran through it, fast as the hurrying footsteps of the storm.

'Summer is over. Autumn is here. Soon it will be winter again. Soon he will be gone and you will be alone, listening every night to the wind and afraid of what it may do, afraid of the dark water and the greedy waves.'

If only John were not so obstinate, she thought, about refusing to go into steamships. Why should he cling to sail, when everyone said that the future lay in steam? She understood his love for his beautiful, birdlike ship; she did not regret that there was less money in clinging to the old ways, but when she knew them to be more dangerous it was hard to bear.

'Don't listen to what people say, Letty,' he would laugh. 'If I put myself, into the hands of an oily engineer, I shall be blown up by his boilers, and serve me right!'

But she knew that he was only trying to lead her away from a subject on which he felt so strongly that argument and persuasion were useless. Putting out her hand she touched the strong limbs so close beside her. He was like a great tree, she thought, like a piece of the well-tried oak from the ships he loved, and the thought of his abandoning those towering masts, with their sails and rigging, was so fantastic that she smiled in spite of her fears.

Sleeping at last and troubled by dreams, she had wakened with less than her usual serenity. The wind was still blowing, and she watched wisps of straw and pieces of paper, remains of the Michaelmas Fair not yet tidied away, whirling about the Cross as she dressed. But at the breakfast table the family chattered cheerfully of the day's plans, and with a cup of hot, fragrant coffee in her hand she felt a reviving confidence. The date of John's return to his ship was not yet fixed, and how foolish and wrong she had been to allow herself any fears when they were still together! The zest that she always felt when she and John went a jaunt in each other's company, returned as she remembered that they had planned to walk over to Llanaber that afternoon to see the Powell cousins. It would be a pleasant walk along the deep lanes, sheltered a little from the wind.

Her mind running thus, she noticed that the Cross was no longer empty. Over John's shoulder she could see Mr Dan Jenkins from next door, slippered and hatless, his coat flapping in the wind, his field glasses held to his eyes.

'What is Mr Dan looking at?' The words sprang to her lips, yet at once she regretted having said them. The pleasant orderliness of breakfast was immediately broken, three of the children already at the window and her husband turning in his chair.

'I expect it's one of his rare birds that he gets so excited about,' Archie remarked.

'He's beckoning,' said Ivor. 'Can we go?'

'No one is to go, except Papa if he wishes,' said Lettice. 'Finish your breakfast, all of you.'

She spoke more sharply than she intended, seeing John rise with a rueful look at his untouched breakfast, and watched him go out and join Mr Dan, where the field glasses passed from hand to hand, excitement lighting up both faces, the wind fanning the hair and beards that framed them. The children were still dutifully ladling porridge into their mouths, their eyes fixed on the window, but next minute John was calling to someone, there was a sound of galloping hooves and the Cross was filled with running people. Discipline round the breakfast table of the Stone House suddenly snapped, and the children were all out of doors, Lettice close behind them.

'What is it, what is it? Tell us what you can see.'

'It's a wreck.' Dread words, like a cold handful of spray in her face. 'She's struck the Bitches! Bod Mawr, she's on top of them!'

Standing in the street, the wind disarranging her curls and buffeting her skirts, Lettice looked down past the old stone Cross, past the grey towers of the Cathedral in the valley below, past the green fields, out to the sea and the island rocks. Even at that distance the great waves could be seen, one every now and then greedier than the others, stretching up a white arm against the island cliff.

'May we go? Mamma, may we go now?'

The voices, the familiar questions, summoned her back to where she belonged, to the little kingdom she ruled.

'Not a yard till you've had your breakfast and put on your boots.'

She had them all indoors again, gulping their food, struggling with bootlaces.

'Matty, you're to put on your warm pelisse and stay close

to Ivor.'

'I'll look after her, Mamma.'

'Archie, you must wash the egg from your mouth before you go. No, Philip isn't coming. He's to stay with me. Oh, what was that?'

But she knew what it was, even as the question was jerked from her lips. The lifeboat gun! Then more shouting and running in the streets.

'Go and find Papa,' she ordered Ivor. 'Tell him to come and have some breakfast and remind him that he is wearing his slippers and no hat.'

'Yes, my dear, so I discovered.' He was already beside her, touching her lightly on the arm as though to show that he knew of her perturbation.

'But I can't wait. Give me something to eat in my hand. I may be of use.'

Silently she fetched his boots. He laced them quickly, took a piece of bread from her hand, thanked her with his eyes and was gone. Matty ran beside him; Ivor and Archie rushed ahead while groups of people hurried on before and behind, all bound for Porthbach and the lifeboat.

They were gone, and Lettice returned to the quiet house, the disordered breakfast table and a plaintive Philip. It was easy to pacify the child by taking him with her about her morning tasks, since there was nothing he loved so much as 'helping Mamma', running to fetch her household keys and assisting her to weigh out sugar and raisins or fill a tea canister.

But it was not so easy to soothe her own thoughts. Her racing mind moved between the wrecked ship and the lifeboat. Fearful thought, to see a wave curling high above the deck, to wait powerless while it crashes and to feel the solid ship, the ship that has been one's home for months, perhaps for years, stagger and split. She shuddered and turned her thoughts instead to the lifeboat and her crew – all of them known to her, at least by name – wearing their little pirate caps and fastening on their cork jackets. Johnny Morris, the cox, was a fine man with his dark romantic eyes and olive colouring, said to be a heritage from Spanish blood – but some of the others were so young. Mrs Williams, the washerwoman, whose grandson had but lately joined the crew would be feeling anxious today.

By now the boat would be nearly launched, but Lettice knew Porthbach Cove all too well. There was no smooth, inclined slip down to the water in those days. If the tide were out, a reach of shore strewn with boulders lay between the boat and the sea. Men, women and children would be tugging at the rusty chains, their feet sliding on the slimy seaweed, struggling to shift the weight of the boat over the stones.

By eleven o'clock a fine rain was falling, blown inland from the sea. Lettice began to worry about the children. Matty had gone without a mackintosh, and she was a chesty child with a tendency to bronchitis. Here at last was something to do, instead of endlessly waiting. She settled Philip with a paint-box and some old magazines, under Catherine Jane's eye, tied a bonnet on her head, put on her old grey cloak and packed a basket with a flask of brandy, some apple turnovers which Marged had just taken out of the oven, a couple of mufflers and Matty's waterproof cape. Then, she slipped out of the house and walked rapidly in the direction of Porthbach.

Now that she was out in the open air, the wind whipping her bonnet strings and tugging at her cloak, her feelings revived. Perhaps by this time the men had all been rescued, she would not allow herself to think anything else as she followed the road under Penbryn Farm and across Rhosfawr moor – a desolate, marshy stretch of country, the home of wild duck. Yellow flags and bog cotton grew there in summer, but today the wind howled over its empty spaces.

How swiftly the autumn had come! Last week the summer had been with them; they had been picking blackberries in the warm lanes and the children were demanding still more picnics, still more bathes, as though they could never have enough of the golden days. But now the wind had risen and blown it all away, all this happy warmth. It was as though someone had opened the door and let in the draught. October scarcely here and already a wreck on the coast! Ruin and wrecks and fresh partings, that was all the winter brought.

To the right she saw the grey double gables of Bryneithin Farm, said to be a haunted house, and then suddenly stood still at the sound of galloping hooves. A pony came round the corner, a farm boy on its back, the loose stones flying to right and left. Lettice drew back against the hedge to let it pass, but the boy pulled up sufficiently to call out in Welsh that the ship's crew could be seen plainly clinging to a rock with waves dashing over them. They must be half-drowned and he was on his way to fetch Dr Parry. If she wanted to see, her quickest road lay through the farmyard. He was off again, urging his pony at breakneck speed, full of the importance of his errand. To some people, thought Lettice, unlatching the farmyard gate, a wreck was like a dog fight – they must be there to see.

If it were not for the children, she told herself, nothing would have induced her to come today. But she did not like the thought of Matty seeing half-drowned men, even if the child were both warm and dry. Ivor could look after her, but with so much to excite him he might be less careful than usual. As for John, he had probably forgotten that the children were there at all.

The muddy farmyard through which she picked her way was deserted. Everyone was by the shore, and now she could see little groups of people straining against the wind at the cliff's verge. As she came to the ragged edge of gorse and slippery grass there were cries of 'There they are!'

'Deio, they've done it.'

'Well done, now! Didn't I say they'd do it?'

'Only twelve men they've got, out of all that crew.'

'Thirteen there were on the rock.'

'Only twelve men!' The words whipped her ears like the wind that was making her eyes stream.

Round the corner of the headland the lifeboat was fighting her painful way. The crew in their cork jackets looked grotesquely broad; their oars rising and falling gave to the craft the helpless air of a beetle on its back. Yet she came on steadily, in spite of the churning waves which seemed determined to oppose and overwhelm her. Crouched in the stern was a huddle of men, the survivors of the ship's crew.

Lettice might have guessed where she would find her family. In the cove below, where a crowd of people awaited the landing of the boat, she picked out the tall figure of the Captain and the three excited children. She clambered down the pebbly cliff path just as the boat grounded, dragged up at the last by a score of eager hands, and the drenched, spent men in the stern were half lifted out. One of them, obvious chief of the forlorn little band, looked round him and then stepped up to John Peters, as one leader to another.

'The master's gone. I'm his mate,' he said briefly.

'Can ye take me to the nearest post-office where I can be telegraphing the owners?'

'I'll give you a hand with that,' said John Peters. 'What's your ship?'

'The *Mystic Tie* of Aberdeen, homeward bound for Liverpool from Cape Coast Castle. There's ten good men gone with the master.'

He was a tall, fair man, his blue eyes – large with a fixed, weary gaze – level with those of the Captain standing before him; his arms hanging limply down from broad powerful shoulders. Suddenly Lettice saw him sway on his feet, and it seemed he would have fallen had not John Peters held him. The next minute she was beside them both, slipping on the treacherous green seaweed, a little breathless from her hurry.

'Here, quick, John! Give him this.'

'You here, Letty!' He put his astonishment quickly aside, taking the brandy bottle from her hands, wrenching out the cork and holding it to the bluish lips of the mate. He revived well enough to walk with the others to the lifeboat house. Here food and a few clothes of a sort had been hastily collected, and thence a farm cart would take them in to St. Idris, where John Peters would help the mate with the necessary business of telegrams and letters to Aberdeen.

'And Letty, we might put up this chap for the night. Can you manage it?'

Lettice nodded. She was busy tying a muffler round Matty's neck, while Ivor and Archie munched their apple turnovers.

'You'd better have one yourself, John,' said Lettice, and dived once more into her basket.

John surveyed her with twinkling eyes. 'Who but you would think of turnovers and mufflers and have the brandy ready in the nick of time? Ivor, take your mother and Matty home at once, and look after them. I must see to these poor fellows.'

Matty was white with cold and excitement, her small hands bleeding from the rusty links of the chain which had dragged the lifeboat to the water.

'Matty hauled like a good one,' said Ivor proudly.

'She must have been dreadfully in the way. I should never have let her go,' Lettice thought to herself, but she said nothing to damp their ardour.

Ivor and Archie were busy telling her the whole story. Just as the lifeboat was being launched someone had brought news that men could be plainly seen, clinging to a rock with waves dashing over them. Thirteen of them had succeeded in reaching that narrow sanctuary, and there they had clung, in constant danger of being dragged downwards by the clutching waves. One of them must have lost his hold, for only twelve men had been brought to shore.

Strangely, but mercifully, Lettice thought, the children took it as a matter of course that half the crew should have been lost, and even one of the survivors on the rock swept to his death. It was as though the rhythm of that battle between man and the elements still held them in a trance. The boys talked excitedly; Matty was silent with serious face and shining eyes. Lettice kept her own mind from dwelling on the sadness that haunted her until her little family were safely home and changed into dry clothes. Then she busied herself preparing the spare room for the rescued mate, and put two hot bricks into the bed.

They came in at last, John and Noah Anderson, the mate, the latter wearing a farmer's borrowed coat too small for those broad shoulders. The two men had been busy telegraphing, and billeting the eleven other survivors on kindly townspeople. Marged had kept a meal hot in the oven, but Noah Anderson was too exhausted to eat more than a little.

'It's verra kind of you, marm, but eating's beyond me,' he said, and accepted a cup of tea instead, into which Lettice had put five lumps of sugar. Then he went upstairs to a hot bath which Catherine Jane, her eyes round with excitement, had carried to the bedroom.

Later, when the mate was sleeping, Lettice heard further details of the ill-fated *Mystic Tie*. She was on her way home from Africa with a cargo of palm-oil kernels and had stranded in the small hours of the morning.

'The captain did all that was possible and went down with his ship, as a man should do,' John Peters finished. Then he added, 'There's another thing left to see to. One body's ashore already – the one swept off the rock. He was a black boy, the only coloured man aboard of her, and it seems that none of the other twelve know anything about him.'

'Do you mean they don't know who his parents are, or where he comes from? There's no one at all they can tell?'

'I'm afraid not.'

'Oh, John, how awful! Think of his father and mother waiting and longing for news of him, and never, never a word.'

'Perhaps his parents are dead and gone before him, and God knows who they'd be anyway.'

Lettice sat silent, her mending untouched on her lap. Then she asked in a low voice, 'Where have they put him, John?'

'In one of the side chapels of the Cathedral. The Dean offered it, and it seemed best for him to wait there till the funeral.'

Lettice pressed her hands close together and looked across at her husband.

'I don't want to go to the funeral, John.'

'My dear, of course not. No one would expect it.'

'But I can't bear to think of him alone in this strange place, with never a friend and never a flower. Would you come with me this evening to the Cathedral, if I took some flowers?'

'Anything you like, my love, if you wish it.'

Late in the afternoon, Lettice slipped out into the garden where wind and rain had made havoc of her flower-beds. Little was left of the summer's wealth; some goldenrod, a few battered dahlias and the last flight of roses, their heads heavy with moisture. They seemed an odd posy for a dusky boy from the burning sunshine of far-off Africa.

Lettice thought of her own voyage in the *Zouave* down the West Coast, the palm-fringed beaches shimmering with heat, and the shore boats pulling out to meet them, crowded with laughing black faces. Remembering the bright colours they loved she chose her gaudiest dahlias, the best of the crimson roses and a last tiger lily from the sheltered corner under the wall. She fastened these together, adding a scarlet spray of Virginia creeper, and told John she was ready.

Together they fared beneath the Tower Gateway, part of the old city walls, and down the worn steps between the gravestones. Wind and rain had ceased, and bands of sunset lay beyond Carn Idris. Round the dark headland the sea was smoothing out its fury, spent and satisfied at last. Was it only this morning they had watched the white spray flying?

Lettice never entered the Cathedral without a feeling of awe and almost excitement. Before her marriage she had seldom worshipped there, and it was to the Welsh Independent Chapel with its slated roof, severe grey walls and iron scroll-work, that she took the children every Sunday. To anyone so naturally religious the place of worship was of small account, yet she preferred the Welsh Chapel because the order of service was familiar and seemed to her right. But the beauty of the Cathedral fabric never failed to stir her heart.

When they entered it was nearly dark, and the oil lamps hanging here and there seemed but to deepen the shadows between the great pillars. No other steps echoed in the marble floor as they made their way to the side chapel where the African boy awaited his burial.

He lay there, it seemed to Lettice, in simple state, not out of keeping, as some might have supposed, in the shade of that venerable place. In the light of the oil lamp that hung on the pillar near by, the brown forehead seemed polished stone, the crisp hair a piece of frozen sculpture.

He was young to have come so far! But little older than Ivor and Archie, thought Lettice, laying the flowers beside him. Strange fate that had brought the dusky savage from his African village to lie beneath those sweeping Norman arches in the company of saints and prelates, crusading knights, learned chancellors and 'that noble Lord, Edmund, Earl of Richmond, Father and Brother of Kings', whose tomb stood near by.

'I hear she broke her back this afternoon,' said John, as they came out into the open air. 'The *Mystic Tie* is a total loss for the underwriters.'

'The *Mystic Tie*,' Lettice repeated to herself. The name fell strangely on her ears, as though charged with a meaning she could not yet grasp. They climbed upwards through the dark graveyard, where an unexpected land breeze sighed past them, bearing the scent of autumn fields, and she wondered if the name of the ill-fated ship was the thread joining the African sailor to that lordly company of the dead.

No barriers of time or space, creed or colour separated them. Together they slept, bound by the *Mystic Tie* of their common mortality.

Chapter 4

'So Farewell, Love, Farewell'

In the third week of October, when the swallows were gathering on the telegraph wires along the road to Westford, Captain Peters rejoined his ship.

The stormy weather that had wrecked the *Mystic Tie* had blown itself out, and St. Luke's little summer came in with still days of gold and purple and a lazy sea. Lettice was so busy that she hardly noticed the coloured world outside. Only the robin singing under the window, as she packed John's trunks, told her of the season, and the children, running in with baskets of nuts, and calling to her that Uncle Jim had driven over from Nantgwyn with a barrel of apples.

Hurrying out of the house on an errand for John, she felt the warm sun on her neck, tasted an air like wine, and was astonished to discover the same sense of excitement that she had known as a child with every changing season. It must be, she told herself, because there was still so much to do, with all John's things to get ready, and friends and relations looking in every day to say goodbye.

On the last day but one, when John had gone into Westford to see the banker and lawyer about various matters of business, and Marged was making pumpkin pie, an itinerant photographer arrived at the door with his paraphernalia and offered to take their pictures.

'Oh, marm, he has the most beautiful likenesses. Something grand!' said Catherine Jane. 'He has taken one of Mrs Jones Parry's daughter and you wouldn't know her from a smart lady, same as the summer visitors.'

'He can't be very good at likenesses if he makes Minnie

Jones Parry look beautiful,' said Lettice. 'You'd better tell him to go away, Catherine Jane. We're too busy today.'

'But, marm, he doesn't come this way more than twice a year,' said Catherine Jane, crestfallen. 'Thinking I was it would be a grand surprise for the Captain to have a lovely picture of yourself, taken in your pineapple muslin.'

'I shan't put on my pineapple muslin for anyone at this time of the morning,' said Lettice, closing one of the trunks with great decision. 'But he might photograph the children. Only you mustn't breathe a word about it, Catherine Jane.'

Catherine Jane clapped her hand to her mouth. 'Deio! you'll see me split first,' she said mysteriously. 'I'll call the children this very minute.' And she was out of the room and down the stairs like a whirlwind.

The children were collected and told to tidy themselves while the photographer, a small, eager man with a nervous manner, was busy arranging his gear in the back yard.

'C-c-could you lend me a sh-sheet?' he asked Marged, suddenly popping his head round the kitchen door. Marged was indignant. 'The best bedspread it is he will be wanting next! Give him an old sheet that needs mending, Catherine Jane.'

A few minutes later he was at the door again. Would the lady oblige with a rug?

'To make an old show,' snorted Marged.

This time one of the brown wool mats was brought from the parlour, and the leather chair that was least scratched about the legs carried out from the dining-room. At last the children appeared, Ivor and Archie wriggling their necks in clean collars, Matty with her hair neatly brushed under a velvet snood, Philip in his tartan frock and buttoned boots.

If an artist is someone with an infinite capacity for taking pains, then the photographer earned the name. The sheet, tacked at its four corners to the stable door, provided a background against which he arranged and rearranged his sitters. When all seemed ready, the wool mat on the ground, the children posed round the chair – Matty and Philip on its broad seat, Ivor leaning against one side, Archie with his arm placed self-consciously on the back, supporting his head – the photographer ran forward.

'One m-m-minute, if you please – the little girl's head should be turned a trifle, so. Excuse me, sir,' this to Ivor, 'the handkerchief would be better showing slightly from the pocket.'

'Glad he doesn't ask me, 'cos I haven't got one,' muttered Archie.

'If you would p-put your arm round your little brother, miss, that would be very pl-pleasing,' went on the photographer.

Catherine Jane, hovering near, flung up her hands in sentimental pleasure.

'Oh, marm, look at the little angels! Indeed they don't look like our children at all.'

'I've got pins and needles in my elbow,' Archie announced.

'One moment, children, it's nearly finished,' Lettice begged. 'I think perhaps if you could take it now at once.' She turned to the photographer, but he had gone to ground again under his velvet hood and the camera clicked and shook and clicked again with his frenzied efforts.

Standing on the kitchen doorstep, Lettice felt a sudden stab at the heart. The four children with their young, grave faces, the shabby chair, the white sheet nailed a little crookedly to the stable door, the autumn sunshine filling the pleasant yard, all these things were being caught and pinned before her eyes, so that John should see them, holding the picture in his hand, on some day of winter gale and grey sea, or more likely, in a strange smelling tropic port on the other side of the world.

There they were, the four he loved so much, their quick footsteps and eager voices stilled for an instant; Matty with her arm round Philip, Ivor and Archie standing side by side – one passing moment held and preserved.

*

The Captain was back in time for tea and had various business matters in which to instruct his wife. Of all the preparations for leaving this was the part that Lettice dreaded most, since in her secret heart she regarded the rules of a man-made world as faintly ridiculous.

She did not go so far as to think that she would run the world better than men could do, but she was quite sure that she would run it differently. In John's absence it sometimes fell that she must consult Mr Davies, the bank manager, or Mr Bevan, the lawyer at Westford, and although, remembering her position as wife and mother she tried to be serious and businesslike, she was struck more and more by the foolishness of these people.

To begin with, what a way of living! No wonder Mr Bevan looked pinched and yellow, spending his days in a frowsty little room where her fingers itched to be at the windows, to clean and polish them and throw them wide open. The very smell of the place, the company of those black tin boxes and the consumptive clerk in the cubbyhole downstairs, were enough to turn a man's brain, filled as it was all day with tiresome, unimportant details.

Mr Davies, the bank manager, receiving her in his room marked PRIVATE, was always gallant and unbending. 'My dear lady,' he seemed to say, 'I know these things are above you, but leave them to wiser heads than yours.' Was he really so wise? Lettice asked herself, piqued by this masculine air of importance and mystery. Was not true wisdom to be found among children – healthy, well-loved, well-trained children; in a clean house full of air and sunshine and pretty things; in a garden bright with flowers?

Sometimes, seated in the bank manager's room, her glance would wander to the blue sky outside the window, and she would think, 'What a day for a picnic! I'd like to take the children to Silversands this afternoon.' Which of them, she wondered, was the foolish one, the man who spent his time considering people's investments, or she, planning a golden afternoon for her family? She knew her answer, but kept these thoughts to herself while carefully observing the rules of the masculine game.

'Pash Cash', she wrote absent-mindedly one day on a cheque, instead of' Pay Cash'. When the pink-faced young bank clerk pointed out her mistake she laughed aloud, and went on laughing all the way down the High Street of Westford. 'Pash Cash' was such a good name, she thought, for all the funny little shibboleths of serious minded men.

There were other things besides bankers and lawyers that women would abolish, Lettice thought, going that evening into the room where the trunks and valises stood ready. St. John knew all about it when he foretold a Heaven with no sea.

'No sea and no partings,' she said to herself, kneeling down to tuck one more little package into the sea-chest, that strong box of polished camphor wood with brass-tipped corners, which John always refused to leave behind him.

Everything was ready now. The new shirts that she had marked so carefully, the socks she had knitted, the suits she had sponged and pressed, all these had been packed as Lettice alone could pack, slowly and very carefully, with small bags of lavender and lemon verbena laid here and there.

But there were other things besides garden herbs that Lettice hid away among the clothes. Here and there in the pockets, folded carefully in soft white paper, she tucked tiny packages of the Captain's favourite sweetmeats. Among these were hard, round peppermints, the size of two-shilling pieces and called 'Extra Strong', kept by the Beehive store in St. Idris. There were also pink and white sugar almonds and, best of all in Lettice's opinion, 'Motto Sweets', shaped like hearts, diamonds and squares, and bearing such sentimental remarks as 'I love you', 'Meet me by moonlight', 'Will you be mine?' and 'When shall we meet next?' Lettice was careful to place these both in the thick overcoats and the thin, tropical suits, so that whatever the course of his voyage, John would continue to find the little surprise packets.

Yet now, perhaps, his surprise would be greater if they were not there at all!

Kneeling before the open chest, folding and smoothing, she smiled to think that John's clothes had been her special care, even before she knew John himself. Her mind went back to an autumn day in Liverpool in the year 1866, when she was staying with Cousin Ann, the minister's wife at Rock Ferry. One day she had been asked out to tea by a friend and neighbour, Mrs Patterson, wife of a Scottish sea captain, and on arriving found the kind old lady dressed for walking and greatly perturbed.

'My dear,' she told Lettice, 'Captain Peters is sailing suddenly. You remember, I spoke of him before – a friend of my husband's, just given his first ship. So young! He has asked me to help get his clothes together, and I have a quantity of things still to buy.'

'But let me help you,' Lettice had hastened to say.

'You're sure you don't mind, my dear? It's most kind of you. Perhaps if we divided such things as there are to do we should be sooner finished.'

To Lettice had been allotted the captain's shirts. She had spent some time in a very masculine shop where, with a list in her hand, she had tried to conceal her ignorance and to appear, at the same time, not too familiar with such matters in the presence of the male assistant.

Returning to the Pattersons' house for tea, they had found Captain Patterson already there, and with him a tall, fair young man who reminded Lettice of pictures of Vikings in their winged helmets. He was introduced as Captain Peters. Lettice blushed to think she had been choosing his shirts, and blushed still more when Mrs Patterson praised her help and Captain Peters thanked her for it.

Oddly, it seemed, he too was embarrassed by the situation, though his eyes sought hers continually across the tea-table. To this day she remembered that room; the Chinese vases on the mantelpiece, the bright fire, and the kind Pattersons pressing their tongue-tied guests to tea and muffins.

Then the walk back through the foggy streets to Cousin Ann's with the tall sailor striding beside her. He was sailing for China next day, and she would soon be returning home to Nantgwyn. There was so little time for anything, yet time had become of such small account. It was not time but eternity that mattered once she and John had met.

Leaving him there on the doorstep of Cousin Ann's house, running upstairs to her room, she had known one thing, inescapable and for ever fixed, that John Peters and no one else would be her husband. She was no less certain then, taking off her bonnet before the gas-lit mirror, her grey eyes shining as though someone had lighted candles in her head; no less sure than now, the mother of four children, kneeling before the open chest, getting her man ready to go to sea once more.

The last day came, and the corded chest, the trunks and the two valises were carried down to the front hall; Tom Pugh's fly was ordered for seven o'clock next morning. The afternoon, shining from an untroubled sky, beckoned John and Lettice from the house for a last walk. They went out by the yard and through the garden where apples hung low on the trees, through the doorway into the back lane, and so by mutual consent towards the cliffs and the sea. Late blackberries still hung from the banks on either side, but they were October ones on which 'the Devil had spat', too ripe for picking.

As they walked they talked of the children, and it seemed to Lettice that she saw them for a moment with John's eyes, not as her clamorous flock, but as growing plants whom she was there to tend. Only John, returning at intervals, could tell if her tending were good and if the growth had been right. How would he find them next time, she wondered?

'Lettice, take my hand. Don't look so anxious!' He had read her thoughts as usual. 'I shall be proud of them if they grow up half as good as you, and none of them will be so good-looking!'

'Oh, John, how can you say so? Matty is distinctly pretty. Everyone says so, though she is perhaps a trifle too pale.'

'Not half so pretty as her mother. I like that frock you're wearing. Will you put it on the day I come back? I shall look for it.'

There was no answer to that except a squeeze of his fingers, and they walked on down the sunny lane in silence for a while.

Then Lettice said, 'I'm glad it's to be India this time. I don't feel so far from you when I know the places.'

'You'll be able to picture it all, won't you ?'

'You must promise to do the same things, so that I can get it right. I shall see you at Bombay, bathing by starlight, diving from the ship's rail at the anchorage.'

'Do you remember our early morning picnics on the sands at Jouhou? I climbed the palms to get you fresh coconuts for breakfast.'

'Then there was Madras. Those Indian singers droning on and on, and you sang them a Welsh hymn, to show that other people could be melancholy too when they chose!'

'You remember everything,' said John. 'I'd forgotten that bit.'

But of course she remembered everything. All else might fade, but she would keep as long as she lived the memory of those days at sea. Dolphins and flying fish leaping the bright waves; men scouring the decks with holystone and great buckets of sea water till it shone snowy in the sun, and mending their clothes with that mixture of handiness and clumsiness that characterises a man's efforts with a needle. And then, by way of stark contrast, the man who fell out of the rigging on a stormy night and was abandoned at long last, because no boat could be launched in such a sea. She had heard his cries; that was something she would like to forget....

'I will look up our old friends in Calcutta, if any are left,' John broke in on her thoughts. 'Which ones, in particular?'

She recalled two or three names and sent messages, but it was like speaking of another life, the life with those people who had been kind to her twelve years ago in the little bungalow on the riverbank at Garden Reach, set in its shady compound with the flaming gold mohur trees by the gate. Would John try to find their old ayah and tell her that Ivor Baba was grown to be a fine boy? 'And that there are three others as well,' Lettice said proudly.

John promised to do what he could, then suddenly left her side and sprang up the bank to an overhanging hazel bush and tossed a cluster down to her. She caught the spray and cracked a nut between her teeth, till he stopped her by clapping his hand over her mouth. They both stood laughing, remembering how she had teased him in the old days at sea.

'D'you remember? Off Cadiz, wasn't it? Your lovely white teeth, that I was always so scared would be broken!'

'They're not lovely now, and I lost one when Philip was born.'

'Philip's worth a tooth, isn't he?'

Lettice laughed her low laugh. 'They're all darlings, but there's something special about Philip. Something specially sweet. I do believe, John,' she added seriously, 'Philip will grow up to be a good man.'

She was to recall those words one day, and the view of Crab Bay below the cliffs at their feet, shot with colours in the October sunshine. Hand in hand they looked out over the dividing sea, murmurous with never-sleeping sounds; this element which was to John Peters daily bread and taskmaster and the first love of his life. Lettice did not think of it in that way. The sea took her husband from her; it would take her sons. But love was an indestructible rock which no waters could devour.

Yet how to face next morning, the fly at the door and the children dancing excitedly in the hall, as though meetings and partings were both much the same, something exciting which broke the monotony of every day?

How to meet John's last kiss with a still face, and to stand waving, waving on the doorstep, Philip's warm hand held tightly in hers? But she succeeded. When the fly had gone she sent the three elder children off to school and set the maids about their work. Then only did she turn swiftly into the parlour, close the door and turn the key.

No one saw her again that morning. In the room where she and John had spent their last evening together she prayed that he might be kept safe, and that she might be given strength to endure.

Chapter 5

Beehive and Choir

Matty stood at the nursery window watching the December rain sweep through the Cross and down the shining slates on the roofs of the houses opposite, while she pondered the puzzle which had long teased her mind, 'How is it that I can see the whole of the Beehive through one pane of glass?' But there, without doubt, enclosed in a single frame were all the changing scenes of that highly varied emporium which supplied the needs of St. Idris, from a shirt button to a loin of veal.

Not that loins of veal and legs of mutton ever dangled above the ribbons of the counter, or disturbed the discreet shadows of the Beehive. When once on a visit to Westford Matty, for the first time in her life, noticed a butcher's shop, the sight so filled her with horror that she had dreamt of it afterwards for many nights.

No, the Beehive managed things better than that. A small boy would come knocking at the back door of the Stone House, 'Please would Mrs Peters like any veal this week?'

'Yes, Mrs Peters would like a fillet.'

A few hours later he might appear again. 'Mr Tudor is very sorry, but he didn't have enough orders for veal, so he isn't killing the calf this week, but he thinks he will have some beef.'

The same evening, as like as not, the small boy would be there once more, 'Mr Tudor is sorry, but he won't have nothing but mutton, and what part will Mrs Peters have?'

During the time their joints were under discussion, the animals grazed undisturbed in their pastures.

Mr Tudor, the owner of the Beehive, was a brisk, kindly man with black eyes and a good tenor voice. His only child, Olwen, some five years older than Matty, attended boarding-school at Westford, from which she returned every holiday as round, black-eyed and merry as ever.

Matty, her nose pressed against the nursery window on this particular wet afternoon, knew that Olwen was home for the Christmas holidays. But would she give a thought to Matty, now that Olwen had so many new friends of her own age? Then the lovely, looked-for thing happened. Olwen, wearing a red frock trimmed with curly braid, appeared at the door of the Beehive waving her hand. Matty waved ecstatically back; thereupon Olwen disappeared into the shadowy shop and was back at the door in a minute, holding up a magazine that was unmistakably the Christmas number of *Chatterbox*. Much pantomime followed, Olwen indicating that she had sweets to offer, and that Matty had only to cross the street to find all these delights.

Philip was happily busy in a corner of the nursery, turning all the things out of the bottom shelf of the toy cupboard. With one swift glance Matty saw that he would have enough to keep himself occupied and Catherine Jane busy clearing up, for some time to come. Downstairs her mother was sewing by the parlour fire, her smooth brow a little puckered over a jagged triangular tear in Archie's jacket.

'Mamma, may I go to the Beehive? Olwen has the Christmas number of *Chatterbox*.'

'Has she invited you?'

'Yes, through the window.'

'Very well, you may go for a short time, but you must put on your goloshes to cross the street.'

'Thank you, Mamma.'

'And don't eat too many sweets while you are there.'

'No, Mamma.'

Matty closed the door carefully behind her. With such

a treat in view she did not want to spoil it, or even blur the pleasure of the moment by one false step, one reprimand. Then she flew to the back passage, found her goloshes behind the door, flung an old brown cape over her shoulders and was across the street like an arrow, leaping the streaming gutters, and in through the magic doors of the Beehive.

The innermost recess of the Beehive, now given over to grocery, had once been the Tudors' sitting-room, for they had taken to shopkeeping only of recent years. Mrs Tudor, in fact, had never taken to it at all. No one had ever seen her serve at the counter. She had delicate health and spent most of her time in a sitting-room on the first floor, full of pretty old china that she had brought with her from her home when she married Richard Tudor. At the top of the tall house was another sitting-room where lived Old Nannie, as they always called her. She had been Mrs Tudor's nurse and had lived with her ever since – a little old woman, whose rheumatic hands could no longer knit or sew. None of Mrs Tudor's brothers ever came to the house without running upstairs to see Old Nannie. One was a parson, one a doctor and yet another a Q.C., who was said to have a fierce way with witnesses up in London. But he was a very humble man when he climbed the stairs and knocked on Old Nannie's door.

The walls of the back room of the Beehive, before the coming of the grocery, had been hung with a paper showing the rival modes of travel – a stage-coach and a railway train. These pursued each other in lively greens and reds across the top of the spice boxes and tea canisters, and Matty always regretted that the sugar bags hid so much of their glory. In vain she told herself that behind the bags there were only more dashing stage-coaches, more steaming trains; in her heart she suspected there were some other episodes, far more exciting than the ones already known.

At the back of the counter burned a roaring coal fire, a much more jovial fire than was customary at the Stone House, where grates were economically 'banked' with slack after breakfast and looked very sulky during several hours of the day. But the Beehive fire always seemed at its best, so that it was pleasant to think of the wind and rain outside, while the flames danced briskly up the chimney.

Olwen and Matty sat on two pulled-out drawers of the counter, which gave Matty a delicious sense of insecurity, heightened when she fell back into the drawer, and lending an air of unexpectedness to everything. *Chatterbox* lay open on their knees, and within easy reach were the bottles of sweets, an array that presented but one problem, 'Shall it be acid drops, or raspberry drops, or bull's-eyes?'

'Where's your papa gone this time?' asked Olwen, her cheek swollen with a large raspberry drop.

'India. And China after that, I think,' said Matty rather vaguely.

'What'll he bring you back? Silk and ivory elephants?'

'I don't know,' said Matty, not very interested. ' Oh, look, Olwen, here's another story about Oswald and Angela and the ruined castle.'

'I don't like that one so much as 'The Rajah's Jewels',' said Olwen. 'That's a beautiful story. If my papa were going to India I'd ask him to bring back sapphires and peacock's feathers.'

Matty thought it would be more exciting to have a papa who stayed at home and kept a shop, particularly if it were the right kind of shop, like the Beehive. But at that moment they were interrupted by a small child tied up in a shawl, who trotted in with a jug and pushed it silently across the counter.

'Is it treacle you want?' Olwen asked in Welsh, getting down from her drawer. The child nodded mutely, and Olwen set the jug under the large green urn, fixed in one corner of the counter.

'Matty, you can turn the handle.'

What pleasure it was to see the thick, black stream oozing

slowly into the jug! Matty wished that a whole string of children would come, bearing empty treacle jars, but for the rest of the short winter afternoon their peace was undisturbed. Bent over *Chatterbox*, the hard edge of the drawer beneath her, the taste of peppermint chasing the flavour of raspberry in her mouth, Matty was aware of extreme happiness. By four o'clock it was too dark to read any more, and Lizzy Owen, the carpenter's daughter, who was helping Mr Tudor with his Christmas stocktaking, bustled into the room to light the oil lamp hanging from a hook in the ceiling over the counter.

'Here's Catherine Jane come to fetch you, cariad,' she said to Matty; 'there's pity you have to go so soon. Next time you must stay to tea, indeed you must. Olwen likes to have your company, don't you, Olwen? for you are both so fond of book-reading.' In the outer shop Mr Tudor was busy counting flannel shirts, rolls of oilcloth and clusters of tallow candles. He looked up to smile at Matty and send a message to her mother.

'Ask your mother if she is coming to the Singing Practice on Friday. Tell her it is very important. St. Idris hasn't competed in an Eisteddfod for three years, and we must beat the lot, certain sure. What about you, Catherine Jane? Have you not a nice little soprano? And Marged too! There's a good steady contralto, I'm thinking. You must not hide all your lights under bushels.'

Catherine Jane laughed and shook her head, but once across the street she grew scornful, to Matty's surprise. 'As though we should all three be out of the house together, the mistress and Marged and me, singing in his old choir! And what would happen to you children, I'm wondering? Tell me that, Mr Tudor Beehive.'

But Lettice, stitching alone in the lamplight after the children had gone to bed, was not so sure what course to take. She had not sung in a choir since her girlhood at Nantgwyn, when she, the least gifted member of a musical family, had

gone with Jim and Martha and the others to the weekly Singing
Practice. Ah, those walks on May evenings through the gorse
scented lanes, with a mild moon hanging in the sky above the
Rhydfelin hills! All the boys and girls together, her cousins
Tom and Howell among them. When those two joined in with
Jim's baritone and Martha's pure, strong voice, Lettice felt her
soul caught up to Heaven.

The thought of the freedom and sweetness of those
early days rushed on her now, as she sat alone, the basket of
unmended socks still before her, for the repairs to Archie's
coat had taken half the evening. If John had been at home she
might have felt differently about the Choir Practice. She would
have persuaded him to come too, to bear her company, though
he was no great singer. But to go alone and sit all evening next
to some giggling girl! (For her voice was still soprano, and
such friends as she found there would certainly be among the
sober, matronly contraltos.) Did she really want to do it?

'Perhaps it will be better than sitting alone every evening,'
she thought, folding back the hearth-rug and turning down the
lamp. Halfway up the stairs she paused at the landing window.
The rain had ceased and a wintry moon shone on the roof of
the Beehive. 'I shall wait till Richard Tudor asks me properly,'
she said to herself. 'He needn't think it is enough, just to send
a message by Catherine Jane.'

There was no lack of asking, Lettice found next day.
Richard Tudor, 'the indefatigable secretary of the St. Idris
Choral Society', as they called him at the yearly speech-
making, walked across before noon to beg her to join the
choir, and 'Owens Bach', the conductor himself, looked in the
same day on his way into the city. He was a miller and small
farmer from a hamlet four miles away. Not much of a farmer
or business man, it was said, and everyone referred to his wife
as 'that poor Mrs Owens'. Yet when it came to music, ah, then
there was no question of his mastery! With his baton in his
hand he became as one having authority, eaten up with the

flame of zeal and knowledge.

But the man whom Catherine Jane showed into the parlour of the Stone House was Moses without his rod. Lettice found him hunched on the edge of his chair, nursing his bowler hat; a small, black figure wearing a greasy mackintosh, one dark lock of hair fallen over his swarthy forehead. On the far side of the Border Owens Bach would certainly have been dubbed a foreigner; compared with the light-haired Celts of St. Idris and with Lettice herself, coming forward to greet him, he seemed what he probably was – the relic of some old, half-forgotten strain of the human race.

He began brokenly in English, but on Lettice answering at once in Welsh, he turned gratefully to his own language, helped out with many a gesticulation of his surprisingly small fine hands. The Idrisland Eisteddfod, as she knew, was to be held at St. Idris this year. Never would it do for the prize to go to a neighbouring choir. Their numbers had shrunk; they must have new blood.

'Now, Mrs Captain Peters, you are a member of the Nantgwyn family. Everyone knows what that means. Will you join us this winter?'

'But, Mr Owens, I do not sing like my brothers and sisters. I wish I did.'

The little conductor pushed away her objection with both hands.

'It is not only the voice. It is knowing how to control it. Mrs Captain Peters, I heard your brother Jim conduct the Nantgwyn choir at Hendre Eisteddfod last summer. I tell you it was beautiful. His pianissimos were so fine, you could scarcely see them – a cobweb of sound strung over a dark cave. Then his crescendos, he drew them up like the waves of the ocean, till it was a sea of song – *mor o gan*. '*Mor o gan yw Cymru i gyd,*' he quoted, '*All Wales is a sea of song,*' and fell into silence, brooding over the memory of the music and the vision it had evoked.

Lettice put out a hand and touched his knee.

'It is nice to hear anyone speak so well of Jim's music. I will come and sing my best. But you must not expect too much of me.'

Owens Bach jumped up, grasped his hat and made for the door. 'Well done, well done,' he cried delightedly and rushed out. Halfway down the front steps he turned back to shout, 'We'll beat them all yet. There is not one choir that will stand up to St. Idris!'

The following Friday found Lettice and Catherine Jane scurrying to bath the two younger children before seven o'clock, for Catherine Jane had been roped into the choir too, and only Marged, who conveniently protested that she would not make an old show of herself by singing in any choir, was left to keep house. Marged now came upstairs to say that Mr Howell Lloyd, Trehafod, had called in and was waiting below.

'Cousin Howell! What a moment to choose,' cried Lettice, who was plaiting Matty's hair. Both children were clamorous to see him.

'Mamma, may we come downstairs?'

'Cousin Howell gave me five pennies when he came one time,' added Philip.

'Shillings, not pennies, silly,' said Matty. 'Mamma, may we come?'

'No, certainly not. You are to have your suppers in the nursery as usual,' said Lettice firmly.

Whatever could Howell be doing here now, she wondered, while she tied a ribbon on Matty's second plait. Then, stopping to smooth her own curls for an instant before the candlelit mirror, she hurried downstairs.

Howell Lloyd was standing in the middle of the parlour, looking very big and jovial. Lettice was suddenly aware of the scent of good tobacco, tweeds and a faint mixture of whisky and the stable that were almost overpoweringly masculine. The parlour, with its carved Indian tables and china knick-knacks, became a dim, frail background for the big man with his bright blue eyes and red moustache. He crossed the room in two strides and kissed her heartily on the cheek.

'Well, Letty fach, how goes it? I can see you're well, for you're prettier than ever! Come and sit down now and tell me all the news.'

'Oh, Howell, I can't! It's the Singing Practice this evening. But it's good to see you again. Will you stay and have some supper, if you don't mind eating it alone? Marged can get it in no time.'

She had turned back to the door when Howell seized her wrist and pushed her firmly into a chair.

'I don't want any supper. No, nor drink neither – I daresay I've had enough of that already. And I don't care about your old Singing Practice. They can get on without that little piping voice of yours for a bit. But I want to hear all about you and the children. What's your last news of John? Now, tell me everything.'

He flung himself on the settee, stretching out his long legs in their well-cut riding breeches.

Lettice laughed. 'You always were a masterful man. But I haven't much news. John was at Cape Town when I last heard, and wrote that they'd had a fair voyage so far. The children are all well. Ivor and Archie are having supper at the Vicarage with the Trevor boys and will be sad to miss you. As for Matty and Philip, they're upstairs and dying to see you,' (and with a sudden inspiration), 'Go up and talk to them a minute, there's a dear. They're having their supper in the nursery. I'll put on my bonnet and then you can walk with me as far as the schoolroom.'

Howell laughed. 'I see you've made up your mind to have me out of this house. All right, I'll go and talk to the brats.'

He tramped upstairs, while Lettice flew to the kitchen and

told Catherine Jane, who was waiting, to go on ahead. Then she ran upstairs, fastened on her bonnet and slipped into her jacket with the high fur collar.

Through the open door of the nursery she could hear pealing laughter and cries of 'Do it again, Cousin Howell! Me next!' and the thought came to her of how much gaiety a household must needs forgo when the master, the fun-maker, is absent. But Howell should certainly marry – he would make an excellent father of a family. She would tell him so today.

Soon they were walking together up the dark street to the schoolroom, and Howell insisted on giving her his arm. Lettice asked in turn about all the relations. How was Uncle Simon over at Cefnmawr? Had he seen Aunt Damaris or any of the Cilau cousins? Was Aunt Rachel's rheumatism any better?

Howell halted suddenly in the middle of the road.

'Lettice, don't go on asking me questions. I tell you I've neglected them all. You and Jim over at Nantgwyn are the only relations I ever see, and that's not because you're related but because I'm fond of you. But you see how it is. I come fifteen miles to talk to you and you turn me out of your house and make me walk up a villainous dark road to a chapel schoolroom.'

'Howell, that isn't fair! You know very well how welcome you are. But why have you stayed so long away? Where have you been all this time?'

'Well, I slipped over to Ireland again to buy a horse or two. I brought back a lovely little mare from Waterford and when I've put some flesh on her bones I'll make a good thing out of her. Or perhaps I won't. I daresay I'll keep her and hunt her myself.'

'How's the farm doing?'

'Well enough, but I let the accounts look after themselves, so it's hard to say.'

'What you want,' said Lettice emphatically, 'is a good wife to run the place for you. Seriously, Howell, why don't you get married?'

'Why not put the same question to Jim? He's the sort of husband a woman wants.'

'You know quite well about Jim. There was someone, once—'

'Oh, that! Hasn't he got over that yet?'

'No, he hasn't,' said Lettice a little distantly. No one must ever question Jim in her presence. 'Jim is not the sort of person,' she added, 'to change his mind on a matter like that.'

'Neither am I. I've as good a right as Jim to remain faithful. Haven't I?'

'Oh, Howell, I never knew. You never told me there was anyone.'

'But you knew very well there was.' The bantering note had gone from his voice as he hurried on. 'Lettice, you remember the Christmas Eve when the fields were flooded and I carried you halfway from Nantgwyn to sing carols at Pentremawr? And those old choir practices of Jim's, all of us walking back through the lanes, and the white owl that flew out of a tree and frightened you?'

Lettice's mind gave a little start. Yes, she too remembered. How short a time ago she had walked the same lanes in memory, recalling the laughter of those fair, free days. Sometimes, when boys and girls passed her window, talking and jesting together, she felt like calling out, 'Make the most of your freedom! Don't be in too much of a hurry to lose it, for you'll never, never find it again.'

But what was Howell talking about? That was something different. He must have had too much whisky, as she had suspected from the beginning.

'Howell, isn't it time you were starting home? Where have you left your horse and trap?'

'At the City Arms.'

'It's a dark night,' said Lettice, thinking of the winding, hilly road to Trehafod.

'That's no matter. The moon'll be up soon, anyway. There's no hurry.'

'It's high time you went home. Thank you for coming with me, and good-night to you, Howell.'

With a swift movement she disengaged her arm from his and hastened forward to join the dark groups of people entering the schoolroom porch.

'Lettice! Lettice!'

She heard him call twice, but she did not answer, hurrying out of the darkness into the bright lamp-lit room, with its smell of paraffin and recently scrubbed wood, and with rows of hard narrow benches suited to the small frames of Sunday School scholars, and a brown map, hanging on the wall, of the mission field in the Khassia Hills of India.

The room buzzed with chatter, and for a moment Lettice felt confused and shy. Then she saw Mrs Jenkins, the new minister's wife, smiling, nodding and patting the bench. So she was soprano too! Lettice took her place beside her, exchanged greetings with two or three others near by and looked round.

Catherine Jane was sitting in the front row of all, with three other girls who had the traditionally frivolous air of all sopranos. On the opposite side sat the contraltos, looking like a flock of elderly sheep into whose midst one goat had strayed.

The goat was Mr Price Powell, a thin man with sloping shoulders, who bore his falsetto voice like an infliction. He sat between Miss Roberts, the milliner, and the governess from the Vicarage. Behind them were ranged the basses – Mr Lewis Edwards, the squire of Tremadoc, a jovial, burly man and a great breeder of cattle; beside him Johnny Morris, the lifeboat cox; Evan Evans, the tailor, Richard Tudor of the Beehive, the chemist's assistant and a batch of farmers' sons. Lettice could not see the tenors without turning her head, but a swift sideways glance told her, what she had already guessed, that the wooden-legged weaver was immediately behind, a man with so sweet a voice that Ivor once, when a little boy, had asked if a sham leg would make him sing like Shôn Ellis.

With each new arrival the hum of chatter and laughter rose higher on the air; the front line of sopranos were trying to stifle their giggles with handkerchiefs pressed tightly to their mouths; the first row of contraltos was in earnest conversation with the row behind, all except Mr Price Powell and the Vicarage governess, who continued to study their scores, while the men at the back of the room were laughing and stamping and calling out to each other in a mixture of Welsh and English.

Suddenly a sharp, quick step, and the voices and jests falter and fade – 'Owens Bach' is stumping up the gangway and climbs on to the little platform at the far end. In the room below him there is a last moment searching for scores, and a few murmured remarks which Owens Bach quells with a rap of his baton.

With his black lock of falling hair and his stooping shoulders, the conductor looks like an old bear roused from his cave, snuffing the air before he starts his hunting. But when the hunt begins, ah, then he is a bear no longer, thinks Lettice, but a young god moving to the chase, harnessing them all to his chariot.

Owens Bach does not beat time with his arms alone, but with his whole body, while with his hands he calls forth the music, hushes it, soothes it, returns it whence it came, and then gathers all four parts together in one triumphant whole.

Lettice steals a glance across at the basses. The chemist's assistant is a small man with poor teeth, but his face is transfigured now; as for the Vicarage governess, her eyes are shining like stars, and Miss Roberts, the milliner, has not noticed that her own bonnet is crooked. Owens Bach has them all in the hollow of his hand, yet even now he is not satisfied. He taps on the music stand and brings them to a halt, his face creased with the effort of finding words.

'Listen now, I am wanting *silks*; what you are giving me

is *alpaca.*'

Mr Tudor Beehive will appreciate that, thinks Lettice, smiling behind her score; but for Owens Bach, the miller, it would surely have been more natural to say, 'I have asked for the finest white flour and you have given me *wholemeal.*'

After the glees there is a short rest, filled with the buzz of talk and an exchange of peppermints; then Owens Bach is calling them to take their copies of *The Messiah.* 'The Mezziah', he calls it, dwelling reverently on the word. Lettice has an old copy of Jim's, scored with little marks of his own. They are like a lamp in her hand and she gives herself more closely than before to the music and to the eternal words of the Scripture.

'Surely, surely,' they sing, 'He hath borne our griefs and carried our sorrows.' What heavy burdens they must be, the sorrows of the world!

'And with His stripes we are healed.' But there were so many incalculable griefs to heal; disappointment, loneliness, broken hopes. Jim's still face when the girl he was to have married suddenly died; Philip saying 'Bwoken, Bwoken!' in a low voice, over and over again, when Archie had smashed his little glass musical-box; Howell calling her name when she had left him that evening in the street.

'Now we shall practise the Hallelujah Chorus.' A little note of expectancy runs through the room and the old hands, who have sung it many times before, prepare cheerfully to lift the roof. Owens Bach is quick to scent this over-confidence. A few bars and he stops them with a gesture of despair.

'*Think* of it, *think* of it,' he implores them. 'Picture to yourselves Heaven open, God Almighty on His throne with the Holy Angels crying, 'Hallelujah!' round Him, and *sing*, *sing* as if you saw it all, not as if you were coming home from a fair.'

Lettice would have liked to walk back alone when it was all over, with the great choruses still ringing in her head, but there were too many kind neighbours anxious to see her home. She parted from Mrs Jenkins, the minister's wife, on the opposite side of the Cross and turned towards her own door. The moon had risen and sailed serenely in the sky, beyond the quiet huddle of roofs and the dark tower of the Cathedral in the valley below. She saw Catherine Jane leave her little company of friends and run round to the back door. Was Howell safely home by now at Trehafod? Lettice wondered, and their conversation of that evening came to her as something faraway and quite unimportant.

From her handbag she drew the big front door key and fitted it to the lock, then turned to have one more look at the wintry sky. She and John had once made a pact that whenever they looked at the moon each would think of the other. However far apart, the moon was something they still could share. Turning her face to its brightness she thought of him now.

'Heaven open, God Almighty on His throne, with the Holy Angels crying Hallelujah!' had said Owens Bach.

It seemed to Lettice, standing there, that Heaven's doors were always open, and if only John and she could be together they might find a way in. John would certainly be made welcome, but he would never go inside without Lettice. She smiled at the very notion, then suddenly realised that Mr Tudor Beehive was waving good-night from the other side of the Cross, and hurried indoors.

Chapter 6

The Chough's Nest and a Journey

Spring was back at St. Idris.

Down in the Cathedral Close the rooks were clamourously nesting, and the lanes were suddenly hot with sunshine and the scent of gorse. Speedwells opened eyes of brilliant blue under the sheltered banks; along the fields cowslips shook in the wind, and blue squills flung starry carpets to the very margin of the cliffs.

Here, on the last stronghold of the land, the gorse made shining ramparts. Matty, running between the bushes, skipping and jumping to avoid the fierce prickles, thought they were like the golden chain armour of Welsh princes. There were several princes buried in the grass-grown side chapels of the Cathedral, their faces battered by time but their limbs still shapely and the pattern of their jewelled belts cut deep into the stone. Yet no princely gold or jewels could have shone more clearly than the colours of sea, sky and flowers on these May mornings, when thrift and campions and white moon daisies cascaded down the rocky slopes, showing their loveliness to the wasteful ocean, and to adventurous boys who climbed, unheeding, down the steep cliffs in search of eggs.

John had written from Rangoon that he might be back by the end of the summer, and Lettice, feeling that summer had already come, decided to buy herself a bonnet for Whitsuntide and to give Matty a new frock of dove-grey poplin, trimmed with Vandyke braid. Early one afternoon she and Matty walked over to Miss Preece, the dressmaker, for the first fitting.

Miss Preece lived in a cottage that was coloured pink and white outside like apple blossom. On the walls of her sitting-room hung a picture of the Bay of Naples, painted on glass, and another of the clipper Spindrift, in which Miss Preece's father had been mate. The model of a sailing ship in a bottle stood on the sideboard, and a couple of flying-fish in a glass case on the mantelpiece. In the front garden, sheltered from the sea wind by a stout whitewashed wall, primulas and columbine grew with veronica and flowering currant.

The scent of the currant flowers came deliciously through the open door to Lettice, as she sat in a low rocking-chair watching Miss Preece fix her pins in Matty's new frock. But Matty, fidgeting as Miss Preece's pins just missed her skin and dreading the final moment when the stuff, bristling with a hundred points, would be drawn upwards over her shrinking person, scowled at the sunshine on the garden path, where a tabby cat was cleaning its paws. The miserable unfairness of being a girl lay once more heavy on her heart, for here was she spending this perfect afternoon in Miss Preece's cottage while Ivor and Archie were searching for eggs on St. Idris Head.

Lettice roused herself from a pleasant dreaminess to attend to the business of the day.

'Don't you think, Miss Preece, that the yoke drops a little on that side? Matty dear, are you standing quite straight? No, you see, you weren't! How can Miss Preece fit you properly if you stand on one leg?'

Disconsolately Matty stood on two legs. What fun it would have been to run along the top of the cliff, with the wind in her hair. When they clambered down the side Ivor would help her over the difficult bits, and perhaps let her climb on his shoulders to reach an egg in some cranny high up on the rocks...

On the garden path the tabby cat was beginning her second paw. Someone came running along the road outside, the sound of footsteps flapping in the dry air. The gate at the bottom of Miss Preece's garden, which always stuck a little, was pushed quickly open and there was a young man, his shirt open at the

neck, the sweat standing on his forehead. He came up to the
doorway, suddenly filling it, and called out in Welsh, 'Is Mrs
Peters there?'

Miss Preece, kneeling on the floor with pins in her mouth,
stared with round eyes, but Lettice rose from the rocking-
chair and came forward in one swift movement.

'What has happened? Tell me quickly.'

The young man was so out of breath that he stood for a
minute, holding the door-post. Then he said, 'Your son has
fallen over the cliff at Penwern. They sent me to tell you to
make ready.'

Lettice's hand went up to her mouth, and for a moment
there was silence except for the noise of the young man trying
to find his breath. Then in a small, harsh voice that was not in
the least like her own, Lettice asked, 'Who is it, do you say?
Which of my sons?'

'I am not knowing his name, but it was the bigger boy of
the two. Fell over the old cliff, he did, going after the eggs.
There was a man swimming in the sea, one of the visitors
from Hendre, and he has gone round carrying a rope so that
he may draw your son up to the top of the cliff. They are
bringing him to your house, and sent me running to tell you.
But I could not find you. It was your maid Catherine Jane who
told me where you were. She is a niece to my auntie over at
Clogfan.'

But the last words were spoken to Miss Preece and Matty,
for already Lettice had gone. She did not run, nor even hurry
very much, but she walked without seeing anyone or anything
as she passed.

'Oh, dear anwyl, what troubles there are in the world!'
cried Miss Preece. She wished the young man would go, for
how could she take Matty out of her frock with him standing
there catching his breath?

'Would it be your brother who has fallen over the cliff?'
he asked, looking at Matty. Matty did not say anything. She

wanted to cry out and to run after Mamma. But she was pinned tight in the stuff and her own frock was lying on a chair.

Presently the young man went away, closing the stiff gate very carefully behind him, and Miss Preece pulled the poplin dress back over Matty's head. She did not mind that the pins scratched. All the time Miss Preece was talking to herself, lamenting Ivor's misfortune and scolding the young man for the way in which he had broken the news.

'Has Catherine Jane no sense at all in her head that she should let him come running like a wild bull to frighten your poor mother? All that hurrying and scurrying won't mend the poor boy's bones! There you are, child, you'd best go after your mother. That yoke's still crooked and the pins anyhow, but there, what's the use? Maybe it's a black dress I'll have to make for you, after all.'

It was more than an hour before the men brought Ivor home. In the house Lettice was preparing with so still a look on her face that no one, except Marged, dared speak to her. First she had sent Catherine Jane with a message to Dr Parry, and Matty was dispatched to Mr Rhys, the chemist, with a list in her hand. Next she carried blankets and pillows down to the sofa in the dining-room and set Marged boiling kettles of hot water. Old linen she fetched from the cupboard upstairs and tore into long strips, brought arnica from the medicine chest and brandy from the sideboard cupboard. Then she sat down and waited. If Ivor came back to her alive everything that she could prepare was ready. Now the only thing left was prayer.

They came at last, bringing Ivor on a farm cart, with a white-faced Archie trotting behind. Not till afterwards did Lettice recognise the men who had brought back her son and hasten to thank them. For at the moment she saw only Ivor, his blue eyes eagerly seeking hers from under the blood-soaked handkerchief round his forehead, and heard his quick words as they lifted him down, 'All right, Mam fach. I'm not really hurt.'

Then he fainted away as they carried him indoors and Lettice flew for the brandy.

That evening, sitting in the boys' bedroom, her chair close to the window to catch the last light of the spring dusk, she wrote to John:

Dr Parry says he will soon be mended. The collar-bone is broken and one rib is cracked, but in one so young these will not take long to join. For the rest, he is but cut and bruised, and I think is bound to suffer a little from the shock of the fall.

From Archie's account it seems that a piece of rock gave way and he fell a fearful distance. Had the tide been out they tell me he would certainly have been killed, but the water broke his fall; yet he might have drowned had not this stranger, who was swimming a little way off, come to help him and fasten the rope round his body so that he could be drawn up the cliff by the farm men at the top. Poor Archie, thinking he was dead, ran all the way to Penwern farmhouse.

It has been a sharp lesson for both of them. For Ivor I have no more fears. I know his body may undergo many dangers, but I now have an assurance that he will grow in goodness. While I waited for him to come home I prayed that he should not come back to me alive unless his life were pleasing to God. Now I know that Ivor will grow up to be a good man.

The light had gone and the square of paper gleamed wanly under her hand. The boy in bed stirred on his pillow and Lettice rose quickly and went over to him.

'What are you doing, Mamma?'

'Writing to Papa. Shall I send him your love?'

'Yes, please. And oh, Mamma, you might tell him one thing from me.'

'Of course I will. What is it you want to say?'

'Tell him that Archie and I found a chough's nest. There

were five eggs in it, five beauties. I only took one and Archie was carrying it, so it didn't get broken!'

As Dr Parry had predicted, Ivor was soon about again, with his rib and collar-bone well strapped, and a scar on his forehead. Whitsuntide came and went, and soon afterwards came a letter from Great-aunt Phoebe inviting all the family to pay a visit to Great-uncle Simon and herself at Cefnmawr.

'I am sure,' she said in her letter to Lettice, 'that you are in need of a change and rest after the fright of Ivor's fall. But please think too of the pleasure it would give your Uncle Simon and me to see you all again under our roof.'

Lettice debated with herself whether so many visitors would be too much for the kind old couple, for Uncle Simon was a minister with three chapels in his charge, and no woman was more occupied with good works than Aunt Phoebe. But they were a childless couple, and what greater pleasure, thought Lettice, looking down the table at the four children all eating their porridge, could a mother give her friends than by occasionally lending them her jewels?

She therefore wrote to Aunt Phoebe accepting the invitation, and the three elder children pranced with joy at the thought of missing school for at least two whole weeks. No one thought of going as far as Cefnmawr for less time than that, and Matty recalled with shame that she had once caused loud laughter in school by asking Miss Carlyle if she might have a half-holiday 'to go to Great-aunt Phoebe's for a fortnight.'

Uncle Simon and Aunt Phoebe lived just over the Carmarthenshire border, among the blue shapely hills that guarded the promontory of Idrisland. On the day of departure Lettice and the children breakfasted early and set off at seven o'clock in Tom Pugh's fly for the three-hour drive to the railway station. The day bore every promise of being fine, with a soft haze veiling the sun and filling the little hollows through which their road dipped and wandered.

At Croesty the three elder children jumped down from their seats to climb the long hill, while Lettice stayed in the carriage with Philip. The horses reached the top long before the straggling children and stayed to rest. Lettice was glad of this. She never wearied of that last view of the sea before the road turned inland. There it stretched, a slowly turning line of silver on the empty sands, and beyond lay the islands, remote and indestructible in their morning beauty. After long absence from home that was the first outpost of St. Idris to greet the returning traveller. In years to come the three children, now idling on the dusty road, stopping to pick a flower, to tie up a bootlace or chase a butterfly, would hail it like a dear lost friend, or watch its fading sky-line with homesick hearts.

To newcomers that view of Croesty seemed the end of the world and they were astonished to find that St. Idris lay beyond even this Ultima Thule.

At ten o'clock in the morning, when the sun had sucked the last mist from the hollows and stood high in the sky, they clattered through the streets of Westford, crossed the old stone bridge over the river and drew up at the confectioner's, a pleasant, clean shop with bow-fronted windows, standing between the bridge and the square keep of the Norman castle on the hill above.

For Lettice there was continual pleasure in the ritual of life. She liked to observe it, even in trifling things: small ceremonies that were repeated till they grew rich in associations and charged with memories of 'last time'. Now one piece of the journey, inseparable from the arrival at Westford, was the taking of refreshment at Owen's shop. Whenever she gave her unvarying order for tea, jam sandwich and Queen cakes, Lettice recalled other occasions – hurried journeys to Liverpool and Belfast, Dundee and London, to meet John's ship; often alone, sometimes taking the children; once or twice with John himself, though these times were so few and so precious that she hugged them to her heart. One thing was certain: to enter Owen's shop, to say good-morning to short, black-eyed Mrs Owen and her two plump, black-eyed daughters, was the beginning of all good adventures. Only today there was a difference, for their train would bear them deeper into kindly Wales, towards the sound of Welsh voices and the friendly welcome of relations. The little spice of apprehension that usually accompanied a journey was missing this morning from Mrs Owen's Queen cakes.

At White Abbey, the sleepy junction where they changed trains some hours later in the day, the children sat in a row on a station bench and considered with disapproval an advertisement painted on the opposite wall. It heralded a 'sale of raincoats from stock, also overcoats', set out in a mixture of English and Welsh, as follows:

Cyflawnder o Raincoats
Mewn Stoc
Ac overcoats

'Why don't they stick to one language?' asked Ivor. '"O raincoats" sounds so silly, like Dr Prout making us decline nouns in Latin.'

'And "Cyflawnder" makes you think of lots of people floundering about on a very wet day,' added Archie.

'The signal's gone down. She won't be long now.'

From White Abbey to Cwmbach the journey was very leisurely. Philip fell asleep, his head on Lettice's knee, while Ivor and Matty read their story-books and Archie, head out of window, kept the others informed of all that was happening.

'Here's the level-crossing and the stoker's got down to open the gate. The man with red hair, you know, the one that smiled at us. Now we're through and the guard's shutting the gate. What a joke if they left him behind one day!'

Slowly the train gathered steam and puffed between the green banks; wild roses and elder flowers almost brushed the carriage windows, and where the little streams ran by was the shining gold of kingcups. Then with a doleful groaning of brakes the engine pulled up once more, and Archie reported that an old woman was hailing the train from the top of the bank with her umbrella.

Lettice, remembering the long drive still before them and Aunt Phoebe's excellent tea, sighed a little at these vagaries. On the Cwmbach railway cows were said to scratch themselves on the buffers of the engine, and when passing fields of mushrooms, passengers, engine-driver and guard had been known to descend and gather the crop.

'Anyway, it's too early for mushrooms,' said Lettice to herself, growing drowsy, while with slow deliberation the train made its way upwards into the narrowing hills.

They were there at last, climbing down with their bags on to the little wooden platform. Foxgloves grew thick on the bank above and the hill air tasted sweet and heady after the dusty railway carriage.

'There's Uncle Simon!' called the children, and ran to meet a man in a minister's long black coat, a big man with so kind and reassuring a look on his round, clean-shaven face, that no one in his company could possibly continue to feel either cross or anxious.

'Well done, well done, Letty fach,' he said, holding her hand in his great warm one. 'You've brought them all and not one missing. That's the way it should be and glad we are to see you.'

Stowing their bags in the bottom of the dog-cart they climbed in, Lettice and Philip in front with Uncle Simon, and the three elder children in a row on the back seat where they could watch the dusty road run out like a ribbon from under their feet. After the bare rocks of St. Idris the country was astonishingly green and heavy with summer. On the hillside above their heads hung little woods of dwarf oaks, ghostly with grey lichen. The ferns on each side of the high-banked lane were so tall with the full growth of June and the lane itself in some places so narrow that the ferns met in the middle and seemed to block the passage of the dog-cart. Here and there, at the bottom of a steep pitch, a little stream crossed the road and they had the joy of splashing through the water.

One of these places was already sacred to a special rite invented by Ivor, and Uncle Simon pulled up Doli, the brown mare, so that the elder children might observe it. Scrambling down from the trap, they ran ahead to a spot where a tinkling brook ran out of the ferns and hastened across their road to disappear beyond in a green hollow, guarded by foxgloves and tangled with honeysuckle. This was the boundary between two counties, and the three children, following Ivor's inspired lead, drew up on the near margin, chanting 'Now we are in Pembrokeshire!' A flying leap landed them on the other side, crying 'Now we are in Carmarthenshire!' Then they straddled the stream with a leg on either bank, shouting 'Now we are in Pembroke and Carmarthen!' Matty's short legs were hardly equal to this part of the ritual, and her feet, in their elastic-sided boots, were sliding into the water until Ivor pulled her across to the further side.

After this, the road climbed another hill, and Doli mended her pace before coming to a full stop in front of a plain farm gate. They had arrived.

Uncle Simon and Aunt Phoebe lived in a long, low house covered with the glossy leaves of a magnolia, and there on the doorstep was Aunt Phoebe, very small and neat, wearing a white lace cap. She kissed them all warmly, sent the children to wash their hands in the back kitchen, and led Lettice upstairs to the spare bedroom which had been prepared for her coming. A great tester bed stood in one corner against the wall and there was a little trundle bed for Philip at its foot. The two small windows with their deep window-seats were shadowy with the movement of leaves in the afternoon sunshine; the warm water in the thick blue china basin was deliciously soft and so was Aunt Phoebe's fine linen towel, smelling of lavender.

Aunt Phoebe herself moved about the room like a small bird fidgeting in a bush.

'Is Ivor really well again?'

'Yes, thank you, Aunt Phoebe, but he mustn't climb any more rocks before his bones are mended.'

'Tut, tut, I should think not indeed. Well, well, he'll find no rocks here. Poor thing, poor thing, what a time you've had! But never mind that now. Ann Jane has the kettle boiling and there's glad you'll be to have tea.'

Every house has a claim to fame for one reason or another. But Aunt Phoebe's house differed from others for a multiplicity of reasons. Nowhere else did you get such paper-thin oatcakes, much too thin for the golden butter that was spread on them. No other house on a wet day contained so many amusing puzzles and games for the children; Halma, with men of scarlet, green, black and yellow; a solitaire board of polished mahogany with green glass balls; tiny ivory dominoes in a heart-shaped box; and a Chinese puzzle which Aunt Phoebe's sailor brother had brought from Canton. Then how amusing it was to watch the maid make the bed with a long stick, for that was the way in which Lettice's great bed was straightened each morning. The frame was too heavy to move from the wall every day, and so the huge featherbed upon it, after vigorous pummellings, was turned, flattened out and its blankets tucked in by Ann Jane's dexterous use of the stick with its crooked handle.

The day after they came to Cefnmawr was Sunday, and the whole household attended morning service at Rehoboth, which was the nearest of the three chapels in Uncle Simon's charge. His grandfather had built it on his own land, and the date 1784 stood over the sturdy, whitewashed porch. The outside of the chapel was pink, the soft pink of 'bye-and-byes' (Aunt Phoebe's name for peonies), or the inmost curve of a sea-shell, which Matty thought the prettiest colour in the world. But within the chapel was austere with the austerity of whitewashed walls and stone-flagged floor. High-backed seats flanked both sides of the pulpit and on these sat the Cefnmawr family; the rest of the space was filled with backless wooden benches. A 'set fawr' (big seat) for the deacons stood under the pulpit, and behind it, written on the wall in two languages, Hebrew and Welsh, were the words 'Cry Aloud and Spare Not'.

In the quiet graveyard outside, where no crying could disturb them, were the headstones of Uncle Simon's people, who were Lettice's people too. Preachers, farmers and master mariners lay here with their wives beside them – Lettice and Margaret, Martha and Damaris – while the tide of summer turned from cowslips and cuckoo flower to sorrel and white moon daisies round their graves.

The two doors of the chapel stood wide open on Sunday mornings to the green world outside, and this world was full of innumerable small noises, the murmur of insects, a curlew's call and the distant bleating of sheep. But the interior of the chapel was as cool and swept as a sea cave, and silent but for the clatter of clogs on the stone floor as the worshippers made their way to the benches at the back. To Lettice it was a benediction even to sit waiting in Rehoboth. Perhaps she had been there only in summertime, for in her mind the doors were always open and the gentle, living world flowing in from outside seemed to help Uncle Simon, as with voice raised in earnest prayer he searched for the great simplicities of Love and Truth.

In this bare, sun-filled room spirit met spirit. Lettice was sure of it, and she reflected that this was so because the preacher's religion did not stop on the threshold. With Uncle Simon and Aunt Phoebe the pattern of holiness was woven into the very stuff of their lives. One-tenth, the ancient portion, of Uncle Simon's modest income was regularly set aside as not belonging to him: it was God's property and must be used for His work and His poor. To this kindly, childless couple it seemed indeed that goodness was as natural as breathing. With a little smile Lettice reflected that Uncle Simon had only one vanity, his astounding knowledge of the Bible. He would allow the children to test him by opening the Book at random and beginning a passage. Nearly always he could complete it and they could trip him up only by resorting to the dreary wastes of the Books of Leviticus and Numbers, or to such other stretches of country as they knew already to be out of bounds.

Vanity of any sort was lacking from Aunt Phoebe's nature. Her dress had a Quaker simplicity and no event or season varied her grey frock and white cap. Yet Lettice knew that in her youth Aunt Phoebe had been the belle of the neighbourhood, and had worn a tall Welsh hat and scarlet cloak on Sundays and holidays. That was how Uncle Simon had first seen her, with her short skirt showing her neat ankles, and her black eyes dancing under the brim of her high hat. The hat was still upstairs in Aunt Phoebe's wardrobe – an expensive hat made of the best silk beaver and marked 'Christy's, London'.

But now that bravery was put away and Aunt Phoebe had need of every thrifty device to make Uncle Simon's income do all that was required of it. One of these devices was the saving of coal. The fires at Cefnmawr were scientifically 'banked up' after breakfast to last the day. Not until evening did they break into flame and give a cheerful glow. It was told in the family that an old friend and brother minister of Uncle Simon's once rang for the maid on a winter's day and said, 'Please bring a shawl to put on the fire, it looks so cold.'

Sunday was a busy day at Cefnmawr. Morning service started at ten; at two o'clock came Sunday School and after Sunday School half an hour's Singing Practice. Then at six o'clock there was Evening Service, followed by Seiat, a meeting of Church members and their families, when the children of the congregation were expected to rise in their places and recite aloud such portions of the Scriptures as they had prepared. Presiding at the midday meal, Aunt Phoebe spoke of the pleasure it would give them to hear Ivor, Archie and Matty repeat some of the verses they knew, and the three children exchanged rueful glances.

Kind Uncle Simon spoke next. 'If they come to Evening Service and then take part in Seiat, that is enough for one day, Phoebe. I shan't expect to see them in Sunday School this afternoon. Young limbs were not meant to sit still all day in holiday time.'

The rueful glances vanished, and Lettice thought with relief that there would now be time to hear the children rehearse their verses, so that they would not disgrace themselves before the Seiat. When the meal was finished, she called them all to her room and asked what they wished to recite. Ivor chose the fifty-fifth chapter of Isaiah: *Ho, every one that thirsteth, come ye to the waters!* and repeated the first half-dozen verses very steadily. Matty had known the whole of the Long Psalm at the age of six, but tended by this time to confuse the order of its hundred and seventy-six verses. With her mother's help she now chose and polished some of them, beginning

> *Wherewithal shall a young man cleanse his way?*
> *By taking heed thereto according to Thy word.*

Archie's case was more difficult. For some time he had been learning the Apostle's vision of the New Jerusalem from Revelation, but for one verse only could he be trusted with certainty, that one which refers to *'the fearful and unbelieving and the abominable; whoremongers, sorcerers, idolaters and all liars'*, over which Archie smacked his lips with relish.

Seated on his mother's lap, little Philip repeated the first lines of *'The Lord is my Shepherd'* without any prompting. Satisfied at last, Lettice released them into the golden afternoon and sat down to write her Sunday letter to John.

Now, at the back of Uncle Simon's house was a large, green duck-pond, the colour of rich pea soup and overhung by thorn trees, crooked with age. Near by, almost hidden with nettles, lay a tub which Archie's observant eyes had noted on the evening of their arrival. He told Ivor of his discovery, and both boys ran to the spot, their imaginations fired with a single glorious idea.

Ivor, arm in sling, was unable to do more than direct operations, but no one could do it better. Between them, and in spite of many stings on hands and legs, Archie and Matty succeeded in dragging the tub from its green resting place and trundled it down to the water's edge. They found two pea-sticks in the woodpile to serve as oars, and then Archie gingerly stepped aboard. Balancing himself with great skill he managed to propel the unwieldy craft half-way across the pond.

'Me too! Oh, take me too!' Matty implored. 'Archie, don't be a pig. I helped you roll her down and I'm all nettle stings. Let me work one of the oars.'

'You'd better not, Matty,' said Ivor prudently. 'She'd capsize with two on board.'

But Archie was optimistic. 'All right. There's been a mutiny,' he said. 'The crew have captured the ship and cast off the captain and mate in one of the ship's boats. I'm the skipper and you're my mate, but you'll have to keep quite still and you'd better let me handle the peasticks.'

He manoeuvred his craft back to the shore under an overhanging thorn tree, and Matty, holding the trunk with one hand, carefully inserted herself beside him.

'Heave-ho, my hearties, and mind your head,' said Archie as they pushed out under the low branches.

'Look out!' called Ivor from the shore. 'She's beginning to sink.'

His words were all too true. For many years the tub had

lain in the dry seclusion of the nettle-bed, nursing its cracks like grievances, and now that at last it was launched upon the wetness of the pond the water started to seep gently through every crevice. When Matty stepped on board and her weight was added to Archie's it filled rapidly and sank. Before they had so much as reached the centre of their ocean, skipper and mate found themselves seated ignominiously at the bottom, with the oily green water up to their chins, while Philip, standing on the shore, burst into loud wails, thinking he would nevermore see his brother and sister.

It was Ivor, suddenly conscience-stricken, who pacified Philip and told them what to do next. Archie, for once silent and obedient, carried out directions and dragged his sister ashore. As for Matty, her wretchedness was complete. She had no idea it was possible to be so wet all over, while the new poplin frock clung to every limb. Worst of all was the strong, unmistakable odour of the duck-pond. It was a dejected little party that returned quietly to the back door of Cefnmawr, and delivered themselves to authority.

No words from their mother were needed to point the enormity of their wrong. As she sadly reminded them, Uncle Simon had freed them from Sunday School, and this was the way in which they had broken the Sabbath and his trust in them. Archie and Matty, stripped of their wet clothes, must go straight to bed, and that this would be their portion for the rest of the day was a decision that neither of them questioned.

From her little room under the eaves, Matty watched the sunshine, splintered by the leaves of the pear tree outside the window, and heard the pigeons scrape and coo on the roof. Presently she heard the family – all except Archie – set out for the evening service. Soon they would be holding the Seiat, and Ivor and Philip would say their verses. Sitting up in bed, hands cupping her chin, Matty repeated the words of the psalm she had prepared:

Wherewithal shall a young man cleanse his way?
By taking heed thereto according to Thy word.
With my whole heart have I sought Thee:
O let me not wander from Thy commandments.

What had she and Archie done? They had not taken heed
and so they had wandered from God's commandments.

It was a black occasion, yet it did not spoil the visit to
Cefnmawr. Uncle Simon was so particularly kind that Archie
and Matty almost believed he knew nothing of their misdoing.
But one day at dinner he helped them both to over-generous
platefuls of green peas, fresh from Aunt Phoebe's garden.

'I have always understood,' he remarked, twinkling a little,
'that ducks and peas agree very well together. And ducks and
peas are better than duckings; eh, Matty and Archie?'

Matty's poplin frock never quite recovered from the pond,
though dear Ann Jane did all she could with her washing and
ironing and hanging-out on a lavender bush. But when the
time came to go home, Aunt Phoebe gave Matty a length of
beautiful dark brown material, woven from the wool of her
own black sheep. Miss Preece made it up into a new frock for
the autumn.

Chapter 7

The Echoing Past

Matty was reading her story-book in the Bishop's Palace and had chosen her favourite seat, one of the windows of the Banqueting Hall, now a broad grassy ledge where, with feet tucked up and the book open on her lap, she could look down into the green courtyard below. Compared with the Palace all other playgrounds were dull and common place, and the four Peters children were well aware of their good fortune. Leaving out consideration of its glorious past, of the prelates who lived like princes within its walls and entertained kings and noblemen to their feasts, the Palace was the best place in the world for Hide-and-Seek and every sort of game.

Only boys, it is true, could climb the lofty chimneys and break their limbs occasionally by falling down them. The girls' many petticoats forbade such feats, but Matty had once taken part in an exploring party along a secret passage with Ivor, Archie and two guttering candles for company; an expedition that ended in all of them being wedged for a time in stifling darkness and then crawling back a little frightened to the light of day.

Quite ordinary sights and sounds took on a special meaning during an escapade in the Palace, and this was because every game they played within those walls held an echo, not the empty echo of voices, but a ghostly octave doubling everything they did and said; an uneasy Fear that could be roused from sleep like the bats clinging to the walls and roofs of the vault below.

When in the course of their games the children chased each other with flying feet down broken stairways, hid themselves behind a spiral bend to watch, through an arrow slit in the wall, their pursuer's stealthy approach, or leapt into the dark mouth of a vault, then it was well to lay a firm hold on the present; to listen for the friendly sound of a cart crossing the Deanery bridge, or remember that Marged had been baking and that there would be fresh bread for tea. Anything at all to keep at bay the thought of men being hunted for their lives, of places slippery with blood, and dripping prison walls from which there was no return to sun and air and cheerfulness again.

But on this summer's day Matty would not have changed the company of the Palace for any other in the world. As she sat quietly reading her book she could fancy that others stood just behind her at the window-sill looking out into the courtyard – knights in armour, ladies wearing wimples and long pointed sleeves, and pages in slashed velvet. They would still be there, if only she could turn her head quickly enough. Their laughter had scarcely died on the breeze; or had it died five hundred years ago, although in the great Palace kitchens the chimney-pieces were still blackened with the roasting of the Bishop's oxen and venison?

Matty decided against turning her head, in case they were startled, or worse still, were not there at all, and went on reading, soothed by the noise of endlessly cawing rooks in the sycamores of the Close, and half entranced by the loveliness of old grey stone and tender grass, by the airy arcades and the blossoming of a rose-window at the end of the Banqueting Hall that had endured in stone all the changes of time and the greedy carelessness of Bishops.

Only when the shadows began to lay long fingers across the turf of the courtyard did Matty close her book and slide down from the window-sill to take her way home past Hall and Solar, Chapel and Vestry. But when she reached the Great Gate she turned back, suddenly remembering that she had forgotten to drop a pin into the Wishing Well. Back she ran, glad of an excuse to linger in the Palace, and yet sorry that the little dark pool of magic powers should be in one of those vaults where already the shadows were deepening. But it would never do to omit her wish, so tiptoeing into the dark corner she dropped her pin into the sunless pool and muttered, 'I wish that the boys may take me with them to the top of Carn Idris next Saturday.' The black water received her votive offering in unruffled silence and Matty ran home.

Between Cathedral and Palace flowed a stream, covered with a tangle of white flowering water-weed and crossed by a stone slab. It was a wide stone with a crack across the middle, and over this Matty took a peculiar leap. She never did this if a grown-up were watching, but in her secret opinion this stone was Llech Llavar, the Speaking Stone. There was a book at home that told the story of how once on a time, when a funeral was passing over it, 'the stone broke forth into speech and by the effort cracked in the middle, which fissure is still visible'. There was the crack on the bridge, plain for all to see, so of course it was still the same stone and might without warning lift up its voice again. Matty's terror that the stone would speak was only equalled by her disappointment when it said nothing.

All this was too strange to talk about, but was part of the magic web of miracles and marvels that hung like morning gossamers round that enchanted country. By this very stream which Matty was now crossing a saint had rested one summer evening and built a small fire of sticks. The straight blue smoke which rose from that fire was a sign of defiance to a heathen chieftain on his neighbouring hill. That was one of Matty's favourite stories, all the more real because the hill still bore the chieftain's name, though both he and his wily wife had perished of their wickedness, while in the place where the saint had built his solitary fire, soared the great Cathedral.

It was still the Saint's Valley, where the wind suddenly dropped as you came out of the bleak sea country into a place of venerable stones and tall trees. At one time people had fled there from the harshness of the world, and had named it the Valley of Roses. There were roses now, prim red and white ones in the Dean's garden, and over the wall of the Palace that a Bishop had allowed to rot and fall into ruins the wild briar blew every passing June. But the Rose of Sharon, the rose of all the world, still flowered in men's hearts when they left their affairs behind and came to St. Idris. Even the most careless felt themselves to be on holy ground.

The children took these things for granted. Near the edge of the cliff was the place of the saint's miraculous birth. Here a well had gushed forth and stones had risen up around it to comfort the blessed mother, and there they were still, both well and stones, in the middle of a green field, half smothered by blackberries and wild thyme. The young Peters often stopped to drop pebbles and pins and confide their secret wishes to the bright water.

Further along the coast and facing the Island stood the chapel of the Murdered Martyr, its grey symmetry roofless and open to every wind that blew. Even the altar had gone and nothing was to be seen except a little winding stair in one corner, and everywhere the growing grass. The children would play there on their way back from watching a lifeboat practice in the cove below; but it seemed a desolate place, well suited to the unhappy martyr who had fled from the world to the Island, only to be plagued by devils and finally beheaded at their bidding. Nothing daunted, the holy man had picked up his head and, holding it under his arm, had crossed back over the water, landing at the spot where now his crumbling chapel stood.

It seemed that the Wishing Well in the Palace had real potency, for on the following Saturday, while the Peters family sat at their midday meal, Ivor asked Mamma if he and Harry Trefnant might take Matty with them that same day to the top of Carn

Idris. Archie had sprained his ankle while climbing after a jackdaw's nest in the Palace, so he was out of it; but Harry Johns, a distant cousin known always, from the name of the farm in which he was bred, as Harry Trefnant had come over for the day. Ivor and he discussed the best way of climbing the hill, whether they would prefer to go from Silversands after a bathe, or choose the nearer way by Tybryn.

Matty said nothing, though it was difficult to remain silent when so much was at stake. Would Ivor remember the promise he had made long ago? If he and Harry chose the longer way and the bathe, then there was no hope of her going too. The pudding stuck in her throat at the thought of being left behind, but she managed somehow to swallow it. If Mamma saw that she could not eat her dinner, she would never agree to the project. Matty took another mouthful and thought hard of the Wishing Well, seeing with her mind's eye the falling pin and the dark inscrutable face of the water.

Ivor spoke again. 'If we went up by Tybryn, Matty could come too. I said I'd take her one day.'

'Do you think she can walk so far?' asked Mamma.

'It's a long way for the child, and I remember a great many gorse bushes. I don't want her over-tired.'

Matty held her breath as Ivor answered, 'I promise she won't be, Mamma. She's a good little walker now, and Harry and I can hoist her over the worst of the bushes.'

'Very well,' Mamma agreed, and added, 'Take some cake and apples in your pockets.'

O joyful words! Was it possible that the dark water of the Wishing Well, still floating in Matty's mind, winked to itself for one scarcely perceptible moment?

Some time in the afternoon they set off, going first by the dust-powdered road but soon leaving it for ways of Ivor's devising, between the green fields of springing wheat and along the tops of walls where foxgloves and campions grew with pale convolvulus and lady's bedstraw. Then they began to climb, with the hot sun on their backs, first the stony lane through Tybryn farmyard, with a great sow lying asleep and the dreamy cheep-cheep of chickens wandering in the dust, and then over the gorsy hillside straight towards the rocks of Carn Idris. Matty began to wince a little as the bushes pricked her short legs, but Ivor was as good as his word. He and Harry made a chair of their linked hands, and in this fashion the two of them carried her over the fiercest prickles. Then came the last scramble up the rock, with Matty being pushed and pulled, till at last all three of them stood on the summit and looked around them.

For the first time in her life Matty saw the kingdom of her world stretched at her feet. Beside her the two boys were discussing other matters, but she scarcely heard them. At first one proud reflection occupied her mind – she had climbed to the top of Carn Idris and could tell the girls at Miss Carlyle's of her achievement. But this thought, pleasant though it was, gradually gave place to one that was even better – complete satisfaction and delight in what she saw.

It was all there, everything that made her universe. She could see the grey city climbing out of the Cathedral hollow, the green treeless country and scattered farmhouses, pink, white and yellow, to each of which Ivor and Harry could put a name; the winding road to Silversands, along which they had driven Shoni's donkey the day before; the jagged rocks of the Island; and everywhere, round each curve and corner of the land, the curded edges of the sea. That was surely the right arrangement of things, for even Miss Carlyle's map of the two hemispheres showed that there was more sea than land in the world. Would it be possible, Matty wondered, to exist in a place where you couldn't see the sea?

They sprawled on the short turf of the hilltop, under the sun-warmed rocks, and Ivor emptied the apples out of his pocket, picked the rosiest and threw it over to Matty.

'The Island looks grand with the sun on it,' said Harry,

with his mouth full of apple. 'What are the cliffs like to climb? They look steep enough.'

'They're worse on the far side,' Ivor answered. 'William Benbow rowed me over in his coastguard boat in the spring, but when I wanted to go near the edge he made me crawl on my hands and knees. My word, the waves were monsters! They came crashing into the caves and sounded like the bass of the Cathedral organ. That's why they call it Ogof Organ, I suppose.'

'Did you get any eggs?' asked Harry.

'Too early for eggs. But we saw guillemots, and kittiwakes and puffins and I don't know what else. They were like a fall of snow on the rocks; thousands and thousands of them. On the way back we had tea at the farm with Mr and Mrs Richard Lloyd. Those two and the farm servants are the only people on the Island.'

'They must be a bit lonely in the winter,' Harry remarked. 'Suppose they're taken ill? What happens then?'

'There's a beacon built high up on the rocks over this side, and a tin of paraffin kept handy. They can light it in five minutes, and that's the signal for the doctor.'

'The doctor would have a rough passage in winter.'

'He can't always do it,' said Ivor. 'There are three different currents in the Sound, you know, and when its rough no one will risk it. Sometimes he hasn't got there in time, and there's a graveyard just behind the farm. Nine people buried there out of that one house'

He finished his apple and aimed the core dexterously at his cousin's head.

'Good shot,' said Harry calmly, and then asked, 'Who makes the coffins and who takes the services?'

'Depends on how long the rough weather lasts,' said Ivor, and added inconsequently, 'There's a moon tonight. I wish we could stop here and watch it rise.'

But Matty went on thinking about the Island and how grand

it would be to have a funeral to oneself, with no strangers and all the seagulls wheeling and screaming round the graveyard.

They munched their cake and then fell silent, as children sometimes do on a summer evening, till the West turned to rose and they could see the Irish mountains, caught in the net of the sinking sun. The light was beginning to grow tricky, and the Druid circles on the headland below were being sucked into the dark pool of shadow when at last they picked their way down, sure-footed like all children bred on that rocky shore, among the tufts of gorse and heather and half-hidden rabbit-holes of the hillside.

Their young voices called to each other and then faded on the breeze, and Carn Idris was left to itself once more and to its long vigil. One generation after another climbed to its summit and went home again, unmindful of the past, for past and present had a way of growing inextricably confused in that country. The green mound of an early British camp was the favourite place for a picnic, and children played 'I'm king of the castle' on the stone sepulchres of a forgotten people, raced barefoot over the sandy dunes that hid a Roman city, and paddled at low tide among the stumps of forest trees, the edge of that lost land that lay under the waves, the Cantre'r Gwaelod.

There were fishermen who said they had seen the drowned roofs of those forgotten cities, lying under the water, at sunset and in the half-light of early morning. If the houses were still standing, Matty wondered, were there chairs and tables, beds and children's toys in the rooms? And who was left to eat and drink, to sleep and play?

Were there Lost Children in the Lost Land? Or young mermaids? Or only brightly coloured fish, sliding in and out of doors and windows, and up the marble steps of those deserted palaces?

Chapter 8

Saying Goodbye to Betsi
and Locking Out Miss Carlyle

The children of the Stone House, as befitted a sailor's family, accepted as a matter of course their father's sudden appearances and their mother's hurried journeys to distant seaports. When they looked out of their windows on to the Cathedral city there was often nothing to be seen but a collie dog sleeping in the middle of the street, yet it would still be true to say that in some respects the four young Peters were citizens of the world, familiar with monsoons and trade winds, coolies and lascars, rupees and dollars, revolutions in Brazil and gun-running in Spain. Was not the best farm in the neighbourhood owned by Captain John, who had grown rich by running the blockade in the American Civil War? The wide ocean was the world's highway and they lived by it.

So, for that matter, did most of the people of St. Idris, and perhaps a community with its windows 'opening on the foam of perilous seas' could ignore the fussy ways of contemporary life. For although ostrich eggs and flying-fish, Chinese curios and sometimes a profane old parrot were common objects in the cottages; although the sea claimed one or two men out of every family as a matter of course, yet many of the city's inhabitants had never travelled by train or even seen one.

It took three hours to drive to the nearest railway station and the passing of a steam threshing machine through the street of St. Idris was a nine days' wonder. A troop of children followed it and all the old folk came to the doorstep to see the Machine-Tân, 'the fire machine', as they called it.

Strange and incomprehensible were the ways of the railway. One of the Miss Lloyds of Pwllglas, an elderly spinster lady, on making her first train journey had studied with interest the appearance of sundry guards and ticket collectors in smart uniforms, and then remarked tartly that she did not think any of them so attractive that they need proclaim on their caps that they were all married men. The badge, you see, was that of the Great Western Railway, and the Welsh word for husband is 'GWR'. But of course most people knew better than that and could afford to laugh at poor Miss Lloyd.

All the same, a journey was an adventure and anyone undertaking it needed strengthening and encouragement, so that when Lettice engaged Betsi Reynolds' daughter, Lizzie, to go into service in England, it was natural that Lettice should walk over to see her and her family on the eve of departure. She took Matty with her and carried a small package of six new pocket-handkerchiefs, as well as some labels, neatly and clearly written.

Long ago Betsi had been a servant at Nantgwyn, and now her daughter was making the great plunge of taking service as a housemaid with one of the Nantgwyn family, married and living in England. Lizzie would start at daybreak next morning in the carrier's van, which took four hours to reach the railway station.

Betsi's cottage stood in the little hamlet of Trefihangel, a collection of houses coloured pink, yellow and blue, according to their owner's fancy, with roofs of thatch and whitewashed slates. The short cut from St. Idris lay along a grassy lane with high banks where Matty as usual ran aloft, while Lettice picked her way more carefully, holding her skirts in both hands above the drenched grass, for it was July and treacherous, thundery weather.

Betsi was waiting for them at the cottage door, a short, stout woman whose face had a way of breaking into a broad smile. Her treatment of this smile was peculiar – she would hastily cover it with her hand and wipe it away, leaving a sober expression in its place. Matty sometimes looked at her hand half expecting to see a smile on it. Curtseying, smiling and removing the smile, Betsi welcomed them in voluble Welsh and ushered them into the spotless room which was at once bedroom and parlour.

Along one side was the closed 'gwely cwpwrd', the cupboard bed in which Lizzie and her mother slept at night. The kitchen on the other side of the passage held a similar bed in which Lizzie's father slept with his two sons. Kitchen and passage were flagged with slate, but the floor of the room where Lettice and Matty sat on two shining chairs was of beaten earth, brown and hard and decorated by Betsi in a traditional green pattern. This pattern Betsi renewed whenever she washed the floor by rubbing it with fresh dock leaves. Squares and circles were ingeniously adapted to the size of the furniture, and Matty, who thought the effect very fine, wished that Mamma would do the same thing in the drawing-room at home, in place of the dull carpet.

Meanwhile, while Mamma talked, Matty's eyes were busy picking out the ornaments on the chest of drawers which was Betsi's special pride. Its front was bright as a mirror and every inch of the top was covered with china. Matty had discovered the cups which once belonged to the breakfast set at the Stone House, and the green glass vase that had recently stood on the spare room mantelpiece, when Betsi asked suddenly in English, 'Well, Missie, are you looking at my pretending ornaments?'

This filled Matty with confusion. She it was who had noticed one day that the breakfast cups were there because they had lost their handles, and had been filled with a desire to discover the flaw in each piece of china, so cleverly placed as to look perfect.

'Oh, Betsi,' she had begged, 'do let me look at every one of your pretending ornaments!'

Dear old Betsi had thought this amusing and was fond of repeating it, but Matty by this time had begun to feel ashamed of her curiosity and now hastily withdrew her eye from the china, listening instead to the conversation which had begun afresh in Welsh.

'Lizzie has got a candle ready to take with her, marm.'

'A candle ?'

'Yes, and a few matches in an old box.'

'What for, Betsi ?'

'In the basket in her hand I mean, marm.'

'What made you think of that?'

'Well, Ann Preece was telling me about the tunnel and we were thinking that Lizzie would be frightened to go through it so fast in the dark. And Ann said that when she and Margaret Ellen went to see their brother James that lives in Swansea, you remember, when they thought he was dying, they took a candle with them and lit it in the tunnel, and she was telling Lizzie to do the same. That will be all right won't it, marm?'

'Lizzie can certainly take a candle if she wishes' said Lettice slowly, 'but I think I shouldn't if I were you, Lizzie. There will be nothing to fear and none of the other passengers are likely to have candles. They will trust you and I advise you to trust them. Hundreds of people go through that tunnel every day quite safely in the dark.'

'Good gracious, marm! Hundreds of people every day! Well, well, why doesn't somebody put a lamp for them, poor things? Well, Lizzie, don't bother about the candle.'

The next thing to be discussed was the trunk. It stood, very new and shiny in its bright yellow paint, and the rope with which it was to be corded lay coiled on top. Lettice took from her bag the labels, already addressed, which she had brought with her, but at that moment heavy boots sounded on the flags outside and the shadow of Twm, Betsi's husband, fell across the sunny threshold.

In every way Twm was the opposite of his wife, a dark, sour man, silent and reserved, with melancholy black eyes. After a brief 'Prydnawn da' (Good evening) he stood listening to the conversation, then pointed to the labels and remarked suddenly, 'There's no need of those; Mrs Jones the Shop gave me some last night and Lizzie has written on them herself.'

Lizzie shyly took two labels out of the bodice of her dress. On them she had written in a large hand, 'Elizabeth Reynolds basenjar from Trefihangel.' Lettice looked hard at them in silence for a few seconds, then said gently, 'But they do not say where you are going, Lizzie. That is the important thing.'

'I see no reason,' said Twm obstinately. 'What business of anyone else's is it where Lizzie is going? Those labels will do very well, and Mrs Jones the Shop would be offended if we did not use the labels after her giving them to us.'

Lettice yielded the point, but later when Twm had gone out to his garden she slipped her own labels into Lizzie's hand, advising her to add them to her trunk as soon as she reached the railway station. Then there was nothing left but the good wishes, exhortations and goodbyes, with messages to Lizzie's new mistress, who could be trusted to preserve all the old Nantgwyn ways although fate had bestowed on her that doubtful blessing, a 'mixed marriage' with an Englishman.

The evening was sultry with thunder when they came away from Betsi's cottage: great damson-coloured clouds had rolled up over the sea and the tall dog-daisies and glowing poppies on the roadside were motionless in the still air, as though a spell had been cast on them. Lettice glanced at the sky and told Matty not to loiter, yet she herself found it difficult to hurry. The languor of deep summer was on her, weighting her limbs, while the sense of approaching storm gave her an alarmed feeling of expectancy. Had she caught the sensation from Lizzie, poor little 'basenjar', setting forth next morning from the only spot she had ever known to a place where even her own tongue would never be spoken, save by her mistress, and where every word she spoke to others must be carefully put into English before utterance?

Betsi would miss her girl, though no word of any such

thought had escaped her, but husband and sons – especially such a husband as Twm – could not fill the gap left by a daughter. Sons are our pride, thought Lettice, the crown of life, the flag flying at the helm, and if a woman lost her sons there would be no crowns and flags left for her. But a daughter is closer; she speaks the same language of the heart, she is the apt pupil, quicker than any son to learn the lessons handed on from generation to generation.

Watching Matty's lithe limbs as she ran along the top of the bank, free and untrammelled as a seagull in its flight, Lettice felt vexed and rebellious at the thought of parting one day with her daughter. It seemed to her pure misfortune that there should be a cousin in Yorkshire, head of a famous school, whose eagle eye was already fixed on Matty. Yet no one knew better than Lettice the limits of Miss Carlyle's little school in St. Idris, where in the days of Miss Carlyle's father Lettice herself had been taught, together with her brothers and sisters and numerous cousins.

'Matty!' she called to the child running ahead of her. 'Has anything been said yet of holidays? When are you going to lock Miss Carlyle out?'

'Soon, Mamma, quite soon. Lydia Roberts, Cefnyglyn, brought some ears of corn this morning and put them on Miss Carlyle's desk, and the big girls were all talking of it each time Miss Carlyle was out of the room.'

'If the Cefnyglyn corn is ripe, it won't be long now,' remarked Lettice, and added with a little laugh, 'I should like to be locking Miss Carlyle out again. How cross she was if ever we did it a day too soon!'

Lettice was right, as next day proved at Miss Carlyle's school. The bunch of ripe corn from the Cefnyglyn field, laid on the mistress's desk, was the sign of a general revolt among the pupils, for the farmers wanted their children home in the busy harvest time, and the pent-up excitement of the summer days rose to bubbling point.

The school year at Miss Carlyle's was not divided into terms, but into quarters, and no dates were fixed beforehand. Corn harvest decided the time of the summer holiday, and according to an age-old custom it was an act of rebellion – the 'locking-out' – that gave the signal of escape.

Strange and riotous event! The pupils would seize a moment when Miss Carlyle had left the room, locking the door and barricading it with benches dragged from their place and piled one on the other. This done, the pupils danced, jumped and shouted within, waiting the dramatic moment of Miss Carlyle's return. Soon she would be hammering at the door, demanding to be let in. 'Not until you promise to give us holidays!' shouted the rebels.

'Yes, yes, you shall have your holidays.'

'How long shall we have?'

'Three weeks.'

'No, no, we must have a month!'

'Well, a month it shall be.'

Then the barricades were removed, Miss Carlyle entered smiling and her pupils gathered their books together and ran home with the news that the holidays had begun. Perhaps the event was not really so unforeseen as it seemed to the excited children, and came as no very great surprise to Miss Carlyle or their parents, but school never broke up without the riot.

There were, of course, terrible occasions when Miss Carlyle was locked out before that lady was ready for her holiday. Then wild was the pandemonium. Outside the door she sternly cried, 'Open!' while inside her pupils danced and hurled defiance. Of course in the end she had her way, and once inside the room she was the same terrifying autocrat as of yore, but the frightened little subjects were never punished for their ill-timed rebellions. On this one day on the long road of learning the children were given at least the semblance of power.

Tall, strict and commanding, Miss Carlyle ruled her small kingdom with a firm hand. Reading, writing and spelling were the three subjects for which her school was justly renowned in the neighbourhood. Anyone who had spent a considerable time repeating those lengthy columns of words under Miss Carlyle's stern eye was grounded for life in the knowledge of English spelling. In arithmetic her pupils were provided with small books called Tutors. These gave a sample sum, while immediately below stood another sum of a precisely similar type. This jugglery was imitated slavishly and the result compared with the answers in Miss Carlyle's book, by which method pupils worked through the whole of the Tutor, solving problems under the mysterious headings of Discount, Profit and Loss, Partnership, etc., without gaining the faintest idea of what they meant.

No maps hung on the walls of Miss Carlyle's school. Geography was acquired from a diminutive book which contained six small maps, one of the two hemispheres and others of the five continents; the letterpress, in minute print, once learnt by heart was repeated verbatim.

History, General Knowledge and Scripture were taught by catechisms. In these cases the pupils learned the answers and rarely troubled themselves with the questions. But this, no doubt, was just as well, for how otherwise, if any use of intelligence were required, could Miss Carlyle have retained her reason, when it happened that her piano stood in the middle of the schoolroom, so that the sing-song noises of two dozen girls and boys, reciting their columns of spelling, mixed with the sound of scales and five-finger exercises? No wonder that when the little fingers struck the wrong notes they were sharply rapped with a long pencil. For serious faults Miss Carlyle reserved the use of the ruler; minor offenders found themselves in the corner.

In one thing above all others Miss Carlyle's pupils excelled. Every afternoon the drab schoolroom blossomed into an oriental riot of colour when the big girls spread out their antimacassars, and the little girls stood patiently holding on their outstretched arms gay skeins for the winding. To become a winder of wool, instead of a mere holder, was the most envied promotion of the school. Matty had not yet attained to this glory, but she had made a sofa rug from long strips of knitting sewn together in diagonal patterns of purple, emerald and rose; and she had nearly finished her sampler, every letter of the alphabet, capital and small, repeated twice and surmounted with a succession of traditional patterns, such as the strawberry border and the rose border.

It was quite a creditable sampler, but a poor thing compared with the one which Lettice had worked in that same school, and which hung in one corner of the parlour at the Stone House. All round was the famous border, and within the border texts of scripture alternated with gigantic roses. In one corner a plump girl in a blue frock walked across a boggy meadow, her arms full of flowers, between butterflies as large as herself. In another corner crouched a rabbit, twice as big as the girl. Black-and-tan terriers, baskets of flowers, and stiff little birds perched on stiff little trees, enlivened the scene, and in the midst of all, beautifully worked in the finest lettering, stood these words:

> *Now in the heat of youthful blood*
> *Remember your creator God*
> *Behold the years come hastening on*
> *When you shall say my joys are gone*
>
> *Behold the aged sinner goes*
> *Laden with guilt and heavy woes*
> *Down to the regions of the dead*
> *With endless curses on his head*
>
> *The dust returns to dust again*
> *The soul in agonies of pain*

Ascends to God not there to dwell
But hears her doom and sinks to hell

Eternal King I fear thy name
Teach me to know how frail I am
And when my soul must hence remove
Give me a mansion of thy love

Appalling words! Yet the child who had embroidered them in those finest of stitches had grown to a woman with excellent eyesight and a most happy assurance of God's goodness. No thought of endless punishment troubled her: it was something she had been taught in childhood that teased her no more than did the lack of proportion between the rabbit, the butterflies and the trees.

Had she been asked her opinion she might have said that the promise of the last verse meant more to her than any threat of curses. Like the girl in the sampler she trod the boggy meadows, with her arms full of flowers, serenely unafraid.

Chapter 9

Ship Overdue

The end of that summer was fine and dry and the harvest was gathered early from the fields round the scattered farmhouses. Clear September weather hung like a blessing over the land from the far blue outline of the mountains to the Island rocks, where every scar and cranny lay revealed in sunlight. Blackberries were so thick that Lettice wearied of jelly-making, and the children lamented that they had to go back to school while the golden days still spoke to them of picnics, and the summer sea beckoned from every sandy bay and murmuring inlet.

Lettice went about her tasks with a slight undercurrent of anxiety. John was on his way home, but no news of him had reached her since June. She who could not abide a newspaper and had never, all her life, read one through, now looked eagerly for each day's *South Wales Gazette* and searched its pages for a short list headed 'Ships Spoken'. But all through those fine warm weeks there was no mention of the clipper *Zouave*. Nor did the mailcart, when it clattered in from Westford every morning, bring any word from the owners, Messrs. Bagshaw and Lock of Liverpool, concerning the *Zouave's* arrival at her next port of call.

At last Lettice wrote to Liverpool and received a polite intimation that the *Zouave* had not yet reached Cape Town. She was overdue, stated the letter, but as yet there was no cause for anxiety. Messrs Bagshaw and Lock undertook, as usual, to let Mrs Peters know of her arrival. The letter was signed Henry Bagshaw, whom Lettice knew to be senior partner of the firm. She recalled him to her mind, in his comfortable office with its thick blue carpet and mahogany furniture. A precise man with piercing grey eyes and a mouth that shut like a trap. He was a widower and it was said that he had adored his wife, so perhaps his words were not as dry as they seemed.

'As yet no cause for anxiety.' Lettice repeated the sentence to herself as she sat in the parlour mending the frill of a curtain. The needle poked in and out of the stuff, and the words fell dully on her mind like the strokes of a pendulum. The stillness of afternoon lay on the house, wrapping it round so that there were no sounds but the occasional noises of the street coming in through the open window: a child running, bowling an iron hoop, and someone calling out in Welsh, 'When is he coming back?'

'When is he coming back?' The words rung in Lettice's ears as she threaded her needle afresh. Normally she liked a quiet afternoon of sewing. To sit with work in her hands, best of all in the company of her sister Martha, while (pleasing accompaniment to their task) the tinkle of teacups being set out sounded from the next room, this was one of Lettice's many recipes for happiness. Even to sit alone, knowing that the children would soon return, brimming the house with their voices and footsteps, was a pleasure. But today she was restless and wished the afternoon were at an end. Philip had gone with Catherine Jane to fetch a basket of eggs from Penbryn, and the three elder children were at school. Marged had just finished her week's baking. In her mind's eye Lettice saw the spruce kitchen with the door standing open to the sunny yard and Marged dozing in her chair, while the bread rose under its white cloth and filled the room with a sweet smell.

She was half inclined to leave her sewing and slip into the kitchen, just to see if all were as she fancied, when the noise of hooves and the rumble of wheels sounded outside and finally came to a stop at her door. Then, even as she ran to the window, the knocker was lifted and a gay voice, which she knew at once for her cousin Fanny's, called, 'Lettice, Lettice, are you at home?'

Outside in the sunny street stood the Hendre Evan phaeton, with a pair of chestnut ponies, and there, holding the reins and doffing his hat to her, with Eliza sitting beside him under a red sunshade, was her cousin Thomas Walters.

Now the very sight of Thomas was an invitation to enjoyment and a banishing of care. It was known that in New Zealand he was a man of substance, with several complicated businesses under his control. But no one would have guessed that any weight of responsibility hung on his shoulders when Thomas, on one of his whirlwind visits to Europe, descended on the quiet home of his people and stirred them into life. He was staying now with Eliza at Hendre Evan; Lettice knew that already, and she now guessed with certainty that Thomas had suddenly wearied of the sleepy farm and persuaded his two sisters to drive out for a call. 'But I should have written to tell Lettice we were coming,' she could hear Eliza's slow voice admonish. It was so unlike Eliza to do anything in a hurry; so like Thomas to leave no one any time.

Now from the air he had conjured up a lad to stand at the ponies' heads and was lifting a great parcel out of the phaeton, and all of them were trooping into the parlour, Eliza exclaiming at their good fortune in finding Lettice at home, and begging her to join them for a picnic tea. 'Eliza has packed up enough food for a Sunday School treat, so you'd better help us eat it,' said Thomas, at which Eliza protested, and Fanny added that they had brought their bathing things.

'We haven't had a bathing picnic all summer. Eliza was always too busy. Oh, Lettice, say you'll come!'

'But first open my parcel,' said Thomas.

'No, no!' Fanny objected. 'The afternoon will be gone. Open it when we come back.'

Like Thomas, Fanny Walters had a way of getting things done. Almost before she knew what was happening Lettice had summoned Marged and told her to give the children their tea when they came home, and to see that Catherine Jane put

Philip to bed in good time if she should be late. Then, with Fanny abetting and prompting her, she gathered together her bathing clothes and a light wrap, tied on her hat of leghorn straw, picked up her green parasol and stepped into the phaeton.

The lad, obviously rewarded by Thomas above all expectations, stepped aside from the ponies' heads and away they bowled through the Cross, past the little houses where golden-rod and dahlias sheltered behind stout, whitewashed walls, and up and down the curving road to the sea.

Lettice, seated in the place of honour beside Thomas, the rush of sun-warmed air fanning her cheeks, was charmed and exhilarated. Eliza and Fanny, on the opposite seats, their bonnets dodging the reins which looped through a flourish of metal-work surmounting the dashboard, wished to talk, and Lettice tossed back the ball of chatter as often as it was thrown to her. But she would have liked to be silent and to give her whole attention to the scene which became so enchantingly different when viewed from a rapidly moving carriage. Ducks and geese scattered before the ponies' feet, and a white cloud of dust hung behind them on the green banks. As they passed Penbryn Farm a yellow, bow-legged corgi, waddling in the yard, and the bright water spilling from the hooded well, were as fresh and new as though she had never before set eyes on them. In the blue air above them a buzzard wheeled slowly and was gone. For Lettice the dim parlour, the torn curtain and her own sad thoughts had turned to gossamers.

At the crossroads they took the way to Porthcarreg, so that Silversands lay below them, the waves turning lazily on the shore. Thomas pointed with his whip.

'Do any of you remember catching sand eels there by moonlight?'

Eliza and Lettice both said yes, while Fanny exclaimed that she had always longed to catch them, and never yet had the chance.

'Moonlight and a spring tide, that's the time to try,' said Thomas. 'And of course you must go in couples: one to hold the can and the other the spade. Who's your choice of a companion, Fanny?'

But Fanny would not tell.

'And barefoot,' said Lettice. She was remembering the cold moonlit foam between the toes, and the firm wet sands under the soles of her feet.

' Frying them afterwards in the kitchen at midnight, that was the best part,' said practical Eliza.

'I always felt like a conspirator,' added Lettice, 'creeping into the house at twelve o'clock and stirring up the kitchen fire.'

Howell Lloyd and the four Trehafod boys, and of course Jim, had been the keenest pursuers of moonlit eels and of all the fun that went with them. Suddenly Lettice wished that she and John had grown up together, that they could have shared not only the cares of a family but the free foolish years when even the most ordinary days smelt as sweet as wild thyme, and she would wake every morning at Nantgwyn in a rapture of happiness.

Thomas and Eliza were still discussing the best way of cooking sand eels.

'Plenty of vinegar,' said Eliza, 'and then eat them with thin slices of brown bread and butter.'

'I met something like them once in Monte Video, and another time in Barcelona,' remarked Thomas, 'but not nearly so good. Spaniards will eat anything out of the sea and they're very coarse cooks. Our sand eels were real delicacies, and what beats me is that I've never met anyone else in this country who's even heard of the things.'

They were in sight of the sea again and Porthcarreg lay before them. Thomas drew up the phaeton for the ladies to alight; then drove to a neighbouring farmhouse to stable the ponies. Eliza, Lettice and Fanny, carrying their baskets and parasols, set off for the cliffs by way of a narrow footpath. Green tufts of mare's-tail grew along the bank, and Lettice, plucking it as she passed, broke the jointed stalks into a dozen little separate sticks, just as she had always done as a child.

From this path they could see all the islands scattered on the calm sea. The lighthouse on the South Bishop was a fairy citadel, white and shining; while the North Bishop, like an old prelate on a tombstone, lay sleeping on the blue water. The three rocks of Trecarreg, where so many good ships had been wrecked, looked innocent enough today; beyond them, very small and dark, lay the island that is named 'Gwahan', which means 'separate'. Lettice had always felt sorry for this island; it looked so lonely, and because it was called 'Gwahan' it seemed that it must remain alone for all time, alone as she would be if anything happened to John. Suddenly her fears for John returned and she hurried after Eliza, unable to keep this anxiety any longer to herself.

Kind Eliza was all concern and reassurance, and immediately recalled several cases of missing ships that had turned up safely in the end. There was the case of Mrs James of Croesgoch whose son had not been heard of for many months: Eliza could not exactly remember how long, but it was certainly a long time, from the hay harvest until nearly Christmas, and Mrs James had been very anxious indeed. She remembered her saying so at the Chapel bazaar, which was sometime in November; but then of course it had been all right and young William had turned up again as well as could be. 'But indeed I'm sorry for you, Lettice fach, with all this old waiting.' Eliza finished in a burst of sympathy. 'I've often wondered what I should do if Sam were to go to sea.'

Lettice could not help smiling at the thought. Sam Rhys without his fields and barns and his shrewd eye for stock was as unthinkable as John in a farmyard. By the time they had reached the shore and approved Fanny's choice of a cave for undressing she felt more cheerful again.

Because this was not her own familiar piece of shore the cave was almost as exciting to Lettice as a new house. Caves varied so much. There were the homely ones where the children undressed every day for bathing, taking care not to go far back because the water dripped from the walls; strange, inaccessible caves into whose hollow depths great waves boomed and whose secrets they alone knew; caves which had been the haunts of smugglers, and others where the huge seals lifted their glossy heads out of the sea, lived and bred their young; caves in the face of the cliff which could only be reached by ropes, and where crystals sparkled on floor and sides and ceiling.

Just as the caves were different, so were the creeks. It was remarkable how methodical the sea was in sorting its gifts. Here a cove was completely carpeted with shells; there with boulders; here pebbles. In one place the sands were golden, in another black. But everywhere there was seaweed; yards of shining brown satin ribbon, strips of green watered silk, much prized by Matty and other little girls for playing shop; juicy bunches of yellow grapes, and small delicately-fronded pink-and-mauve seaweed which Lettice, in her childhood, had taken home, floated in her wash-hand basin and lifted carefully on to sheets of paper to preserve for ever. 'For ever,' she had thought then, but none of them had outlived the next spring cleaning. It was only Aunt Hephzibah's sea trophies that withstood the rot of time, dried in all their feathery grace and mounted with deft fingers in tiny fairy wicker baskets on cardboard where she wrote in her fine Italian hand, 'Call us not weeds, we are flowers of the sea'.

So many things flowered for Aunt Hephzibah; it was not surprising that the seaweed she gathered behaved well under her influence. She was a Merion of Nantgwyn, talented and cultivated, with some of the energy of James Merion, the preacher. She spoke Italian, French and German, enjoyed reading the Georgics in their original tongue, and was a

nimble harpist. No picnic party ever found her without her
water-colours and sketchbook. She would think us an idle set
today, Lettice reflected.

The tide was out, and had left behind it many little pools among
the rocks. These rocks, washed and worn by the fretting sea,
were most variously coloured – some rosy red as the vivid
campion in the hedgerows, others dove grey and lilac like
the walls of the Cathedral. But it was the pools that delighted
Lettice, each one teeming with wonders; tiny shellfish,
delicate seaweeds and deep red sea anemones clinging to
their sides. Yet no sooner had she set eyes on them than her
conscience smote her that she should have come away without
the children.

Here was a pool the very shape and size for Philip's round
limbs, where he might poke a fat finger into the middle of
an anemone till the red flower that had been in full bloom
would be hurriedly withdrawn and become a red bud once
more. What was Philip doing now, she wondered? Had the
corners of his mouth drooped when he got back from the farm
and found that his mamma had gone? Would all four of them
feel that they had a grievance? At least she must take back
something for the two youngest, and immediately she started
searching till she had found some of the things they liked best
– a battered purse of skate's eggs (there was gold inside if
only you could discover the right way to open it); a mermaid's
sponge, a shell like a fairy's fan, and a piece of white cuttlefish
bone which Matty found so useful for rubbing out the blots in
her copybook.

'Lettice, Lettice! Aren't you ready yet? Why, you haven't
even begun to undress!' called Fanny reproachfully. She was
wearing a scarlet flannel bathing-suit, much frilled below
the knees and with a white anchor jauntily embroidered on
its front. Lettice laughed a little shamefacedly and hid her
gleanings on a shelf in the cave. Fanny was unmarried and

Eliza childless: neither of them would really understand that little heap of treasures.

In the sea she forgot for a time everything: John, the children, and all her loves, fears and anxieties. The sea, that had been her playfellow as a child, what was it now? Did it grow older in her company? It took her man away from her, yet it could soothe her cares like someone wise and ancient. Floating on her back she felt the strong sunshine on her face; turning lazily to swim back to shore she saw the familiar coastline before her, stretching wide arms of welcome.

Eliza, good soul, had left nothing to chance. She had brought a bundle of dry sticks with her in the bottom of the phaeton, and when these were alight the kettle, filled at the farmhouse where Thomas had stabled the ponies, was soon singing. While Eliza and Fanny unpacked the tea Thomas stretched himself beside Lettice on the warm rocks.

'Tell me about the children, Lettice. I wish they'd come today, but it was the last chance of seeing you. Does Ivor know yet what he wants to do?'

'Oh yes, he knows,' said Lettice.

'To follow his father, I suppose?' Thomas queried. Lettice nodded. She was plucking at a sprig of samphire which grew on the rocks and held it to her nose, snuffing the pungent leaves. Always that scent excited her, making her think of tarred ropes and spicy, far-off places; explaining better than any words what it was that drew men and boys to follow the sea.

'And Archie? What about him?'

'The same, I'm afraid, Thomas.'

'That's a pity,' said Thomas. 'Archie is the kind of boy who would do very well in business. He's quick and enterprising.'

He certainly gets into trouble quickly, thought Lettice, but aloud she asked, 'What sort of business do you mean, Thomas? I'm afraid none of us knows anything about it.'

'I'd like him to come with me,' said Thomas suddenly and surprisingly. 'There's a lot of things moving in New Zealand now. A boy like Archie, with his wits about him, could easily make his fortune.'

Lettice sat still, the samphire still pressed to her nostrils.

'It's very kind of you to think of it Thomas but…'

'Fudge, my dear girl, it's not kind at all! Tell John what I say when you write to him next.'

'Of course I'll tell him, but it's Archie who will decide I expect, and I'm not really sure…' She hesitated.

'What are you not sure about?'

How could she explain? If only the samphire could tell, for somehow the samphire explained it all to her.

'You see, I don't know that Archie really wants to be rich. I don't mean,' she added hastily, 'that Archie doesn't like nice things to eat. He does, much more than the others. But he hates sitting still. You can't think how difficult it is to get him to finish his homework. I don't believe he'd ever sit still in an office for more than ten minutes!'

'What's that about not sitting still?' asked Eliza. She had been blowing the fire with pursed lips and was pink in the face from the exertion.

'It's we who are sitting still and letting you do all the work,' said Lettice with contrition.

'Nonsense,' said Eliza. 'But I don't see why I shouldn't play Mary as well as Martha at this picnic. What is Thomas talking about?'

'He is suggesting very kindly,' said Lettice 'that he might take Archie into his business.'

'Well now, that's a good idea, Letty fach,' said Eliza promptly in her comfortable voice. 'He would make a lot of money, I shouldn't be surprised, and not be going to sea at all.'

Fanny, who had been quietly buttering scones, looked up suddenly and remarked, 'I don't believe Lettice wants any of her children to be rich. Do you, Lettice?'

Lettice found herself blushing. It seemed almost as though Fanny were accusing her of rudeness. Thomas was always spoken of as the possessor of untold wealth, and everyone knew that Eliza's husband was a thriving farmer and a 'warm man'.

'I haven't thought about it much,' she said. 'What makes you say that, Fanny?'

Fanny smiled and looked mysterious. 'I've just noticed, that's all. The poor cousins all go and stay with Lettice, but when the rich ones come she's nowhere to be found. Not unless they go and drag her out, as we did today.'

'Indeed, she's the same to everyone,' said Eliza indignantly. 'So stop talking foolishly, all of you, while I make the tea.'

Thomas, propping himself on an elbow, surveyed them all with amusement. 'Fanny's right,' he said. 'When Lettice shuts the door in my face I shall know that I'm too rich for the Kingdom of Heaven.'

'As though I should ever do such a thing!' cried Lettice.

It was after tea – Eliza's excellent tea of barley bread, home-made cakes and scones – that Lettice made the awful discovery. She was sorting in her lap the little collection of sea treasures for Matty and Philip, when something naked and unfamiliar in the look of her hands arrested her attention.

'Eliza, I've lost my ring!'

'What ring? Not your wedding ring!'

'Yes, yes, my wedding ring!'

She was on her feet already, searching the rocks, looking among the shells and stones she had gathered for the children. But even while she searched, while she heard Eliza's and Fanny's exclamations of dismay and saw them shaking out the bathing wraps, she knew the hunt was useless. The sea had taken her ring; it had never fitted her slim finger tightly, and now at last the waves had stolen it. She and Fanny went back to the cave where she had undressed; Thomas scanned the shore, but the tide had come in while they talked, blotting out their footsteps and brimming all the pools. Eliza, with a troubled face, continued to peer among the rocks and even to turn out all the picnic baskets, until Lettice, taking pity on them, cried out that she would have no more of it and begged to be taken home.

'Oh, Lettice, I would rather anything in the world had happened than this,' said Fanny as they climbed back to the top of the cliff.

Lettice slipped a hand into hers, 'You are not to mind like that, Fanny. Those are not the things that matter, as you'll find out yourself when you marry. John will give me another when he comes back; one that will fit better.'

But there was no consoling Eliza and Fanny, and it was Thomas and Lettice who had to keep the talk going on the way back. John Peters' ship was overdue, and his wife had lost her wedding ring. That was the thought that hung with threatening gloom over the two sisters every mile of the return journey. Their brother's jovial conversation and Lettice's untroubled face did nothing to solace their feelings, for was it not an omen, dread word to anyone of Welsh blood? They were, of course, all kindness and concern, yet Lettice felt their thoughts racing round her, like dark mice on fearful feet. She was glad to think she would soon be home.

At the sound of wheels in the Cross the door of the Stone House flew open and out into the street ran Ivor, Archie and Matty.

'Where have you been all this time, Mamma? How could you go away for a picnic without us?' Those were the unspoken words behind Matty's shy looks as she shook hands with her relations. The boys admired the ponies and the sight of their mother stepping out of so dashing a an equipage. 'So they don't mind my going without them; not in the way the little ones do,' thought Lettice.

The last farewells were said; yet once more Lettice maintained that she had enjoyed herself immensely; Thomas touched the ponies with his whip and the gay little carriage, with two nodding bonnets and two fluttering handkerchiefs, rattled through the Cross and disappeared round the corner. Now at last Lettice could listen to the questions that besieged her.

'Where did you go?'

'Did you find the smuggler's cave at Porthcarreg?'

'Were there any crystals in it?'

'Was it a good picnic, and did you gather sticks for the fire?'

'What are the ponies' names?'

'Is Uncle Thomas very rich?'

Lettice answered them as well as she could, and then asked, 'Is Philip asleep? How is he?'

'He's probably all right *now*,' said Matty with emphasis. 'But he brought back a duck's egg from Penbryn and said he wouldn't show it to anyone except you. He kept saying all through tea that that no one else was even to look at it. But I peeped at it and it's only an ordinary old duck's egg...'

Lettice was already halfway upstairs and shook her head at the others. 'Don't all stand there talking, you'll wake him,' and then, softly turning the door handle, she crept into her room. Philip, asleep in the little bed beside her own, was not in his usual spread-eagle attitude but curled in a ball, his lashes dark and damp against his rosy cheeks. On the table beside him, placed so that he would see it first thing on waking, was a duck's egg. Lettice stood for a few minutes looking down on her small son and then laid beside the egg his share of the sea-trove from Porthcarreg.

Late that evening, after she had given Matty her shells and brushed her hair, and sat with the boys while they had their supper, hearing their adventures of the day, Lettice slipped into the parlour to put away the curtain she had been mending. The window was open to the street and outside in the soft September dusk it was beginning to rain; the first rain for weeks, but falling so gently and with such a scent of water falling on dust that it was as though a water cart had passed by. Suddenly, standing there, the loss of her ring smote Lettice. It was no hobgoblin fear that touched her, but the loss of something dear and precious; something that was part of her, that belonged to her and John; and looking out into the darkening street, still holding the curtain in her arms, she wept quietly. Then, as she turned back, her foot struck against something, and glancing down she saw the box that Thomas had brought and which she had forgotten until now.

She carried it to the lamplit hall, wishing she had remembered to open it before the children went to bed. What could Thomas have thought of giving her? Inside the wrappings was a foreign-looking box, made of papier-mâché and bearing the name of a Paris house on its lid. Opening it, Lettice came upon a number of mysterious small compartments. From one of them she drew out a wooden egg cup with an improbable blue egg inside and a still more improbable scarlet one fitting over it like a cap. Next came a box with a false bottom, and under the false bottom the elaborately smashed fragments of a watch.

Holding these in her hand Lettice suddenly laughed aloud: Thomas had brought her a box of French conjuring tricks. Here was a magic dice and here a bundle of bright-coloured silk handkerchiefs and a little black wand. The boys would adore it; already she foresaw Archie's excitement in each device. But it was the astonishing childishness of men that made her laugh now. That Thomas should have spent time and money, quite a lot of money too, judging by the look of it, in bringing that elaborate box of foolish tricks from Paris to St. Idris was all part of man's incurable oddness.

She remembered Thomas's remark that afternoon, 'When Lettice shuts the door in my face I shall know that I'm too rich for the Kingdom of Heaven.' She had cried out then that she would never close her door to him, and now she knew the real reason.

'If he's as rich as Dives,' she said to herself, 'he'd still be a child.' And with that she closed the box and carried it to the window of the dining-room where the children would see it at once when they came downstairs to breakfast next morning.

Chapter 10

Llanmadoc

The news that Lettice had lost her wedding ring while bathing at Porthcarreg soon reached every friend and relation in the neighbourhood. It even grew to be the cause of visits of condolence, while the most surprising people, meeting her in the street, would murmur, 'Indeed, Mrs Peters, we were sorry to hear of your loss.'

Lettice accepted their sympathy, but found it hard to bear the thought lurking behind their words, as it lay behind Marged's anxious face and Catherine Jane's dismayed glances, 'Captain Peters' ship is overdue, and his wife has lost her wedding ring!'

Her own confidence was steady, upheld by faith and strengthened by the conviction that if anything had happened to John she would have known. But it was difficult to explain, even to Martha who had hastened over with horse and trap from Nantgwyn to visit her on a blowy morning.

'I know they're all full of superstitions,' Lettice told her, 'and perhaps you'll think me superstitious too. But there it is; if the worst had happened I do not think I should have this strong feeling that I must not worry, that it would be even wrong for me to be troubling myself all the time. Yet it almost seems, Martha, as though people expected it of me!'

'Pay no attention to what anyone says; still less to what you imagine they are thinking,' advised Martha, and then began searching in her handbag.

'I have something for you, Lettice,' she said, 'for I did not like to think of you without your ring. Here is Mamma's wedding ring for you to wear till John buys you another one.

Father agreed it was right for you to have it. She had small fingers like you, so I am hoping that it will fit.'

While she spoke Martha unwrapped a small package. Inside it was the broad gold wedding ring which Lettice remembered on her mother's hand. She had not seen it since she died, and the heavy gold band, so much heavier than her own when she slipped it over her finger, seemed weighted with care. She had a sudden sharp memory of her mother, slight, delicate and harassed by the many concerns of her large family, and wished that Martha had not brought the ring. In some way she could never explain to anyone, it had broken into that region of the spirit which she had inhabited ever since the day at Porthcarreg; a world where her thoughts and John's lived lightly in each other's company. But her mother's substantial ring was an anchor dragging her back to reality.

'You will spend the day, Martha? It will be lovely to have you.' But Martha could not stay. Aunt Rachel at Sarnau was ailing (Aunt Rachel who had had so many troubles in her life that Lettice often wondered how she went on living at all) and Martha was on her way there with presents of chicken broth and a pumpkin.

With kisses, and promises that they would meet again soon, the sisters parted and Martha drove away, her spare figure sitting erect in the high dog-cart. Lettice watched her go, knowing two things with certainty: that after John this sister was the chief pillar of her life, and that if anything happened to John it would be Martha's grief no less than her own, so completely did this dear elder sister share her joys and sorrows.

'And yet,' thought Lettice in honesty to herself, 'it is the sorrows that are chiefly shared. When John comes home it is I who have all the fun and glory of it.'

The bathing picnic at Porthcarreg was the last one of the year. The rain that had fallen that evening ended the long

fine summer, and now autumn weather settled in with clouds
of mild yet penetrating rain blown in from the sea, and the
lighthouses booming all day. It was in such weather that the
St. Idris Flower Show took place in the City Hall. Lettice
allowed the two elder children to go, but was glad to stay at
home herself with the little ones, who were nursing their first
colds of the season. She felt no enthusiasm for the stuffy hall,
smelling of vegetables, and the perennial sight of Mr Jenkins
of Gwasted carrying off the first prize for dahlias and swollen
vegetable marrows.

But she wondered, all the same, whether her cousin
William Humphrey would be as successful as usual with the
Llanmadoc apples, and asked Marged to make light cakes for
tea in case he, or anyone else, looked in on the way home
from the Show. Sure enough at half-past four in the afternoon
the front door bell clanged and Catherine Jane admitted Mr
William Humphrey of Llanmadoc.

William was his mother's only son and had remained a
bachelor until middle age. Reserved and deliberate in manner,
he walked with a slight stoop that made him seem older than
his years, wore a high white stock, and side-whiskers. He was
a man of pronounced conservative opinions and took *The
Times*, which he read from beginning to end every day. This
habit of his annoyed Lettice whenever, on rare occasions, she
visited Llanmadoc, for at the end of his exhaustive study of
the newspaper he had never been known to retail one item of
news of even the slightest interest.

Today when he crossed the threshold of the Stone House
he carried a basket of very large red apples. Lettice came to
meet him.

'And they took first prize again, William! Won't Aunt
Humphrey be pleased! And the children will enjoy them too.
Now come and have some tea and tell me who was there
today.'

The apples were an annual present to the Peters family,

one of the few that William Humphrey was known to make; but today it was clear that he had something else on his mind, and when he had bitten into his third light cake the matter was at last broached.

'We were sorry to hear that you are without news of John. Mother wished me to tell you so, and to say that she hoped you would come over to Llanmadoc one day and bring the children with you.'

Stiff old William! Lettice knew it was not he, but his kind, formidable mother who had devised this plan, but she accepted it as a joint invitation, thanked him warmly and fixed the day of the visit before William took himself off in his gig with his empty basket and his first prize.

One day in the following week Tom Pugh's wagonette drove them all over to Aunt Humphrey's in time for the midday meal. Llanmadoc, where she and William lived, stood close to the church at the end of a short drive of beech trees, with the weather-beaten gravestones of the churchyard on one side of the bordering wall. It was a long, low, yellow-washed house, flanked on one side by the orchard where grew the famous apple trees. Beyond the house was the kitchen garden with hedges of clipped box, and at the end of the garden was a lake with an island in the middle. Two swans floated majestically on the water, or waddled less majestically among the reeds and rushes of the shore. They had a little house of their own on the island, so it was no wonder, thought the children, they were proud.

These things were the subject of pleasant anticipation to the four young Peters in the course of the drive, tempered particularly in Matty's mind with the alarmed expectancy of so soon meeting Aunt Humphrey. She was not there to greet them when at last the horses turned into the beech avenue and drew up before the square yellow porch, for Aunt Humphrey was crippled with gout and moved heavily about the house leaning on a stick, or remained seated in a specially large chair. On this account she had a great bath, encased in mahogany with brass handles, fixed in a room on the ground floor, and also a watercloset, much set about with solid mahogany; all of which things, being of a splendour unknown to the Stone House, impressed the children with their dignity and grandeur.

But if Aunt Humphrey could not come to the door to welcome her guests, Catrin was always there to do so. Catrin had been in the family service since she was a small fair girl, and now she was a woman of forty, with yellow locks, that were beginning to show a few grey hairs, plaited in a heavy coronet above her broad brow and level grey eyes. Wearing a dress of dark woollen stuff, she stood in the doorway and made a little curtsey to Lettice as she crossed the threshold.

'I hope you are well, marm,' she said in Welsh, 'and are not cold from your drive, and all the children well too. The Mistress will be pleased to see you. Mishter' (that was how she always spoke of William) 'has had to go out on business. But he will not be long and sends his excuses.'

She led them through the dark hall, with riding-crops hanging in a bunch from the wall, to a door at the end of a short passage. This was the drawing-room, and here they would find Aunt Humphrey, at which thought Matty, who had been walking with Mamma and Philip, fell back and got behind Ivor.

'Mistress, they have come!' cried Catrin, suddenly opening the door. Through the doorway they saw the large, low room with its panelled walls painted green and the two windows that looked over the lake. Seated in a wide chair before a small fire was that imposing person, Aunt Humphrey.

'How are you, Lettice my dear? Well? That's good then. Now let me see the children. Tut, tut! How they've grown! Matty looks pale. She should try an iron mixture. How are you, Ivor? No bad effects from that fall? Archie is growing very like his father in looks. Come and kiss me, Philip. *You're* rosy enough, anyway. Well, I'm very glad to see you all. Dinner is at one o'clock, so you children can go and play while your mother and I have a little talk. Draw up that chair, Lettice.'

'Why has Aunt Humphrey got such a scratchy face?' asked Philip in a piping voice as Ivor closed the drawing room door behind them.

'Hush, Philip, you mustn't say such things!' said Matty, greatly shocked.

'Let's go to the kitchen and find Catrin,' suggested Archie, who had a lively memory of Catrin's store cupboard.

The kitchen at Llanmadoc was a great room running the length of the house. In addition to the fireplace, where the household cooking was done, there stood in a corner of the room a round black pot hanging from an iron bar. In this the calves' food was heated over fires of burning gorse, and nothing was so dear to the children's hearts as to feed the fire with more and more crackling pieces till the leaping flames licked the black pot, and the dead gorse, that had been so fierce and golden at its prime, lived again in all its glory for a brief instant.

Today, because it was autumn and there were no long-legged little calves standing in the yard, there was no fire under the pot. But Catrin was in the kitchen, ordering about the two maids who were busy preparing the dinner under her eyes. One of them basted the goose that hung from the jack in front of the fire, giving out a rich smell that made the children suddenly realise how hungry they were after their long drive. The other stood ready to hand to Catrin such things as she needed for her pastry, for Catrin was engaged in nothing less than the making of apple turnovers, and the children stood round watching the plump deft hands on the rolling-pin, and the swift shaping and pinching of the edges of the pastry before it disappeared from their sight into the oven.

'Well, now, I didn't think the boys would be wanting a cooking lesson,' she said, smiling and wiping the flour from her fingers.

'Are they for dinner today?' asked Archie when the oven door was closed on the turnovers.

'Of course they are, cariad, but you must wait for them. Here is something to be going on with for a bit.'

She had moved to the dark corner-cupboard and took down from it a tall glass jar like the ones in the sweetshop at St. Idris. But this jar was full of ginger fingers, crisp and frail as autumn leaves and rolled round into a hollow stem up which you could slip your thumb as you nibbled it. Munching in a golden silence, the children ran out of the kitchen to discover afresh farmyard and garden, windfalls in the orchard grass, and the damp, delicious edges of the lake.

Dinner passed off without event. William sat opposite his mother at the head of the long table and carved the goose with great precision. Nothing, Lettice decided, as seated on his right hand she started one topic after another, could make William really likeable; yet in his own house and at his table there was a certain fitness about him that almost, but not quite, amounted to dignity. That was a quality monopolised by his mother.

The children all behaved well, and there was only one bad moment when Aunt Humphrey, a great disliker of waste, looked down the length of the table as the plates were being removed and asked in a loud voice, fixing her eye on Matty: 'Why has that child taken mustard?'

All eyes were immediately turned on the scarlet Matty and the offending blob on the side of her plate, taken in a mixture of alarm and absent-mindedness when William had pushed the cruet-stand in her direction. Then, as suddenly as the question was put, kind Catrin, who always stood behind her mistress's chair during meals, whisked away Matty's tell-tale plate, and the matter was forgotten while Lettice asked William whether his dairy cows had won any prizes at Westford Show that summer, and Catrin brought in the apple turnovers.

After dinner Aunt Humphrey took a nap. That was her unvarying custom and no incursion of visitors, either friends or relatives, deterred her from it. Lettice welcomed the respite from conversation and found that she had been secretly looking forward to Aunt Humphrey's nap ever since her arrival at Llanmadoc.

After the closeness of the house the mild air of an autumn afternoon was a luxury, and so was the sense of escape with which Lettice stepped out of the long window in the breakfast-room and crossed the mossy lawn. The children had run on ahead, she did not know where; she thought vaguely that she must go in search of them, but now her steps led her under the fruit trees where damsons hung, sweet and dusky among the leaves, and the lake lay before her with the two swans, carved and motionless on the dark water.

Then suddenly, as Lettice stood there watching them, her mood changed from one of pleasure in the fresh air and pretty scene to an alarmed sense of foreboding. The anxiety she had felt for John during the last weeks, the fears of which she had made light to Aunt Humphrey but an hour ago, enveloped her, blotting out all else.

It was, she told herself, a trick of light that did it; that queer copper colour that had spread over the sky, the dark water and smouldering autumn leaves. But just as she had been convinced before that John was alive, so now she knew that somewhere he was in instant need of her, that life had become intolerable for him. The thought was suffocating, burning her throat with a thirst of which she had never before dreamt, and she tore from her the scarf she had thrown round her neck on leaving the house. Useless to tell herself that this was pure panic; that here she was at Llanmadoc – peaceful, prosperous Llanmadoc where nothing ever happened except the ripening of crops and the breeding of animals. Her body was here indeed, but her spirit was beside John's at that instant, in some dark region of the soul.

'God help him and comfort him,' she prayed. 'God give him strength to endure, and hold him in the hollow of His hand.' Blind to all around her, her lips moving in prayer, Lettice hurried on she knew not whither and found herself in a little wood of ash and sycamore, grown small and crooked from the sea wind. Beyond the wood was a stile leading into a lane and this she crossed, hoping it would lead her back to Llanmadoc. There were nut bushes in the lane, thick with clusters among the yellowing leaves, and the sight was soothing to her. She remembered the road to Crab Bay a year ago, and John tossing down the nuts to her from the bank above. For a moment it was as though he walked beside her again, and when the next turn of the lane revealed the ricks and barns of Llanmadoc she had found strength to go on, and a calm face with which to greet the children, to persuade Archie to come down from a perilous place at the top of a haystack, to console Matty for being scratched by a bad-tempered farm cat, and rescue Philip from the edge of the duck-pond.

Then, when she had duly admired a water-wheel that Ivor was building in the stream below the churchyard wall, she left them to go indoors, to hold Aunt Humphrey's wool for her and wonder, with a pang, what it felt like to be a widow for thirty years, to have been a widow longer than a wife. Perhaps at that distance of time, thought Lettice, stealing a glance at her aunt's composed face, nothing mattered any more. Perhaps even true love and marriage became like a tale that is told, their joys and griefs alike obliterated. Only Catrin, coming to say that tea was ready, roused her from these mournful reflections.

The last light cake was eaten, the last farewell said; Tom Pugh's wagonette was at the door once more and Philip had been persuaded to kiss Aunt Humphrey's bristled cheek. William stood on the doorstep watching them drive away between the golden beech trees and over the crackling beech nuts, with

Catrin standing at a respectful distance behind him.

On the way home Ivor and Archie still discussed their water-wheel, and Matty was telling Philip a long story about a princess and a swan who lived on an island in the middle of a lake.

'They lived all alone,' Lettice heard her say in tragic tones, 'with no father and mother and no brothers and sisters.'

'Who put them to bed at night?' asked Philip anxiously.

'No one did,' said the heartless Matty. 'But did nobody never wash them?' Philip persisted.

'Swans don't need washing because they're wet nearly all the time. And the Princess bathed in the lake.'

'What did they eat?' asked Philip.

'Mushrooms and blackberries and beech nuts and apple turnovers,' Matty improvised rapidly. But at this point the story was interrupted by Tom Pugh, who turned his broad back round on the box above them and fixed Lettice with his blue eyes.

'Does 'ee want to go same way home, or shall I go by Vawnog Moor, so's to make a bit of a change?' he asked, and added, 'There's nothing in it.'

'Surely Vawnog Moor is longer?' Lettice queried in surprise.

'Not much, I reckon, but as you please, marm.'

'Oh, let's go that way! Please, Mamma, let's go by Vawnog,' the elder children chorused, and Lettice assented.

'Very well. I don't mind, if Mr Pugh thinks it no longer.'

But she wished, all the same, that he had not suggested it. Vawnog Moor was gloomy and she did not desire to feel its melancholy today. Yet she acknowledged the beauty of the place when the bare road, without bank or hedge, stretched before them over the darkening heath. The glow of sunset lay beyond the last loop of the road, and on their left a young moon rose in the quenched sky. But there was another light on the heath this evening, as well as sun and moon – a curious glow growing like a red flower, while two dark figures moved round it with lifted arms. Were they the witches of Vawnog, weaving a spell on the place and all who passed that way? Why had they come by Vawnog at all? What spirits were abroad, and why did fears feed so readily on her heart today?

Tom Pugh turned once more on his box and pointed with his whip. 'Bara tan mattau' ('Peat fire bread'), he said laconically, and Lettice gave a shamefaced laugh. For she saw now that the red glow was made by a pile of burning peat, and the witches' cauldron was a black iron pot turned upside-down in the middle of the fire, with the glowing peat piled over it. As for the two weird sisters, they were the two Cefnmawr girls, Annie and Minnie. Annie, the tall angular one, stood to the windward side of the fire with her pitchfork. Minnie, the younger one, called out a greeting, but Annie, with a brief nod, continued her task, moving the burning turfs aside and lifting the cauldron.

A delicious scent of warm peaty bread reached their nostrils as they passed by and saw the loaves turned and put back beneath the pot. The two sisters were piling fresh peat with deft hands round the cauldron when they lost sight of them.

'It is late in the day to be making bara tan mattau,' said Lettice, and Tom Pugh remarked that the Cefnmawr people didn't know how to stop working. They were so thrifty they'd skin a mouse if they could sell the skin to anyone.

'Very different, I tell you, to the Vaughans of Brynrorin t'other side of Vawnog. There's a place now where things are left to go anyhow and no shape at all.'

He knew all about it because Sarah Ellen, his wife's niece was there in service and didn't care for it. She would likely be leaving at Michaelmas. But if Mrs Peters didn't mind he would stop for a minute to give a little package which his wife had asked him to deliver.

No, Mrs Peters did not mind, and smiled to herself at old

Tom Pugh's artfulness in choosing to go home that way. Mrs Pugh was a sharp-tongued woman and would no doubt rate her husband soundly if he neglected her commission.

Outside the darkling barns of Brynrorin they waited, while Tom Pugh shouted to a man who was rounding up some ducks for the night. The farmhouse with its plain whitewashed front, square porch and grey outbuildings, was like a hundred other farms of the district, but there was something disturbing to Lettice in the place, some troubled memory that eluded her.

The man, a farm hand, came up alongside the carriage to take the parcel from Tom Pugh. He was elderly and ill-clad, with a white face and loose slobbering mouth. When Tom Pugh spoke to him he made inarticulate noises, then ambled off into the shadows without returning Lettice's good-evening.

'Deaf and dumb, he is,' said Tom Pugh in explanation. 'Fancy having that old scarecrow about the place still. That's a thing I don't understand.'

And with that, shaking his head to himself, he turned the horses and whipped them up for the last stage of the journey home. But suddenly Lettice knew the story for which she had been searching her memory. Like a dark bat, escaping from the house they had left, the recollection came with her on the way.

At Brynrorin, when she first remembered hearing of it, had lived a young Mrs Vaughan. Nantgwyn was too far away for any friendship between the families, but Lettice could recall a sweet-faced woman whom she had once seen, holding her little boy by the hand. He was her only child, a lively four-year-old running about the fields and rickyard. One evening a farm servant, who was deaf and dumb and feeble-minded but able to drive the animals, took the child with him to fetch the cows from milking and set him to ride on the back of one. In some way or other the child slipped off, the herd jostled on through the narrow muddy lane and trampled the little body to its death.

Then the poor deaf-mute, but half aware of what had happened, ran to the house and found the gentle-faced mother. Pulling at her skirts, gesticulating and mouthing, he led her through the farmyard and out to the place where her child lay. She never recovered, it was said, from that hour, bearing in her face until she died soon afterward the look of one who has taken fright at life.

Mother and child had been dead now these many years, but the half-wit servant lived on at Brynrorin, and every evening fetched the cows home at milking time.

Lettice, remembering the story, with Philip asleep in her lap, sat very still, thinking of all that life could bring and take away. When they reached home there was still no letter from John, and no tidings of the ship from the owners.

Chapter 11

News from Afar

Michelmas Fair once more at St. Idris! The stalls were set up round the grey Cross, and Ivor turned out the money-box on the nursery chimneypiece and divided the contents honourably in four parts, to be spent on toffee apples, bull's-eyes and pink rock. Archie came home from school announcing that there was a two-headed woman on view in a tent, but Mamma refused to take the two younger children to see her. Matty could not get the thought of what she might be like out of her mind, particularly at night when the flares from the shows lit up her bedroom ceiling.

But there was one event which could be plainly seen from the nursery window. The poor boys from the city for a prize of sixpence competed to eat boiling pudding, seated on a raised platform and before a cheering crowd of onlookers. The platform stood in front of the big tent, and there were three men playing a fife and cornet and banging a drum to attract the people.

Among the boys who strove to swallow the steaming portions in the shortest possible time were two young Flanagans, younger brothers of Wallie now loafing in the crowd with other hobbledehoys of the place. Lettice disapproved strongly of the whole practice as foolish and barbarous, and more than likely to ruin the boys' digestion. But although she remarked several times that it ought to be stopped, she nevertheless stood with the children at the nursery window watching the antics of the boys and the movements of the jostling throng.

A week had passed since the visit to Llanmadoc, another newsless, leaden-footed week. One part of Lettice's mind was numb with waiting, yet she did not wish to rouse it lest the agony of returning consciousness should bring worse in its trail. So now she stood with the children at the nursery window and heard with half her attention their eager comments and the blare of the music.

The grey Celtic Cross, worn with centuries of wind and weather, stood in the midst of the Fair, just as it had stood in the days when mediaeval pilgrims came thronging to St. Idris. They would have been a gay crowd in those days, thought Lettice idly. Even a few years ago the women in their tall hats and red cloaks must have been a cheerful sight. But now it seemed that all the men were crowned with dark bowler hats, and so many of the farmers' wives chose to dress in black. Lettice herself never wore black because of John's dislike.

'Letty, take that old black thing off. I can't bear to see you in it!' he had said to her one day when she was economically making use of a cape of her mother's, and she had never worn it again. She thought of that now, watching the farmers' wives in their sober garments, and then clenched her hands till the fingernails drove into the palms, thinking that she might one day be dressed as they.

'But John is still alive! I *know* he's alive!' she cried to herself. 'O God, make me strong! Take away my doubts!'

At that moment she noticed a familiar figure detach itself from the crowd in front of the booths and cross the street. It was Mr Davies the Post – the quiet, dark-eyed man who ruled the post-office at the lower end of the Cross. He kept also a shop that sold rolls of cloth and homespun for men's suits, though no one ever seemed to buy any, and as there was only one post in to the city and one out of it every day, there was plenty of time for Mr Davies to indulge his taste for reading. His brother, who came back to St. Idris for his summer holiday every year, was a Greek scholar of repute and principal of a divinity college. It was said that Mr Davies the Post could have done great things and gone far in scholarship, but lack of ambition and fondness for a quiet life had kept him in his native place, where he carried out the duties of Postmaster with an air of great dignity and reserve.

This was the man who crossed the street and who even now approached the front door of the Stone House. The distant peal of the bell downstairs a moment later confirmed what Lettice's eyes had seen. Beside her the children were calling excitedly upon her to watch the pudding-eaters.

'Billy Flanagan has won! Mamma, did you see what a funny face he made? Now they're giving him the prize. Oh, Mamma, you're not looking!'

No, she wasn't looking. She was listening instead to Catherine Jane's urgent footsteps on the stairs.

'Mr Davies the Post to see you!' were the words she heard, but Lettice remembered nothing more of that moment of the day until she found herself at the bottom of the stairs facing the Postmaster in the hall.

'Prydnawn da' ('Good evening'), he said. 'I thought I would like to bring you this myself, Mrs Peters,' and he held out a telegram. She thanked him and succeeded in opening the parlour door and going in before him. The room was misty as she tore open the envelope, but something in her own beating heart and in Mr Davies' face calmed her so that she was able to read the words, written in the Postmaster's small, scholarly writing. The cabled message came from Aden and read:

> *All well. Zouave burnt out in Indian*
> *Ocean. All my love. John.*

Mr Davies put out a steadying hand. 'Mrs Peters, may I be the first to congratulate you? You have been in the thoughts of all of us at St. Idris these many weeks, and though I have not spoken to you of the matter I have watched the post every day for a letter from abroad. Now, praise be to Almighty God, your husband is safe. No, no, do not come to the door with me.'

He was gone and Lettice was left to herself. With one swift movement she turned the key in the parlour door, sought John's chair by the fire and fell on her knees beside it.

In the morning came a telegram from the owners in Liverpool, repeating the news that the *Zouave* was burnt and that captain and crew were landed safe at Aden.

For the next day or two Catherine Jane was kept busy answering the door to neighbours and relatives who came to share the news. They ranged from the Dean, who delighted in the thought that he and John Peters would one day continue their geological discussions, to Jimmie Dugan, a ragged old Irishman whom Lettice found at the back door two days in succession, pledging the 'Captain's salvation' in Marged's cups of tea, and assuring the company that 'all the Saints in Heaven and the Holy Mother herself was looking after Captain Peters the way he wouldn't be burnt or drowned neither'.

It was clear to Lettice that most people had given up hope of John's return. They received her news as a cause for whole-hearted rejoicing, but Lettice, even while she exulted in the thought of his safety, knew that John was very far from exaltation. He had lost his ship. This thought haunted her day and night, and of all the visitors who called at her house none was so welcome and so understanding as William Bowen, John's old steward. He had walked the six miles from his cottage to see her, bringing a present which, with the careful handiness of a sailor, he now started to unpack from its brown paper wrapping.

'I thought maybe, marm,' he said, 'that you might like something to remember the old ship by, seeing as how she's a total loss, and that's a thing I can't bear to think of.'

The brown paper was off at last and Bowen set before her on the table a heavy silver-plated cruet-stand.

'You'll recall it, marm,' he said eagerly. 'It's the one we always used in the saloon. When I left the *Zouave* Captain

Peters asked me if I'd like it to keep as a memento. I'm not saying that I haven't been proud to have it all these years, but when I heard what had happened to the old ship I said to the wife, 'There's someone needs that memento more'n I do', and I came along with it.'

There was, Lettice reflected afterwards, something laughable in old Bowen, with his red grizzled beard and his gold earrings, presenting her with a cruet-stand, but at the time she was nearer to tears. Had Bowen brought her Aladdin's lamp instead of a saltcellar and pepper pot, he could not have cast a surer spell over Lettice, for as she searched for words with which to thank him she saw, with memory's heightened vision, the ship's saloon with the mahogany table beneath the skylight and the tumbler-rack hanging overhead, jingling a little in stormy weather. Through the hooked-back door of the saloon she saw, too, the big cabin, fitted from floor to ceiling with shelves of teak (John had them made by a Chinese carpenter at Rangoon), with the light falling on the books that filled every inch of space.

'Burnt out,' the telegram had said, and that meant the loss of many valued possessions. If John were alive his sextant and chronometer were safe, but what of the sea chest of camphor-wood, filled with his clothes? And worse than any loss of money and kit would be the loss of the books. He had spent more on them than he could properly afford, Lettice had always known that. Books on politics and history there were, for he was interested in all things of the mind, but especially books of science and natural philosophy, since he was himself an enquiring and well-equipped scientist. There would be files of correspondence, too, she knew, with learned men – geologists for whom he brought back specimens from the countries he visited, and others who shared his restless passion for aeronautics and the possibilities of flight. He would miss those letters, and the books which had been collected over many years, and were the precious companions of a man who passed days, weeks and months in his own company.

'Tell me, Bowen, do you think everything has gone?' The tears had brimmed over now, and she wiped them away as best she could.

'Marm, I reckon he had his instruments,' was the answer. 'I can't see the Captain abandoning ship without 'em, and they'd be the crew's salvation in a manner of speaking.'

Little by little the two bare words of the message were being clothed in her mind by all the likely circumstances of the *Zouave*'s end. Because Bowen evoked the ways of the sea, which she realised she had been in danger of forgetting, these images now grew clearer.

Did the ship's company, she asked herself, fight the fire for days and nights, the flames licking upward from the holds, driving the sweating men from the pumps, until at length masts, spars and rigging, a flaming canopy, crashed to the sea? Then, when the fight was over and John had ordered the crew to the boats, she saw him coming last over the side, his chronometer and sextant in his hand. But what was the look on his face? Even with her mind's eye she did not care to peer too closely at that moment.

Was it in the glare of day that it happened, or under the soft southern stars? And did the boats float on quiet seas, or must master, mates and crew strain every sinew to keep their craft afloat amid surging waves? Most important of all, had water and provisions lasted until their rescue?

Lettice tried to imagine what her own feelings would be if the Stone House and all its contents were lost, but that a man's ship meant more to him than any house on earth she knew well. John had sailed in the *Zouave* for years, ever since that first voyage to China for which she had helped buy his kit. Because he loved the *Zouave* he had refused the command of larger and faster ships, and had stopped his ears to any talk of abandoning sail for steam. The *Zouave* was part of himself; her caprices were as dear to him as the beauty of her lines.

'He was proud of her, wasn't he, Bowen?' She continued her thoughts aloud. 'Do you remember how he used to say to me in rough weather, 'Aren't you glad we're safe at sea, and not in a dangerous street with chimney-pots falling on top of us?' It always made me laugh when he said it, and I forgot to be frightened. For I *was* scared sometimes, you know, Bowen, of those great seas.'

'I don't wonder, marm. I've felt scared myself. But a thing I've noticed is that it's the good times one remembers. Fair days, when we ran before the Trades and everything went right. The men got to their washing and mending, and there was no complaining. It used to look just right, if I may say so, marm, to see you settin' on the after deck with your sewing in your hands.'

Dear days of sun and smiling sea and constant, purposeful wind. Days that passed noiselessly from blue, unconfused morning through white noon to the first blossoming of stars; amber evenings when the flying-fish at their bows seemed to spring in rhythmic obedience to some law of the universe, and men and ship, bent together in one purpose, followed their destiny round the world.

For the old steward such days were the core of his being; for the Captain's wife they wore the bloom of early married love and her first sharing of her husband's life.

All hardships were dismissed as they talked on, nor did they speak of those weeks when the ship loitered, in the Doldrums, full of mysterious creaks and sighs, or ploughed shuddering through wintry seas. Had Lettice really forgotten the time they ran out of flour and ate weevily biscuits? (She had learnt to remove the weevils and say nothing, though it cost her an effort every time.) It seemed, too, that she had quite overlooked the hours of sickness in her first pregnancy, when the smells of cooking, tarred ropes and lamp oil were her daily undoing, and the odour of foreign ports too intolerable to be faced.

Now, because they would never again see the ship that had been their home, they remembered only sunlit decks and the shadows of the great sails, and heard the sailors chanting their songs.

> *The Yankee ship went down the river,*
> *Pull, boys, pull, jolly boys!*
> *And who d'y' think was captain of her?*
> *Pull, boys, pull, jolly boys!*
> *But old Jehankin Jones, the nigger.*
> *Pull, boys, pull, jolly boys!*

'Do you remember,' said Lettice suddenly, 'how the men used to bait their hooks with bacon when they were fishing over the side for sharks?'

'Ay, that I do,' answered Bowen. 'And there was a hook with bacon on it that was lost, and drat me if it didn't turn up two days later inside a shark that had been a-following us.'

When at last Bowen departed Lettice sat for some time, her hands unaccustomedly idle in her lap and her eyes on the flickering coals in the parlour fire. In her heart and mind the *Zouave* lived again, and it was proof to Lettice, if proof were needed, of the destructibility of things. The ship that John had steered across the Seven Seas; the home that had been the first home of her married life; the china, glass and polished brass and wood that had been Bowen's charge, all these had vanished, as utterly as a dream. But the skill and love and care that had been lavished on the old ship; the beauty of her spreading canvas and the clean lines of her, which for those who knew her would always be the standard of beauty, these remained.

The *Zouave* would never grow shabby, to end her days maimed and unloved as a hulk or slowly disintegrate in a breaker's yard. John's books would never find their way to a second-hand shop in a seaport to be knocked down – like so many other books, once a captain's chosen companions – for a few foreign coins. As Lettice remembered them they were still a brave company, the sunlight on their sturdy backs, the smell of good tobacco among their leaves.

The ship and all that she contained had become a thing of the spirit, and the spirit is never lost. To that truth Lettice knew she must cling.

Chapter 12

Home Again

The time of waiting for John to come home seemed to Lettice a season of drought. The rainy days of deepening autumn did not alter this feeling: it was as though the very roots of her nature were parched and cried out for her husband's return. Strangely, it seemed to her who had waited so calmly while nothing was known, she was scarcely able to endure the six weeks that might elapse while John was on his way from Aden to London.

It was unfortunate, too, that just at this time Ivor and Archie should have broken the wooden model of the *Zouave*, made by the old ship's carpenter, with every spar and bit of rigging in its place. It stood on top of a chest in the boys' bedroom, until one wet Saturday afternoon, when time hung heavy on their hands, Ivor invented the game of circling the room by jumping from one piece of furniture to another, it being a point of honour not to set foot on the ground. Archie, taking a flying leap from washstand to chest, sent the ill-starred model crashing to the floor where Lettice, running upstairs in alarm, found it a jumble of broken cross-trees and rigging. Nor did it mend matters when Ivor remarked calmly, 'After all, Mamma, she's still better than the *Zouave*, for all that's left of her is a cinder!'

Carrying the poor wreck to her own room, Lettice's vexation was increased by the thought that the boys were getting 'out of hand' in their father's absence. Archie had been more than ever difficult of late, not altogether on account of naughtiness, but because of a consuming love for mechanics, which his mother found hard to bear and difficult to understand.

A few days earlier he had taken the two eyes out of Matty's new doll, Guinevere, to see how they pivoted and to discover, if he could, what it was that gave them that look of slight astonishment. But the round brown eyes were easier to take out than to put back, and lay on the table, looking more astonished than ever, while Matty wept over her sightless Guinevere.

Another time it was Ivor's watch that suffered. Archie had taken his own watch to pieces and then, failing to remember how the wheels fitted, dismantled Ivor's and, using it as a guide, succeeded in putting his own together bit by bit. Ivor's watch, without a model to assist, had then remained in fragments.

'He's my elder brother, and his watch should set *my* watch an example,' said Archie.

But there was worse to come. The day after the disaster in the bedroom, Archie and Matty bickered, on their way home from morning Chapel, as to whose turn it was to carry the velvet bag which held the family hymn books. Lettice reproved them both for quarrelling at such a time and over such a matter, but upheld Matty's claim. To pay off the score Archie, in the vacant hour between Sunday School and tea-time, glued up the pages of the book which his sister was reading – a large copy of *The Arabian Nights*.

Books meant nothing to Archie, and he thought it a good joke, but to Matty, discovering the crime next day, it was as though he had closed the gates of Heaven. Beside herself with fury, she flew at Archie like some possessed spirit. Once more Mamma intervened and sent the culprit straightway to bed. And now behold the case reversed, for the tender-hearted Matty could not bear to know that Archie was barred from grace, and spent the evening sitting outside his locked door, while Ivor and the Vicarage boys were baking potatoes in the raked embers of the outside kitchen – one of the most exquisite forms of entertainment known to the family.

But now, at last, the head of the household was on his way home. A cable announced his arrival at Suez, and by the

overland route he would be in London by mid November.
A week before his expected arrival Lettice received a letter,
written on the steamship which had brought him and his crew
from Madagascar to Aden. Very simply it told his story.

The *Zouave*, homeward bound from Bombay, had taken
fire in the Indian Ocean. The fire, which had broken out in
the cargo, beat all their efforts, and captain and crew watched
from the boats their ship's fiery destruction. There was enough
food in the boats, but they were short of water. 'It had to be
rationed carefully,' wrote John, 'but we managed.' He had
kept the boats together and the men in good heart for three
long weeks of burning weather in an empty sea, until a French
packet, bound for Madagascar, had sighted them and brought
them to port. Thence they had come by steamship to Aden,
where John cabled his news.

There was, Lettice heard afterwards, some small trouble
about this with the owners, for John, on reaching the cable
office, had sent, his first message to Lettice, and the second
to Messrs. Bagshaw and Lock of Liverpool. In the opinion. of
Messrs. Bagshaw and Lock it was to his owners and not to his
wife that the first intimation should have gone. Lettice hugged
this to herself with quiet satisfaction.

'It has been a bad business,' wrote John, ' but we are saved
to sail again. Not one of the ship's company is missing. Of
the *Zouave* there is nothing left. We watched her go blazing
to her end. I cannot trust myself to write of her, but you will
understand. I shall never know another like her.'

On a still day in November, so mild that spring seemed but
round the corner, Lettice walked down to Nansi Richards'
cottage to request her services once more to look after the
Stone House while she went to meet John in London.

The distant sea round the Bishop Rock showed calm
and blue, and there were roses still in bloom behind Nansi's
whitewashed wall. The door at the end of the passage, running

the depth of the little house, stood open as in summer-time and showed a gay patch of late snapdragons and marigolds in the back garden.

In one corner of the passage stood the ladder by which Nansi climbed to the loft where she stored her potatoes. On the left was the door into the living-room, the only room in the house, containing, beside Nansi's quilting frame, her wardrobe and chest of drawers (there were always peppermints in the top drawer), her armchair and three-legged oak table, and the huge oak cupboard bed, with sliding doors, so large that when they were closed it was a little dark room in itself.

Lettice found her, as usual, seated at her quilting frame on which were stretched the two layers of material with their interlining of sheep's wool through which Nansi's little blue-veined fingers deftly pushed her needle in elaborate tracery of leaf and flower and scroll. As Lettice crossed the threshold she finished the curling petal of a flower, rose from her work and offered Lettice the armchair with grave courtesy.

The two women understood each other perfectly. Nansi was the only person to whom Lettice entrusted the children when she went away. She was also, and this was important, the only other authority from whom Marged would take orders. The Richards family, in spite of the poverty of this last survivor, were held in high respect in St. Idris, nor was it forgotten that Nansi's mother had helped to keep away the French invasion. Precise and gentle, and no great favourite with the children, Nansi Richards was compact of faithfulness and devotion.

Now, although she knew quite well why Lettice had come, and although Lettice knew that she knew, the two did not mention the matter for some time, but talked instead of Nansi's rheumatism, the mild season and the comings and goings of St. Idris people. At last Lettice came to the point.

'Nansi, I've had a letter. He will be in London in two days' time.'

A slight flush crept into Nansi's thin cheeks. 'You will be

going to meet him?'

Lettice nodded as though it were quite a new idea, this thought of running off to London to meet her husband. 'The day after tomorrow. Do you think you can come and take charge?'

Nansi glanced at her quilting frame as though seeking an answer in the elaborate pattern drawn there, sucked in her cheeks with a peculiar sound which the children always connected with the smell of peppermints, and then intimated that she would come. Lettice gave a sigh of relief, though indeed it had never crossed her mind that Nansi would do anything but say yes, and the skies of St. Idris would have fallen had she refused. Then the two settled down to discuss the details of the children's underflannels, Matty's chest-mixture and the right time for the administration of Gregory powders.

When Lettice took farewell of Nansi and walked back to her own house it was with the conscious feeling that the most important step of preparation had been taken. There was nothing now, except the packing of a trunk, between her and her journey to meet John, nothing but the last details and instructions which long usage would help her to carry out faithfully and precisely until, like a bird on the wing, she would rise in the dark at five o'clock, breakfast hastily by lamplight, kiss the excited children goodbye, and find even Tom Pugh's best horse and the London train itself too slow for her flying thoughts.

Seated at last in the corner of the railway carriage on that long journey, Lettice pondered for a while on this central core of her life, her love for her husband.

In the first years of her marriage, even while she was still able to accompany him on his voyages, she had been pursued by the thought of John's dying. He was ten years older and exposed to far greater dangers than she. If ever they were separated in a foreign port and he unduly delayed, panic would seize her, suggesting misadventure, murder or sudden onslaughts of yellow fever. Even when she put such fears away as unworthy, it was impossible to cure the melancholy that sometimes haunted her. Unless the ship went down, she reasoned, with both of them on board, one was bound to survive the other. Love itself could not prevail, and the grave was the end of all love stories. At this point she turned to religion, but even faith would sometimes falter. John was better and wiser than she was. Would he be sure to wait for her? Supposing, among the 'many mansions' they were no longer considered necessary to each other in the scheme of God's universe?

But of late years these thoughts had ceased to trouble her. Even the earthiness, the very mortality of their love, became a consolation. Earth and Spirit, she discovered, were not really divided; one reflected the other. From their union sprang the surest happiness, even as children were born from the rapture of spirit and flesh; and little children to Lettice's thinking, were near perfection, the one sure and recurring token of God's continued love.

This explanation of things did not tally with most of the sermons and prayers to which she had listened, except perhaps Uncle Simon's at Rehoboth, but it gave her heart peace. She could even think calmly now of the grave, hoping that she and John would be together, the grass and flowers growing over them, while their spirits voyaged in realms of light.

All this came back to her on that November day towards the end of her journey. But she thought she would like to change the phrase 'realms of light', which suggested something hard and brilliant, like the dazzling air of tropic cities. Watching from her carriage window the branches of winter trees pencilled against the fading sky and the gleam of water beyond dim hedges, she recalled the rapture of her girlhood whenever some frolic or errand took her out of doors on a winter evening. To escape into the gusty twilight was to be filled with unspeakable joy. The lighted windows of house or chapel meant confinement and the heat and smell of oil lamps, pinning attention to the task in hand. But out of doors, in the cool darkness alive with scent and sound, the dry leaves scampering at her feet, there was a freeing of the spirit which had its birth in her early childhood when she stood in the rickyard at Nantgwyn and first saw the winter stars. Death, in spite of all the solemn things that were said about it, might well be like that when it came – an escape and a flinging of cares to the winds.

Looking now at the lamplit carriage and the anxious, expectant faces of her fellow travellers as they gathered their baggage together, the women straightening their bonnets, the men glancing through their small change in preparation for porters and cab-drivers, Lettice put the last touch to her private picture of Life and Death.

It was a journey, she said to herself: all of them travelling together through unknown country, with bundles and baggage for cares and responsibilities. But at the end of it all, for her, John would be waiting, and that was all that mattered; just as that was all that mattered now when at last the train ran into Paddington, and there, under the gas light, rather gaunt about the cheek-bones, his eyes eagerly searching the carriage windows, stood John Peters.

He took her in his arms and tried to speak, but found he could say nothing. Finally it was she who put her arm through his and led him away into the comforting darkness.

Chapter 13

Christmas

In the kitchen, where the flavour of mincemeat spiced the air, the maids were making a Kissing Bush. Throughout the bare, sea-girt country of Idrisland, where no mistletoe grew and very little holly either, no household considered Christmas properly kept without a Kissing Bush. Two wooden hoops, tied together at right angles to form the framework of a sphere, were hung from the ceiling and covered with red flannel, red ribbon or anything else that could be found of that colour. Across these were fastened long sprays of ivy, though first the ivy berries were dipped in flour and water so that they gleamed white as snow. Last of all, oranges were threaded on strings and shone through the dark leaves.

Matty and Philip, seated on the broad kitchen windowsill, thought the Kissing Bush the most beautiful thing they had ever seen.

'What is a Kissing Bush *for?*' asked Philip, who was fond of questions. Catherine Jane evidently thought this very funny and laughed so much that she could not answer Philip; but Matty did not want to know anymore about it. For her it was enough that so lovely a thing existed. Besides, she knew quite well that it was a Fairy Tree, and the fruit that Catherine Jane threaded with such nimble fingers was not a dozen oranges bought at the Beehive, but golden apples which would grant wishes to anyone who tasted them; while at any moment a talking bird might fly out of the spicy heart of that magic bush.

There was never a lovelier Christmas than this one, Matty thought to herself. So many things were different since Papa had come home. It was true that this time, there were none of those wonderful presents for everyone, because they had all been burnt in the *Zouave*. There had been, said Papa, jars of chow-chow and chests of tea, a Kashmir shawl for Mamma, a new carved table for the parlour and little elephants of ivory and ebony. Mamma laughed when he spoke of them and said, 'You don't really think I'm troubling about anything of that sort, do you?'

It was quite clear that she was not, for she laughed while she said it, and indeed she was laughing more often than not these days. Often when Matty wakened at night in the little bedroom over the front hall she would hear the house filled with voices: People seemed to be continually coming and going and a buzz of talk rose to Matty's ears whenever the parlour door opened. She knew most of the voices: Canon Roberts' and Dr Parry's, and the sonorous tones of Mr Jenkins, the minister; Uncle Jim and Cousin Howell (the last two meant singing and laughter); the Pentre Evan family and the Llanaber cousins. Yet although she recognised most of them, the downstairs world, once she was in bed, became a strange land with none of the usual features. How alarming they were, those gusts of talk and laughter from the departing guests, till suddenly they died away because Mamma had said, 'Hush, you'll wake the children!'

Matty knew just how she said it, standing at the foot of the stairs with her finger to her lips. It was the one reassuring part of those nightly wakings.

The Peters family kept their Christmas feast on December the twenty-fifth, known in St. Idris as New Christmas Day. In this they differed from most of the country people round the city who kept Old Christmas, twelve days later. But already times were changing. Eliza and Sam Rhys, at Pentre Evan, had always kept Old Christmas; but now Fanny, running in to see Lettice one morning, announced that this year they would be keeping the earlier festival. This step was an innovation, for the Rhyses had always been conservative.

'Do you hear that Eliza is keeping New Christmas Day?' asked Martha, who had driven over from Nantgwyn.

'Dear me, why shouldn't she?' said Lettice. 'She's had plenty of time to get ready. I shouldn't mind an extra twelve days myself. Martha, if you're driving into Westford tomorrow, could you find some purple ribbon for Nansi Richards' cap? I have a warm shawl for her but I know she'd like the ribbon. And then there's Dorit. Some warm slippers, perhaps? There was a pair I noticed, marked 'Latest from London', in Samuel Davies' window that would do very well.'

Martha left with a list of last-minute commissions in her hand, calling out as she drove away that Jim would send the goose as usual from Nantgwyn on Christmas Eve.

On the day before Christmas Eve Aunt Sarah's box arrived by carrier and was brought into the house. Aunt Sarah, who lived at Birkenhead, was a sea-captain's wife with two children of her own, but there was no one in the world who knew better what a family likes to receive at Christmas. The box, a substantial tea-chest from which the nails had been removed, stood tantalisingly in the dining-room window, and it was as much as the children could do to refrain from peeping within, though such a thing would have broken every rule of family tradition.

On Christmas Eve Matty did go so far as to poke her finger inside and was sure that she caught a glimpse of the glossy back of a Christmas Number, but whether it was the *Graphic*, *Chatterbox*, or *St. Nicholas* she could not be sure. That night she prayed that it might be one of the two last, but later felt ashamed of her selfishness, thinking Papa might prefer the *Graphic*.

After this preliminary poke Matty ran upstairs to the nursery to escape from further temptation. The room was growing dark but for the firelight; Catherine Jane had gone downstairs to fetch the lamp and Philip was alone standing at the window

watching the blue dusk fall on the Cross. Matty ran across
the room and stood beside him. No lamps lighted the streets
of St. Idris in those days, so that the Beehive window, where
Mr Tudor had spread himself over the Christmas decorations,
held the stage. Cotton wool, red flannel, a cunningly concealed
oil lamp and glass icicles of a length and thickness unknown
to the mild climate of St. Idris, had made a fairyland of the
usual tea canisters and rolls of calico. Two pairs of eyes gazed
reverently across the street while Matty reflected not for the
first time, on the enviable lot of Olwen Tudor of the Beehive
who lived every day behind so much splendour.

Catherine Jane came in, carrying the lamp, to spread the
table for the children's tea.

'May we make toast?' asked Matty. Catherine Jane said
yes, and cut several rounds from the loaf. Now the nursery
toasting-fork had been invented by the *Zouave*'s mate, Mr
Jenkins, who had a taste for patent devices. Instead of reversing
the bread by hand in the usual way when the first side was
toasted to a pleasing brown, one gave a sharp shake to the
fork, which made a surprising revolution and so presented the
pallid flank to the fire. The prongs of the fork, in order that the
toast might not fall into the ashes, were long and curved, and
tore large crumpety holes in the bread, giving it a distinctive
appearance. Marged would have nothing to do with such a
contraption in the kitchen, and it was only in the nursery that
Mr Jenkins' device found favour.

Matty, leaning over the high guard, dangled her toasting-
fork in front of the burning coals, while Philip sat beside her
on the wooden stool, which in the guise of a horse had carried
them so many phantom miles over the nursery floor.

'Philip, do you know it's Christmas Day tomorrow?' said
Matty. The toast smelt delicious, though it was a trifle too
black in one corner, and she gave the fork a vigorous shake.
'Do you feel excited inside?' she went on.

Philip nodded and for a moment there was silence between

them, while the little black kettle sang to itself on the hob. Downstairs they could hear the sound of voices, Ivor's and Archie's and those of two boy cousins, but here in the circle of lamplight was their own warm nursery world, safe and familiar, and yet with a tingling feel of joys to come that was new and special. Suddenly Philip spoke, sitting round-eyed and rosy on his wooden stool.

'Everything is loverly!' he exclaimed. 'The fire is a lady with long hair, the toast is like toffee, the tables and chairs are rocks and trees and the pictures are birds in the air.'

Matty looked round to see if anything had changed in the room, but saw only the nursery furniture. Yet she could fancy, now that her brother had said it, that everything wore an odd, expectant air this evening.

'What did you say the fire was?' she asked Philip, who had already forgotten.

'What *did* I say?' he asked. But neither of them could remember; the vision had faded, and when Catherine Jane reappeared with the milk and butter she found two hungry children and some blackened toast.

'Deio! There's careless you are, missy, burning all that good bread! Whatever were you thinking of?'

'I think it was *partly* Mr Jenkins' toasting-fork,' said Matty. Other things were responsible as well, but somehow they couldn't be explained.

Catherine Jane snorted. 'It takes a man to invent a silly thing of that sort. Sit down now, both of you, and eat your tea while I draw the curtains.' She paused at the window a moment and looked out into the darkening Cross.

'And if Mr Tudor Beehive isn't careful he'll be burning himself to little bits with his lamp and his old shop-soiled cotton-wool, and the red flannel that he got cheap from Price the Mill, I shouldn't wonder.'

Matty was deep in thought. 'Mr Jenkins' toasting-fork is a *special* thing,' she said, 'and I shall always think so, until I am an old, old lady. So there, Catherine Jane!'

Downstairs in the parlour that evening, when all the children were safely in bed and, it was to be hoped, asleep, Lettice and John filled the four stockings. Many a Christmas Eve Lettice had performed this rite alone, yet now those solitary evenings seemed of no importance. Only the present counted; tonight they were doing it together, with John to help tie up the little packages, stuff an orange in each toe under her direction and try out a new clockwork engine on the parlour floor.

Waking next morning, Lettice heard the shouts of the three elder children and knew that Matty had rushed to share the fun in her brothers' room. Philip sat up suddenly in his little bed, scrambled out of it and pattered across to his mother's side, dragging behind him the swollen stocking that had once belonged to Papa. Lifted up into the big bed and placed between his parents, the trophy lying unexplored before him, he clasped his hands and asked, 'Is that all for me?'

'But of course, cariad! It is thy stocking now,' said Lettice in Welsh. Philip turned quite pale. In a small voice, that only his mother could hear, he remarked to himself, 'Arglwydd Duw! Lord God, it is too much!'

Did the cup of happiness brim almost too full that Christmas? Deep in Lettice's heart there was some hint of this, and she was quick to catch the echo in the words of her youngest child.

On Christmas Day the Peters family attended matins in the Cathedral, since no service was held on that day in any of the nonconformist chapels of St. Idris. Leaving the house, in which a fine flavour of goose was already apparent, they trooped through the Cross, exchanging greetings with their neighbours, and holding fast to their hats and bonnets because of the boisterous wind that came galloping to meet them across the bare land and over the slate and whitewashed roofs that tumble down the hill to the Cathedral Close. Beyond the tall spire of the Methodist Tabernacle they could see the white waves whipping the tail of the Bishop Rock, and when they reached the gateway of the city wall the wind was so strong that Mamma's skirts blew out like a ship's canvas, and Philip's little velvet cap went bowling down the Thirty-Nine Articles, which is the name given to the grey flight of steps that go down to the Cathedral.

But below in the Close there was shelter from the tearing wind, and as always the comfortable sound of rooks in the bare sycamores. They met more people here, all hurrying in to sing and pray: the big family of boys from the Vicarage, the Dean's sister who kept house for him, the two red-haired daughters of the Archdeacon and the young lady engaged to marry the Vicar Choral.

Everyone looked cheerful and Matty thought they had all decked themselves in their prettiest clothes. The Dean's sister wore her sealskin jacket, and the wife of the Minor Canon had bunches of red berries and glossy leaves on her bonnet. Yet no one, Matty was sure, looked as pretty as Mamma in her grey mantle with the chinchilla fur round her throat.

But it was remarkable how little those things counted when once they had entered the Cathedral, and how small and unimportant everyone appeared under the great arches

> *O come, all ye faithful,*
> *Joyful and triumphant!*

sang the choir, and their voices made still more arches of sound. Down through the ages the sweet, shrill voices of boys, those short-lived yet deathless voices, had invited the faithful people to come to Bethlehem; and now once again it was Christmas morning.

Kneeling on her hassock between Mamma and Ivor during the long recital of prayers, Matty's eyes and thoughts strayed up to the carved oak of the roof, hanging like brown lace above the great nave. Strangers came from afar to gaze at its beauty and the wonders beneath it, but the children regarded them as intruders. This was *their* Cathedral, round which they played every day and where they came on high festivals. The lilac-grey stone of it was hewn from their own sea cliffs, and the carved roof, made of Irish oak, was like the brown seaweed that fringed their favourite caves.

No locked doors barred them from slipping into the Cathedral on their way home from paddling in the stream on summer days, or from some delightful escapade in the Bishop's Palace. They might wander at will through the ruined side chapels or steal gently from stall to stall in the choir, quietly tipping up the misereres to find beneath the carved portraits of sea-sick monks and foxes with women's heads.

No fussy verger stopped them, yet it sometimes seemed to Matty that they were watched by motionless figures in the clerestory, high up under the roof. There they were, she suspected, with their shaven heads and brown gowns, and she had no desire to run up the spiral staircase and take them unawares, for she did not like them very much. They were powerful people, she was well aware, for all their quiet ways and their plain gowns. She knew the proud tombs of the bishops in the side chapels, and, even grander than the tombs, the things that had been found inside them, and which lived in glass cases in the chapter-room where the surplices hung on hooks along the wall. There were croziers and rings and jewelled crosses, and while gazing on these objects it was almost impossible not to see also the fat white hands that grasped the golden crozier, with fingers encircled by those tremendous gold rings set with jewels.

Monks, bishops and jewels, shafts of winter sunlight striking between grey pillars, drone of parsonic voice, slight smell of camphor and sandalwood from Mamma's fur, anticipation of more presents and roast goose, mingled in Matty's thoughts, till the sudden ending of prayers brought them all to their feet, and choir and congregation lifted up their voices in *Hark, the Herald Angels sing*.

Aunt Sarah's box, which was opened after dinner, proved to be all that was expected. On top was a goodly collection of Christmas Numbers – *Chatterbox* and *St. Nicholas*, the *Graphic* and the *Illustrated London News*, so everyone was pleased. After them came nuts and tangerines, guava cheese and Elvas plums, with all sorts of luscious dried fruits brought by Uncle Dan from Brazil and Portugal. But best of all were the books at the bottom of the box, books on steamships and railway engines, Hans Andersen's *Fairy Tales* and a big illustrated edition of the *Pilgrim's Progress*, with pictures of everyone concerned from Evangelist to Apollyon with his flaming waist.

It had been the best Christmas of their lives, thought Lettice that evening on her way upstairs to kiss the little ones good-night. They were eating their bread and milk from wooden bowls by the nursery fire, and she paused on the threshold to listen to a story that Philip was telling his sister:

'I walked and I walked and there was the stable with Baby Jesus inside. But, you know, Mary wasn't there at all. Joseph had made a lovely swing for her in the roof and he was swinging and swinging her, up in the dark. But Baby Jesus was alone and he called out to me. He was too little to get out of his cot, so I lifted him out, and his feet were all bare; but it didn't matter at all because I had my big boots on so I could carry him, and we played and we played together, every sort of game we played.'

Christmas was over, and before Lettice had tidied up the house it was Twelfth Night and time to take down the Kissing Bush. John had three more weeks at home, many affairs to see to and letters to write. On fine days, with his geological hammer in his pocket, he would take the children for walks along the cliffs while the wintry sea boomed in the caves below and flying foam was carried inland high across the fields. But even in January there were days when the sea lay fair and blue, as though it were June, and the level sunshine, like golden sherry spilt over rocks and boulders, revealed to the children's eyes ice scratches made by the great glaciers in some dim frozen past of the earth's history.

Still better than these walks abroad were the experiments at home, which Papa so craftily arranged for their amusement and instruction. 'Don't throw away that vinegar bottle, my dear,' he would say to Mamma at lunch-time, 'it will do very well for a kaleidoscope.'

No sooner said than done. A few beads at the bottom, some glass smoked and cut to the right shape, completed the preparations; and the children waited their turn to gaze at the bright revolving colours and to feel that a whole gay world was spinning for their private pleasure. On a day of bright sunlight they were invited to gaze in a ghostly Camera Obscura, arranged in the attic with the help of a closed shutter with a hole in it and a sheet of white paper spread on a table beneath; and after tea that evening the family trooped into the dining-room to sit in a row, with Philip raised on a pile of Encyclopaedia Britannica, so that his eyes were at the level of his brothers' and sister's, while Papa placed pennies in the bottom of a bowl. At first the pennies were hidden from their gaze, but when Papa came with a jug and poured water on them, lo and behold the pennies came into sight in a mysterious fashion! This mirage of wealth was caused, Papa said, by a thing called Refraction of Light, which the two younger ones found difficult to understand though it increased Papa's reputation as a wizard.

Lettice encouraged these pastimes because they kept John and the children happy and busy, and she provided them with the necessary apparatus, ranging from bottles and saucers to beads from her own necklaces, although how anyone could spend their time on such meaningless jugglery often puzzled her.

It was a different matter when, one evening, the whole family gathered in the attic bedroom to look through a telescope fixed in the window-sash, which was reached only by climbing on a chair, then on a chest of drawers and finally on a stool.

Lettice had come upstairs to the icy room to see that the children were warmly wrapped, and that no one fell off the toppling erection, but she stayed to wonder. What were they, those fiery bands round Saturn and those many moons that John was now urging Matty to count carefully? '*Can't* you see eight?' he insisted, while Matty conscientiously counted again and the boys stood eagerly waiting their turn. How would they be, those blazing night skies, with many moons shining together? Were there human wives to watch them? And did dividing seas separate them from human husbands?

Inside the dark room was the cluster of children's heads, and outside the glittering winter stars which Lettice needed no telescope to view with awe and excitement. Suddenly some words of Dafydd ab Gwilym, that poet of the Middle Ages whom Jim was fond of quoting, came to her mind :

> *Da eu gwedd, baderau Duw gwyn,*
> *Yn alanastr heb linyn.*
>
> *Goodly are they to behold, the unstrung*
> *and scattered rosary of Holy God.*

Her head was still full of the glory as she slipped from the room and made her way downstairs to the warmth and lamplight of the house below.

Chapter 14

With Aunt Sarah

At the beginning of February John Peters sailed for India once more in his new ship the *Carabineer*, in which he had purchased a part share from Messrs. Bagshaw and Lock. Lettice and Matty went to see him off from Liverpool, Lettice afterwards returning alone to St. Idris, while Matty stayed on for a visit of several weeks with Aunt Sarah at Birkenhead.

Aunt Sarah's home stood by itself in a neat garden with a vine growing over its front door. In summer the pale-green clusters of grapes hung under the bedroom windows, and Matty could not think why Aunt Sarah ever wanted to live anywhere else in the world. But Aunt Sarah never lived in any house longer than three years. Like her husband she had a roving disposition, but being a wretched sailor she seldom went with him on his voyages, except occasionally to France and once or twice as far as Lisbon. So while Uncle Dan journeyed between Liverpool and South America, Aunt Sarah enlivened her time by moving house. She had a passion for freshly decorated walls and ceilings, and for rearranging her furniture. No sooner did the rooms begin to lose their first freshness than she removed herself to another dwelling in the neighbourhood, with her dogs and cats, her parrot and her game-cocks.

The parrot was a bad-tempered old bird, but Aunt Sarah could make him behave himself, and talk politely in Welsh, instead of swearing in Portuguese, just as she taught her game-cocks to spar by donning a pair of boxing-gloves and giving them lessons in self-defence.

Birds, animals and music were close rivals in Aunt Sarah's affection, and the creatures acquired an almost terrifying amount of character after a few years spent in her company. There was a black retriever who carried her shopping basket, and a tabby cat called Jane who lived to be twenty and brought the letters every day to lay at her mistress' feet. Matty detested and feared her, for she had once wakened in the night with an intolerable weight on her chest, to find Jane sitting there, purring loudly, her green eyes glowing in the dark.

Yet, taken as a whole, staying with Aunt Sarah was a good adventure, although Matty (on whom the choice generally fell because Aunt Sarah preferred little girls to little boys) was often lonely and missed her brothers sadly.

Of course, a great deal depended on whether Uncle Dan was at home or not. Uncle Dan had a curly auburn beard and strong white teeth and was, in the opinion of the Peters children, their jolliest relation. When he was there the house was filled with the scent of good cigars. Good port was also something about which Uncle Dan knew a great deal, and there would be pleasant dinners in the evenings to which the doctor and lawyer, business friends and sea captains were invited. All this lively company ceased when Uncle Dan's ship sailed once more; no one more exciting than the Welsh minister came to tea, and Matty was taught bezique until bedtime every evening by Aunt Sarah.

But there were glorious interludes in these visits, even when Uncle Dan was no longer there, and no doubt the best of them were the Saturday expeditions to Liverpool. Aunt Sarah and Matty would set off in the morning and take the ferry across the river. Since Aunt Sarah felt unwell on any size or sort of vessel, she invariably retired to the ladies' saloon, while Matty on deck was free to watch the world's shipping in the great highway. Big liners and little tramps, dredgers and lighters, schooners and barquentines, with the Chinese crews washing their clothes and the brown Lascars coiling ropes and running barefoot on the decks, were all part of her morning's entertainment.

Then Aunt Sarah, emerging pale but erect from her shadowy retreat, would lead the way to the shore and conduct her niece through the labyrinthine ways of a day's shopping in Liverpool. As they passed through the market Matty saw tomatoes for the first time. 'Love apples' was the name they bore, and Matty thought them so beautiful that she begged Aunt Sarah to let her taste one and was bitterly disappointed with the sharp, surprising flavour.

Later Aunt Sarah, to whom clothes were important, would spend considerable time over the choice of a new bonnet or mantle, and after they had lunched in a restaurant (where Matty was torn between admiration of their fellow lunchers and inability to eat all that was set before her), they would call at Aunt Sarah's dressmaker, who was probably making a new frock for Matty. But although the result was something very much more stylish than Miss Preece of St. Idris had ever achieved, Matty scarcely enjoyed that part of the day's programme.

Mrs Andrews, a widow whom Aunt Sarah employed, partly because she was sorry for her, was a great talker in spite of a mouthful of pins, and it was unfortunate that she should have possessed such particularly good white teeth. Aunt Sarah ventured one day to ask Mrs Andrews what she used for cleaning them. It seemed that Mrs Andrews had always used charcoal, like her mother before her, and henceforth Matty was condemned to the grisly practice and a permanently black toothbrush which was the jest of her elder brothers. Aunt Sarah never gave up hope of making her fair, pale little niece into a 'strong child'. Cold baths were part of her regime, and on this particular visit she had Matty's hair cut short by the barber 'to strengthen the roots'.

But if visits to the dressmaker were trying, everything was put right by the joys of the return journey. Once more the delightful river crossing, and then, to crown the day, they would call at a fish shop where one waited for shrimps to be cooked and then carried them away, pink and warm, in a paper bag, to be eaten at home with one's tea, an exquisite meal and fitting end to the day.

So much for Saturday, but alas, it was followed by Sunday when a small girl had need of all her fortitude. At ten o'clock the day opened with a prayer meeting in the Welsh chapel of which Aunt Sarah was a pillar and support. (For any Welsh person in Birkenhead to attend an *English* chapel, even though it were of the same denomination, was a mark of apostasy regarded with horror. One family of old friends from Pembrokeshire had done this shameful thing and were never mentioned again in Aunt Sarah's house.)

After the prayer meeting came Morning Service, and a long sermon with many depths and heights of *hwyl* from the pulpit, and the full-throated singing known only to those Welshmen who sing the songs of Zion in Babylonish exile. For Babylon may be anywhere from Patagonia to Charing Cross. Just here it happened to be a prosperous suburb of Liverpool.

The midday meal was followed at two o'clock by Sunday School, in turn succeeded by Singing Practice. Then came a short respite during which books of a definitely religious character might be read, and after that Aunt Sarah and her small niece attended Evening Service, sang yet more hymns and heard a sermon that was just as long, and extempore prayer that was just as fervent, as the morning varieties. Finally, at the end of the service came 'Seiat', when the minister came down from the pulpit to the 'Set Fawr' (the big seat), and small trembling children rose in their places to repeat the Bible verses they had learnt by heart.

Matty, torn between sleep and terror, found this hardest of all to bear. Mr Parry Williams, the minister, would pace the aisle, pausing in his walk to point to each child in turn. Matty had never yet failed to repeat her verse perfectly, but her fear grew no less with each succeeding Sunday. At the end of the long day the heat of the chapel and the popping gas-light before her eyes caused an agony of sleepiness. Only Aunt Sarah's presence and the awful warning of William Jones kept her awake. William Jones was a remarkably ugly boy who fell asleep in the pew before her every Sunday. 'You'll look like William Jones if you go to sleep,' warned Aunt Sarah one day, and the dread of that catastrophe kept Matty awake as nothing else could have done.

Blessed days when a slight cold kept Matty at home, but not in bed; when, Aunt Sarah having departed for chapel, Matty carried the big illustrated Book of Revelation into the comfortable kitchen and read aloud from its pages while Ellen basted the joint. The meat turned slowly on the jack, and to the pleasant sound of sizzling, Matty, seated on a sofa in the window, read aloud in Welsh from the open book on her knee:

So he carried me away in the spirit to the wilderness:
and I saw a woman sit upon the scarlet-coloured beast,
full of names of blasphemy, having seven heads and
ten horns.

The coloured picture on the opposite page did full justice to both the woman and the beast, and Matty paused in her reading to study it afresh:

And the woman was arrayed in purple and scarlet
colour, and decked with gold and precious stones and
pearls, having a golden cup in her hand.

'Oh, Ellen, she does sound beautiful, doesn't she?' exclaimed Matty, adding with a sigh, 'It's a pity she was so wicked, isn't it?'

Ellen gave the sirloin another turn. 'Don't you go wasting pity on her, cariad,' she said. 'Parading about, she was, to make an old show. And I wouldn't like to ask how she got all those fine clothes. No honest way that's certain! Go on reading now, Matty fach, for it's nice to hear you.'

It was Ellen who, one summer day, took Matty to a picnic at the lighthouse. Her brother, who drove a carrier's cart, was to bring them back, but the carefully made plan went astray, and no cart appeared at the meeting-place. Matty had run about all afternoon and climbed the winding stairway of the lighthouse to its top. But now, when she was already tired, two miles of dusty road stretched between them and the tram line that would take them home.

The maid set off in consternation while the child, dragging her feet already, walked beside her. Ellen lamented loudly, blamed her brother's carelessness and her own folly in depending on him, and Matty walked more slowly still. Ellen was in despair and decided to sit down on the roadside in hope of a passing lift, when suddenly Matty cried, 'Do you see that carriage coming?'

Ellen spun round but the white road was empty. 'Go on with you, there's no carriage! Is it joking you are?'

'But can't you see it, Ellen? It's a grand carriage with two black horses, and they're stopping here to pick us up.'

'Deio! What has come over the child?'

'Now we're getting in and sitting down, and the coachman is spreading the rug on our knees. Now he's cracking his whip and away we go!'

Every step of those two dusty miles, while the astonished maidservant trudged on, the small girl trotted at her side encouraging her phantom horses and commenting on the beauties of the passing landscape.

'Do you see that castle over there, and the soldiers marching and the swans on the lake?' Ellen saw nothing of the sort and her anxiety increased, but they were getting on fast, all the same; only one more mile.

'I like black horses best, don't you Ellen? And these ones have such shiny coats and long tails. Do you admire my scarlet cushions? I used to have green ones, but scarlet are nicest.' Thus did imagination triumph over dusty life and devour the long road before them; but Ellen, still troubled, put her small charge to bed as soon as they reached home and told Aunt Sarah there was no doubt but the child had had sunstroke.

Fancies abounded, but already Matty was learning to curb them before she harnessed them to her chariot. Walking downstairs in Aunt Sarah's house on winter evenings was terrifying, for the gas-light in the hall did not light the dark well of the staircase and there was one black corner where Matty was sure skeletons waited to clasp her in their bony arms. With a flying leap at this point she eluded their clutches; yet the very act of leaping was a confession of weakness, and the terrified child who had come safely to the bottom of the stairs forced herself to go all the way back and then walk past the fearful spot.

It was about this time that Ellen had the idea of putting Matty's straight hair in curl-papers. The result was an immediate success. The doctor's wife spoke to Aunt Sarah of her 'pretty little niece', and when next they went shopping in Liverpool Aunt Sarah bought Matty a new bonnet ruched with pink which showed off her curls and brought to her pale fairness a touch of becoming colour. But they had all reckoned without Matty. A few days later she refused to have anything more to do with curl-papers. In vain did Ellen coax and wheedle; in vain was Aunt Sarah's authority invoked.

'It's wrong, Ellen. Don't you see it's wrong?' said Matty earnestly. 'If I pretend to have curly hair when all the time it's straight, I'm *acting a lie*.'

Nothing would move her from this decision and the pretty curls were soon forgotten in locks as straight as candle-ends.

The chilly February days were lengthening and Matty's visit grew from days to weeks. 'The child is certainly benefiting from the change of air,' wrote Sarah to her sister at St. Idris.

'It seems a pity to send her back at once.' Her private opinion was that her stricter regime, including Mrs Andrews' charcoal for the teeth, a strong iron tonic and stern insistence that all fat should be eaten up at meal-times, were of great advantage to her little niece.

Then suddenly Uncle Dan's ship steamed into Liverpool and life blossomed once more with light and colour. The rich odour of his cigar, the warmth of his laugh, filled the house. Bezique, which he detested, was banished and a new bagatelle board took its place. Matty was instructed in playing and showed herself remarkably apt.

Uncle Dan was in the highest spirits and taught Gelert, Aunt Sarah's sober black retriever, to jump over the sofas and chairs, until Aunt Sarah put a ban on the sport. He took Matty down to the docks to visit his ship; driving there in a cab among the great drays, drawn by teams of mighty horses with arched necks and streaming fetlocks.

On the wharves they picked their way between cushiony sacks of raw sugar, bursting at the seams so that the brown sweet stuff trickled out on to the ground, past pyramids of loose brazil nuts, and mountains of white cotton bulging through the sides of great bales; while overhead, with creak and rattle of chains and winches, the cranes swung their giant arms to and fro, clawing their booty out of the yawning depths of the holds and swinging it high through the air.

And so to the steamship *Coburg*, plying with passengers and cargo between Liverpool, Lisbon and Maranham, and over the gangway spanning the patch of dark-green water that divided the ordinary world from a place of enchantment. For so the ship seemed to Matty, with her rigging, masts and funnels, queer ventilators like monstrous trumpets, the boats on their davits, the captain's bridge, wheel and compass. Compared with Papa's ship with her intoxicating smell of tar and hemp, Uncle Dan's good steamship *Coburg* was more like a luxurious hotel. Down the companion-way to the velvet upholstered saloon, with its thick carpets, and in and out of the brass-fitted cabins she would wander, until Shenton, the chief steward, came to summon her to the feast he had prepared in the captain's cabin, rich plum-cake, Portuguese fruits and ripe pineapple.

These were days to be for ever remembered, yet sometimes the longing to be a boy and go to sea was unendurable. She was the only girl in her family. Was it possible that God had made a mistake? If only they had been a family of four boys, Ivor, Archie, Philip and the boy who was no longer Matty, they could all have gone to sea together.

Another reason for questioning the decrees of Providence was the appearance of a wart on the thimble finger of her right hand, a small affliction which made sewing painful. She laid the case before Aunt Sarah.

'You see, I don't think that God really *meant* me to sew.'

But Aunt Sarah made it clear that whatever the Divine intention might be, *she* certainly meant Matty to sew, and her mending must all be finished before there could be any more junketing. Only then was she free to go with Uncle Dan on another outing that began in a hansom cab and included chocolate eclairs in a gilded tea-shop. He had undertaken various shopping commissions for friends abroad and Matty must help him decide some delicate question, such as choosing the prettiest mount for a piece of filmy lace, to make up into a fan for a Portuguese lady.

The glittering shop windows of Bold Street were full of magical gifts and strange luxuries.

'Look, Uncle Dan! There's a purse-muff like Aunt Sarah's.'

'Would you like it?'

'Oh, no, no! I didn't mean that.'

Matty's sense of the fitness of things was shocked. At seven years old one did not have a muff like Aunt Sarah's. But already Uncle Dan had swept her into the shop, and the shopman was taking the muff out of the window.

'A very fine sealskin, sir, and lined with the best quality satin. These muffs are extremely fashionable.'

'There you are, Miss Moppett. You can hide your goodies inside when you go to chapel.'

'Oh, Uncle Dan, thank you! It's lovely.' (But whatever would Aunt Sarah say?)

The gold sovereigns clink on the counter and the shopman asks, 'Shall I make it into a parcel, sir ?'

'No, we'll take it as it is. Here, Moppett, keep your cold paws warm in that.' And so out once more into the blue February dusk and the bustling streets.

Dear, warm-hearted Uncle Dan! How odd that your present should survive when so much has perished. You with your curly beard and your warm laugh have been dust these fifty years, and the leisurely life you enjoyed with such relish has vanished as completely as the good cigars you smoked, or the expensive scents you sometimes smuggled from France to Brazil (your steward once got six months for that and came back to you and your ship as soon as he left prison). But the niece to whom you gave that ridiculous present of a sealskin purse-muff possesses it today, and her grandchildren like to snap the fastener and poke their fat fingers into the soft fur. Even the satin lining is nearly as good as ever. Without doubt it must have been of the very 'best quality'.

Aunt Sarah is remembered by a few Lowestoft cups and saucers, prim lilac-patterned, and a Greek Testament, studied in order that she might read the Gospels in the language in which they were written. Just precise and yet steadfastly kind, expecting the highest standard from others but never asking less of herself, Aunt Sarah has remained someone whom it is impossible to recall without a stiffening of the spiritual backbone.

*

February had turned to March in the year 1881, Uncle Dan had sailed once more for South America and Matty was still at Birkenhead, when a letter came from Aunt Martha at Nantgwyn to say that Grandfather had fallen in the rick-yard. To fall down in one's own yard did not seem very serious to Matty and she wondered why Aunt Sarah appeared so troubled. But next day there was a telegram to say that Grandfather was dead, and Aunt Sarah, suddenly remote and red-eyed, shut herself up in her bedroom, while Mrs Andrews, looking very solemn and no longer smiling with her beautiful white teeth, arrived with quantities of black material and ribbons and sat sewing, snipping and altering; while more and more black clothes and black bonnets arrived in boxes from the Liverpool shops, and Ellen at the kitchen fire stood over a black cauldron like a witch's brew.

'For goodness' sake, what is it now?' she cried when Matty peeped in at the kitchen door. 'Afraid I was that you were bringing me more clothes to go into this old pot,' she added apologetically, and thrust in her wooden spoon. A poplin frock, belonging to Matty, that had once been a pretty maize colour, mixed with a pair of stockings, lately tan, rose to view.

'Deio! They're turning green!' muttered Ellen and pushed them back into the cauldron. 'Ellen, are you going to dye all our underclothes black too?' asked Matty.

'For pity's sake, no,' said Ellen. 'This old pot won't hold any more, and there's something wrong with the dye, I shouldn't be surprised. The mistress bought it from a rubbishy pedlar man at the door. Said he was born in Westford and got round her properly, he did. Ruining good stuff, I call it. All your underclothes, indeed! Whatever put such an idea into your head?'

'I don't see why we should wear black clothes at all,' said Matty.

Ellen was put out. 'Don't you say such things, child, with

your grandad only just dead and the poor mistress taking on the way she is.'

'But why should we wear black?' Matty persisted. ' We ought to be glad if he's gone to Heaven. Ellen, do you think that perhaps Aunt Sarah is crying because she thinks Grandad hasn't gone to Heaven?'

This time Ellen really was shocked. 'Matty fach! You know very well what a good man your grandad was. There is not one of the Nantgwyn people who did not speak well of him. And don't I remember him myself at the Christmas parties in the big kitchen at Nantgwyn, and how he would pass round the wassail bowl, smelling so good of raisins and honey. I was only a little girl then, quatting behind my mother's skirts. But the master saw me at the back of the room and got me to join in all those pastimes. 'Shoeing the mare' they were playing, and the master cried, 'Come on, Ellen fach, we'll show them how to do it.' It was because I was small and afraid that he called me out. He was a lovely gentleman.'

But Matty was still pursuing her own line of thought. 'I don't understand why we ought to wear black, but if it's right to do so then we ought to be black all through. I think it's very deceitful to put on coloured petticoats.' And with that she walked loftily out of the kitchen.

Next day they were to set out for Wales, and when they wakened it was to find snow on the ground, muffling the wheels of the milkman's cart and giving every gate-post in the road a neat white cap.

Matty could not fail to be excited by the thought of the journey, made all the more exciting by the new black garments in which she and her aunt were clothed. Even the snow, which for Aunt Sarah added the last touch of melancholy and discomfort to their sad journey, gave Matty a sense of high adventure. Yet later she grew aware of a sense of doom and overwhelming fate when, on reaching the Welsh border, the

snow lay at such depths that their train was frequently brought
to a standstill, while at every station an opening of the carriage
door admitted a blizzard. Their foot-warmer had grown tepid,
and Aunt Sarah's agitation for a new one was at its height
when news reached their carriage – passed from one to the
other of the company in horrified voices – that the body of
a woman had been found in a snowdrift and carried to the
station waiting-room.

Death was everywhere that day: in Aunt Sarah's sorrowful
face, in the muffled world outside, in their own unfamiliar
black clothes and the conjectures of the other passengers as to
the fate of the poor frozen woman.

It was twilight already when they changed trains at
Carmarthen, and the Towy lay black and still under its high
bridge. Then on into the fading light and the white folded hills
of South Wales, while Matty fell asleep and dreamt that she
and Philip were pillow-fighting in the nursery of the Stone
House. But the feathers came out of the pillow and turned to
ice, so cold to the touch that she cried out to Philip that she did
not wish to play any more.

She wakened to find Aunt Sarah shaking her, and the
carriage door open. A bitter wind blew in; someone was
holding a lantern outside and it was still snowing. Their feet
sank into crusted coldness as they stepped out of the carriage.
Soon afterwards there was a drink of hot milk at the Ship
Hotel. First the milk was too hot and then there was skin on it,
and Aunt Sarah was vexed that Matty would not drink it nor
eat any of the food that was set before her. But she was too
tired, and had only one thought in her head, that soon, if only
they could make an end of all this travelling, she would see her
own dear Mamma again.

Everyone was talking of the snow, and the driver of the fly
that was to take them the seventeen miles from Westford to
St. Idris was gloomy about the journey. Yet they got on well
enough for the first part of the way and Matty fell asleep once

more. When she roused, it was with a feeling of deadly cold. Aunt Sarah had opened the carriage door and was climbing out to hold the horse's head, while the driver went to borrow a spade from a neighbouring house. The fly was tipped up so that Matty had difficulty in remaining on the slippery seat; and Aunt Sarah in her voluminous skirt stood knee-deep in the drift.

'This is an adventure,' thought Matty, but she was too chilled and weary to relish it. She found that she wanted to cry, and was ashamed. What was this compared with going to sea and all the trials she would be called on to endure were she a boy?

By this time the driver had returned, carrying one of the carriage lamps, and with him a man with a spade. While they dug out the wheels Matty curled up under the rug on the floor of the carriage and thought of Mamma and Philip and all they would soon be saying to each other.

Sometime after the middle of the night they drove into St. Idris, past the dark shuttered houses, and stopped in the Cross. The snow had silenced the wheels of the carriage so that no one heard their coming, but the front door of the Stone House was not bolted and Matty, pushing it open, ran straight into the lamplit hall.

'Mamma!' she called, and heard someone move upstairs. Her hat had fallen off as she jumped from the fly and she pulled off her wraps in the hall. The door upstairs opened and Mamma came out on to the dimly lit landing. She looked startled and called out, 'Who is there?'

'It's me!' cried Matty, and sprang to meet her. But Lettice, seeing a strange cropped head and black clothes, drew back alarmed.

'Oh, who are you?'

It was only for an instant before recognition followed. Yet even then it was, ' Matty dear! Your hair!'

But at that moment Aunt Sarah mounted the stairs and the

two sisters fell weeping in each other's arms. Matty turned and ran from them into the nursery. It was dark in there, for the fire had long since gone out, but here she could cry by herself, cry bitterly because Mamma had not known her.

Lettice found her and carried her off to bed. But not even the fire in her bedroom and a basin of hot gruel could cheer her spirits. Mamma and Aunt Sarah thought that, like them, she was weeping for Grandfather. But she wasn't. At that moment she came near to disliking both Aunt Sarah and Grandfather: one had cut off her hair, and because of the other she was wearing these horrid black clothes, so that even Mamma, her own darling Mamma, had not known her.

Chapter 15

'Bydd Myrdd o Ryfeddodau...'

Bydd myrdd o ryfeddodau
Ar doriad bore'r wawr
Pan ddelo plant y tonnau
Yn iach o'r cystudd mawr.

Grandfather's funeral was over and the snow still lay on the ground, longer than even the oldest inhabitant of St. Idris, where snow falls seldom, could remember. Lettice drove back from Nantgwyn through an unfamiliar white world with the two eldest children, leaving Sarah to stay on for a time with Jim and Martha.

Ivor and Archie, freed at last from the solemnity of the occasion, talked eagerly to each other about the chances of tobogganing, for nothing of that sort had been allowed since the day Grandfather died. Now they wondered whether the snow would last another day, and whether Fred and Arthur Parry, Canon Roberts' two nephews, would consider a loan of their sledge.

Lettice was glad to hear them talk. After the concentrated sadness of the day, the darkened rooms, Martha's strained face, the long service in chapel and the voices of men and women singing round the open grave, after all this it was unbelievably good to come back to life, to see a string of geese on the roadside and watch the blue smoke of the cottages rise straight against the wintry sunset.

At the Trefelin turning they drew up the horses while a herd of cows crossed the road to a farm gate, their warm breaths blooming motionless in the frozen air, a yellow corgi yapping at their heels. These were sights which her father would never see again, thought Lettice. However one imagined the New Jerusalem, there was no place there for geese and cows and cottage smoke. The homely things must be left behind, and homely things were so often the best. Even today, when they had sung of the mountains of Jerusalem, it was the blue outline of the Preselis that she saw with her mind's eye.

A great company of people had walked along the road from Nantgwyn to the graveyard near the sea to say farewell to James Merion, and as they walked they sang the hymn '*O fryniau Caersalem*', telling how the traveller, at the end of his journey through the wilderness, looks back on his pilgrimage:

> *When all the windings of the way*
> *Fill his heart with sweet content.*

Then, as though there could never be an end to singing, never an end to the sorrow and longing in the human heart, they sang again standing in the snow round the open grave, sopranos and altos, tenors and basses, pursuing each other's voices, generations of poets and singers in their blood, turning their grief into glory, and their lamentation at the common fate of man into a hymn of praise. 'Bydd myrdd o ryfeddodau,' they sang:

> *When on that wondrous morning,*
> *By waves and tempest tossed,*
> *Safe land the sons of sorrow,*
> *Their deep affliction passed.*

So good a man as her father, thought Lettice, would wake very easily on that Morning, for no one was ever more unaffectedly upright in his life. For him there had already been an awakening, and the light that he had seen when he was a young man had never left him. Lettice had once heard the story of how her father, in his heedless youth, had joined the smugglers in one of their escapades along the rocky coast. That very night the King's men trapped them and captured some of their number. James Merion escaped and took refuge in a chapel, where he hid in the pulpit while his pursuers searched without, flashing their lanterns through the windows. When they had gone the young man remained crouched in the pulpit, and there he suddenly realised in Whose house he had taken refuge and saw the wickedness of his ways, resolving thereafter to lead the Good Life.

Lettice remembered the story now and wondered if her father had been ever really wicked – even before he hid in the pulpit.

But there was yet another thought to occupy her mind that day. Not only must she now accustom herself to the idea of Nantgwyn without Father, but also to the fact that Nantgwyn itself might cease to be. For many years, she knew, Jim had stayed there only for his father's sake. It was the family home, but in these days it would never be a prosperous farm. The house was inconvenient, and both the farm buildings and the supply of water were inadequate for modern methods. There were richer, more prosperous farms to be bought or leased in the north end of the county, where Jim's skill in the rearing of stock would no longer be cramped and hindered.

Lettice had known this for some time and Martha had spoken of it today. To the three sisters, Sarah, Martha and Lettice, the contemplated end of their childhood's home was the closing of a door on their youth. Nothing could take the place of Nantgwyn; no other house could match it for charm and happiness.

For the rest of her life Lettice, who despite her sea voyages was deplorably vague about the points of the compass, would fix the relationship of North and East by remembering that if she stood with her back to the stables at Nantgwyn then the sun rose on her right hand over the sycamore tree. Nor would house and garden forsake her in her dreams. It was thirteen years since she had left Nantgwyn as a bride, yet she would wake suddenly from sleep thinking that she heard the creak of the dairy door, or the clip-clop of the donkey's feet on the rocky path that led to the well.

Of course Jim would never sell the house: it would be let to strangers who might come in time to think that was where they too belonged. But that could be their mistake. How could new-comers *belong*, when there were still Merions alive to whom the patterned grain of wood in every door and the notched distortion of certain windowpanes were old friends?

Lettice thought, if you are really in love with a place, then it is for ever new. When she was a child she had loved to be sent on an errand to the kitchen garden because there were two ways of reaching it and each was so pleasant. If she chose to go by the stables there were the sunny spaces of the rick-yard to cross, and a chance of running up the worn stone steps against the granary wall, but that meant foregoing the orchard and the path that began by winding so invitingly past the lilac bushes. Lettice could never decide which journey she preferred; neither of them ever grew stale. But now she would go those ways only in her dreams.

'Mamma, this is *my* pocket-handkerchief, isn't it?' Archie broke into her thoughts, holding up the new silk handkerchief that had been given him for the funeral, with its border of deep black, some two inches wide.

'Mamma, it *is* mine?'

'Yes, of course, Archie. You know that it is.'

'Then can I have it to make a bed for my white rat? The new one, I mean, that's just been born.'

'On no account,' said Lettice firmly. 'The handkerchief was given you for today, because of Grandfather, and it is not to be used for any rat's bed. You had better give it to me to keep for you if you take no better care of it than that.'

'But what's the use of keeping it?' argued Archie. 'We aren't having any more funerals in the family, are we?'

The words were like knuckles knocking suddenly on a door, on a door that was near and would soon open. What did he mean by asking 'We aren't having any more funerals in the family'? Of course they weren't! Here at last was St. Idris, the houses huddling together and the first lamps lit in the windows.

'You understood what I said, Archie. You are *not* to use that handkerchief for any rat.'

Perhaps she spoke more sharply than she intended, but what a day it had been and how dreadfully tired she was, quite suddenly!

Catherine Jane met her in the hall. Philip wasn't well, she said. He had been feverish all the afternoon and complained of a pain in his chest. She had put his feet in hot mustard and water and now at last he was sleeping.

Lettice dropped her heavy cloak and flew upstairs, her heart pounding in her throat. Catherine Jane had lit a fire and the dancing light filled the bedroom. Philip's fair head stirred on the pillow as she entered and she dropped on her knees beside him. His skin was hot and dry, that was the first thing she noticed, she who always judged her children's well-being by the feel of their flesh.

A coal fell from the grate and the child woke from his sleep and called out, 'Mamma!'

'Cariad, I'm here. Mamma is here.' He opened his eyes then, and afterwards fell asleep with his cheek on her arm. She kept it there, cramped and motionless, and shook her head when Catherine Jane crept in to beg her to go down to supper. Marged solved the problem by bringing a basin of hot soup to her side.

During the days which followed Matty found that everything was different at the Stone House. She went to Miss Carlyle's school every morning and described the glories of Birkenhead to her chosen playmates; but the house to which she ran home at midday was no longer the same unchanging refuge. Mamma was often not to be seen at all and Catherine Jane gave them their dinner. Then after two days Nansi Richards appeared, a sure sign of perturbation to the three children, who connected her entirely with Mamma's absences from home. But now, even more perturbing, Mamma was not absent but upstairs by Philip's bedside, with so hushed a look on her face that Archie and Matty forbore altogether to argue or squabble, and Ivor, who had nailed boots of the noisiest, took to leaving them in the hall and creeping about in his stockinged feet.

Dr Parry came twice every day and Aunt Martha drove over from Nantgwyn and stayed on, although she had not expected to do so, and therefore had not brought any luggage. All this time Philip was in bed with a fire burning day and night, and steam kettles to make everything warm and damp; with Marged bringing up hot bricks and buckets of coal and cups of broth that came away untouched, and Catherine Jane crying on the stairs.

The day that Aunt Martha came Matty heard the word 'crisis' for the first time. 'It will be the crisis tonight,' Nansi Richards told Marged. Matty imagined it as something white and glittering, like a fall of snow, but she did not ask anyone what it meant.

That same night when she was in bed and was just beginning to grow sleepy, Mamma (whom she had hardly seen all day) came into her room and knelt beside her on the floor.

'Matty, fach, will you pray God to make Philip better?'

Matty said, ' Yes, Mamma. But of course he will get better, won't he?'

At that Mamma laid her head down on the bed beside Matty and cried and cried. It was dreadful and all the wrong way round for Mamma to be crying and Matty the one to comfort her. She didn't do it very well; only hugged and kissed her and said, 'Don't, don't, Mam fach! Please don't cry any more!'

Mamma went away and Matty fell asleep, but woke once or twice in the night to hear doors opening and closing and people walking about. Next morning it was Aunt Martha, not Catherine Jane, who came to waken her. Aunt Martha was still wearing the clothes in which she had driven over from Nantgwyn. They did not look as though she had taken them off. She had red rings round her eyes. She came and sat on Matty's bed and held her two hands in hers, and Matty was suddenly frightened.

'Where is Philip?' she asked in a loud, jerky voice. Aunt Martha held her hands very tight and said, 'He has gone away from here. He has gone to live with God.'

When she heard that, Matty did a dreadful thing. She wrenched her hands away from Aunt Martha and struck her, Aunt Martha who was so dear to all of them! But Matty did not know what she was doing because she was suddenly very angry. She kicked the bedclothes till she had kicked them all away and cried out, 'I don't want Philip to live with God. I don't want him to go. Don't let him live with God! I want him to live here!'

Aunt Martha tried to make her be quiet, but Matty would not listen. She was furious with these people, Dr Parry, Aunt Martha and Nansi Richards, who had all come to the house and walked about it for days and sent Philip away. So now he was dead, like Grandfather, was he? Why couldn't they have taken better care of him?

'What will Mamma say to you?' she cried out. 'What will Mamma do without Philip?'

'Hush, child, you don't know what you are saying,' said Aunt Martha, and then suddenly the bedroom door opened and Mamma came in. She said something in Welsh to Aunt Martha, and Aunt Martha got up and went away.

Mamma went over to the window and stood looking out for some time without speaking. Matty pulled up the blankets which she had kicked away and tried to straighten them. The anger had all gone out of her and she felt small and ashamed. Suddenly she began to weep, tried to find her handkerchief which was lost, and then buried her face in the pillow; but she could not stop the tears which seemed to rise from some bottomless well inside her.

Then Mamma turned and came over to the bed and knelt down as she had done the night before, but this time it was the right way round for it was Mamma who was the comforter. She hugged her tight and kissed her and rubbed her cheek against hers and said, 'Matty, you and I have got to comfort each other, haven't we? We know that Philip is safe in Heaven, safe and well and happy because he was always so good and such a darling, wasn't he? He won't ever be ill again, and he'll never be sad or tired or lonely. But you and I have got to be the brave ones now. We've got to be good and cheerful, like Philip was, and help Ivor and Archie, and look after Papa when he comes home and keep him from feeling too sad. You understand, Matty fach, don't you?' And Matty, with her arms very tight round her mother's neck, said in a small voice, 'Yes, Mamma. I understand and I'll try.'

Chapter 16

Promise of Spring

Three weeks after Philip's death Lettice drove over to see Aunt Rachel at Sarnau. Day after day she had forced herself to stay indoors and receive the visits of condoling friends and relatives.

'Oh, marm, it's Mrs Jenkins Evans! Suppose now I was to say you are not at home?' Catherine Jane had suggested one day. But Lettice would not hear of it.

'It would be an untruth, Catherine Jane. If people take the trouble to come and see me, I cannot close the door to them.' And downstairs she went to meet her visitors with so sealed a look on her face that they came away subdued and wondering.

But there were others who when they came shared for a moment the load of sorrow. These were not generally the ones whom Catherine Jane showed into the parlour; they came instead to the back door and stood, patient or hesitating, by the well until Lettice came out to them. They were a surprising collection; some of them unknown even to Marged, who did not always approve of such as she knew. Among them were Jimmy Dugan, the ragged old Irishman who had toasted the 'Captain's salvation' so delightedly after the loss of the *Zouave*, and John y Dwrnwr, John the Thresher, as he was called, though no one could remember his working days, whose chilblains Lettice had once cured with periwinkle tea.

Amy Owen, a thin woman with dark eyes and a consumptive cough, whose dinner had been carried daily in a basket to her cottage from Lettice's house for a matter of years, was one of the first to come; and another day it was

Jano Shenkin, the shoemaker's hunchback daughter, and Ellis the wooden-legged weaver who sang so sweetly in the choir. Even Peggy Pwt called at the door with her jaunty clothes and soiled beauty. But there was no bravado in her voice when she talked with Lettice.

Some of them brought little presents of a duck's egg or a bottle of rhubarb wine, but more often they were too poor to bring anything at all and stood holding Lettice's hand while the tears ran down their cheeks. She had helped them, or perhaps only talked with them, in the days of her happiness, and now their friendship came flowing back to her in a way that was strangely comforting.

'Mrs Peters fach, I had rather it had happened to one of mine than to your lovely *bachgen*,' exclaimed Dorit Pugh, the mother of eight children.

'You mustn't say that, Dorit,' answered Lettice. 'You know how much you love them.'

'Deio! And that's true too. Mrs Peters fach, I have borne eleven children and buried three, and I know it is no easier to lose one because there are others left. It is the people who never had any at all who say such things. Indeed, indeed, I wish you had never tasted the bitter waters.'

Such bitter waters they were that often in those days Lettice thought they would overwhelm her. Her body cried out for the child she had lost as though he were still part of her flesh. Her breasts ached for the feel of his head and her hands never ceased pining for the grasp that had once held them. Philip's birth had been easier than the birth of any of the other children, but it seemed to Lettice that the pains of losing him would never end. In a state of mind and soul that was near to despair she ordered Tom Pugh's fly to drive her to Sarnau, for Aunt Rachel was too infirm to move from home and had written asking Lettice to come whenever she should feel inclined.

Wrapped in her cloak, now dyed black, Lettice sat in the

carriage, her unseeing eyes fixed on the familiar landscape, as Tom Pugh's bay mare walked up the long hills and to the sound of the grinding brake descended the other side. On the level her hooves beat out a rhythm, and it seemed to Lettice that it was the metre of the hymn they had sung round her father's grave:

> *Pan ddelo plant y tonnau*
> *Yn iach o'r cystudd mawr.*

> *Safe land the sons of sorrow,*
> *Their deep affliction passed.*

'*Cystudd mawr!*' the words rang in her head and nothing, she thought, could ever heal her deep affliction. Philip's death had broken something deep down inside her, and now she knew how many hopes she had been building round him.

Ivor and Archie would both go to sea. They never had any other thought, and already Lettice faced the day when she would pack their sea-chests and see them go. But Philip was different. Unlike his elder brothers he would sit quiet while anyone read aloud to him; he had an astonishingly retentive memory, and in looks most resembled Lettice's grandfather, the preacher who had ridden so many miles on his white horse and left so fair a name behind him.

Sweet and biddable as he was, already at four years Philip had shown firmness of purpose and a glad confidence in life. She remembered his first steps, and how suddenly one day the babe, who had never yet walked alone, let go her hand and ran from her over the grass, shouting and laughing. The thought of that morning came back to her now, with the scent of gorse and the memory of her own pride and delight, and with it came the words of the stricken disciples on their way to Emmaus: 'We trusted that it had been he which should have redeemed Israel'.

Had she been too proud of this youngest child of hers? Her dreams for him lay like seaweed on an empty shore from which the tide has gone and will never more return; like the crushed weeds that Matty carried home and pressed and then forgot. But Lettice's dreams of all that Philip might have been would lie for ever close to her heart, and just now there seemed room for nothing else there, not even for a small new voice which had been growing more insistent during the last few weeks and which she would like to have shut out.

Their journey was over. The March wind which had been buffeting the side of the carriage suddenly fell away as they clattered into the main street of Sarnau, between the grey and pink houses, and drew up before Aunt Rachel's door.

Aunt Rachel's house was the one in which her father, Alexander McAlister, had lived, and because he had owned several schooners trading up and down the coast, it was a surprisingly tall house with a high loft where he had kept his spare sails and rigging. There was something reminiscent of a Norwegian fjord in the setting of the little town on the deep inlet of sea water, and it was that perhaps which had taken Alexander McAlister's fancy when he first dropped anchor there, to court a Welsh woman and marry her and then settle down for the rest of his life. He was an East Coast Scot with Norse blood in his veins, which may have very well accounted for the long limbs and flaxen beard of his grandson, John Peters, as well as the family inability to keep away from the sea.

Part of that was true of half the inhabitants of Sarnau, which was a nursery of sea-going folk, while the snug houses that climbed the hill with their sheltered gardens, their fruit trees and sprawling hydrangeas, were mostly inhabited by retired master mariners. Under the gorsy hill at the edge of the water stood the grey stone lime kilns, and beyond the quay across the harbour mouth were two chains to which the ships tied up, ships bringing limestone, anthracite and stores of all kinds, and carrying away corn and potatoes to Swansea, Cardiff and Bristol.

The McAlisters had fared to the ends of the earth, and of Alexander's three sons Thomas became a commander in the East India Company's service and died in Calcutta, Henry was lost with his ship and all hands in the Australian Bight, and Alexander the second was shot through the head off Sevastopol in the Crimean War. Rachel, the one surviving sister, married a merchant captain and sent her only child to sea. Father and son died on the same voyage of yellow fever in Rio, and Rachel, widowed, childless and brotherless, lived on in the tall house where she had been born.

Chilled and saddened by her history, Lettice had sometimes found it difficult to visit her relation, but now it was different. Aunt Rachel wanted to see her, and Lettice, suddenly and inexplicably, wanted to see Aunt Rachel.

The parlour of the house at Sarnau had always seemed long and dark, but today the dim light rested her. Aunt Rachel's fires were said in the family to be poor (no one knew quite how badly off she was, and no word of it had ever passed Aunt Rachel's lips), but today the coals glowed warmly in the grate and twinkled on the china that filled every shelf, the Rockingham dinner service and tall dim goblets of Bristol glass. On the wall by the fireplace were the family silhouettes and a sampler worked by Alexander MacAlister's wife. It showed, in the finest stitching, the tall house and the cherry tree in the garden, Alexander's three sailing ships in a neat procession, and the outline of the Black Rock which rises from the sea outside Sarnau harbour.

Aunt Rachel herself, seated by the fire, said little: only insisted that her guest should first eat and drink. She was a large, stout woman with high cheek-bones, and with the slow movements that belong to country people. Her hair had once been red, the flaming red found on Scotland's east coast, but Lettice never remembered it as other than snowy white. Her large hands, the skilful hands of a gardener, lay folded in her lap. While Lettice ate and drank she talked of John, asked how he liked his new ship and spoke of the *Zouave*'s end.

'I dare say he'll never take to another ship so well as to that one,' she said. 'Was it in the *Zouave* that you sailed with John? Well, that's a thing a man isn't likely to forget either. Talk about women being house-proud, it's little compared with what a man feels for his ship.'

'Did you go to sea often with your husband?' asked Lettice. She had never before talked to Aunt Rachel of her youth; it had seemed so far away and tragic, but now she wanted to hear about it.

'Once to South America, twice to the West Indies and three times round the Cape,' said Aunt Rachel. 'I was going with him and Alec that last time and had all my boxes packed, but my father was taken ill suddenly and it seemed right to stay behind. That was to have been the first voyage with both together, my husband and my boy, and I thought it would be like Heaven, going to sea with the two of them. They died in Rio because of the bad nursing in the hospital. That's what the mate told me when he came home with the ship months afterwards. I would have altered that if I'd been there.'

The coals in the grate fell apart and the flames leapt up the chimney. The two women sat silent for a time and then Rachel spoke again.

'I don't know how it is with you, Lettice, but the usual things that are said about death are little use and comfort to me. People tell us to practise resignation, but the truth is I'm *not* resigned and never shall be.'

Lettice glanced across the hearth and thought: She doesn't look resigned, sitting there like an old lioness.

'They call it Christian resignation,' Rachel went on, 'but I never can see that Christ practised it. When people were ill, He cured them, and when they died He brought them back to life. When He had to die Himself He rose again.'

'Are you sure in your own mind that you will meet your husband and Alec again?' asked Lettice.

'So long as I hold to the Christian faith, I am,' said Rachel. 'When I forget it then I'm a black heathen. But not for long. Christ still lives; better people than I am feel His power today. If I can't feel always that Richard and Alec are there, perhaps they sometimes fail me on their side too. I often fail them.'

'But not always?'

'Not always. Sometimes I know they are with me as surely as I know you are in this room now. When Alec was away serving his time, often I'd know our thoughts were together. It's like that still, but far more certain. Not ghostly or fearsome, but just the other way round; something so warm and reassuring that all the other part of life, the cares and the worries, turn unreal.'

'I don't know how it will be with you and your little lad,' she went on gently. 'But perhaps it will be different from what it was before. You used to comfort him when he was hurt. Now maybe he will comfort you. That was surely what Christ meant by the Holy Ghost. He called it the Comforter, but the disciples had to lose Him first before they could receive it.'

Lettice sat very still and the tears fell down as she listened; but they were gentler tears than she had shed before and lightened her heavy heart. She wanted to ask Rachel if there were anything she could do to fit herself for such a visitor, but could find no words. As though she read what was in her mind, Rachel went on, 'There are some things we can do on our side to help. It seems to me that they don't come when we sit down to think about them, but at quite other times when our minds are set on something outside.'

She paused and murmured, more to herself than to Lettice, 'As though we walked out into the sunshine, with nothing in the way.'

'But it's not always like that,' she continued. 'Sometimes a strong rush of feeling, like a great wave, carries us to them.

Then we are compelled to give ourselves up to it.'

'One thing I've noticed, Lettice, and it's a mercy it should be so for us women with all our endless small concerns; it's a fact that *doing* things, if they're right things done in the right way, seems to sweep the path clear: a path where they and we can walk together. We may be busy, and it's best that we should be busy, but all the time we can keep an attentive ear and be ready for them when they knock at our door.'

It was growing dark in the long sitting-room and Aunt Rachel rose slowly and ponderously from her chair to fetch a lamp. Lettice could hear the water lapping in the harbour outside (It must be high tide, she thought), and the sound of footsteps in the street. A man's voice went by under the window singing the words of a hymn:

> *Rhosyn Saron, rhosyn Saron,*
> *Ti yw tegwch nef y nef.*

> *Rose of Sharon, Rose of Sharon,*
> *Thou art the loveliness of the Heaven of Heavens.*

'To be ready for them when they knock at our door,' Aunt Rachel had said. Other fingers were knocking already at Lettice's door. During the last weeks their summons had grown more and more imperative and she had cried out that she did not want to listen, that this was not the voice she wished to hear or the face she ached to see.

But now it seemed that perhaps it was not one but two who stood on her threshold; the child who had left her and the new child who was waiting to come.

The dark shadows of the room wavered and fled as Aunt Rachel came in carrying the lamp, which she set down on a round table. Lettice rose from her seat and stepped into the circle of light.

'I must go, Aunt Rachel. Thank you for all you have said.

I shall remember it.'

She wished to say more, to tell her new secret, but convention forbade it as yet, and Lettice was not one to break down conventions. Only for a moment, as they kissed, she laid her head on the other woman's shoulder as though to draw from her some secret strength.

The way home seemed too short that evening. She would have liked to drive still further, watching the flying vapour vanish in the path of the bright moon and the clear spring sky emerging triumphant over land and sea.

'Right things done in the right way,' came back Aunt Rachel's words, 'will sweep the path clear,' and Lettice thought, no longer bitterly but with a secret exultation, of all the fresh, endless tasks that would be hers with the coming of another child. After all, they would not take her away from Philip: they might even bring him nearer.

On this earth she would not see him again; never more rejoice in his young limbs nor see the light in his eyes. But now she knew, deep in her heart, that those eager feet would not tire on earth's roads; his eyes would now behold God; and his young love flower in the fullness of all Love.

The raw wind of day had dropped, and a thrush, clinging to the top of a twisted apple tree, sang that the long, cold winter was gone and that spring was coming. From distant fields came the wavering cry of lambs, the first, thought Lettice, that she had heard that year; and now ahead of them showed the bold, rocky outline of Carn Idris and the first twinkling of lights in the city.

THE END

Dew on the Grass

by Eiluned Lewis
With a new explanatory introduction by
Dr Katie Gramich

Set in the Welsh borders, this enchanting
autobiographical novel vividly evokes
the essence of childhood and a vanished
way of life. The novel was first published
in 1934 to great acclaim.

978 1870206 808   £8.99

Stranger Within the Gates

by Bertha Thomas
Edited by Kirsti Bohata

A collection of witty, sharply observed
short stories written at a time of great
social change, when the fundamental
rights of women were being questioned.
Bertha Thomas deftly sketches her
characters with a keen eye for satirical
details.

978 1870206 945   £8.99

A View Across the Valley: Short Stories by Women from Wales c. 1850 – 1950

Edited by Jane Aaron

Stories reflecting the realities, dreams and personal images of Wales – from the industrial communities of the south to the hinterlands of the rural west. This rich and diverse collection discovers a lost tradition of English-language short story writing.

978 1870206 358   £7.95

Queen of the Rushes: A Tale of the Welsh Revival

by Allen Raine

First published in 1906 and set at the time of the 1904 Revival, this is an enthralling tale of complex lives and loves that will capture the heart of any modern reader.

978 1870206 297   £7.95

About Honno

Honno Welsh Women's Press was set up in 1986 by a group of women who felt strongly that women in Wales needed wider opportunities to see their writing in print and to become involved in the publishing process. Our aim is to develop the writing talents of women in Wales, give them new and exciting opportunities to see their work published and often to give them their first 'break' as a writer.

Honno is registered as a community co-operative. Any profit that Honno makes goes towards the cost of future publications. To buy shares or to receive further information about forthcoming publications, please write to Honno at the address below, or visit our website: **www.honno.co.uk**.

Honno
'Ailsa Craig'
Heol y Cawl
Dinas Powys
Bro Morgannwg
CF64 4AH

All Honno titles can be ordered online at www.honno.co.uk
or by sending a cheque to Honno, MyW, Vulcan St,
Aberystwyth. SY23 1JH
FREE p&p to all UK addresses